PRAISE FOR
SYNC

A 2025 Texas TAYSHAS Reading List Pick

A September 2024 Amazon Best Book of the Month

An August 2024 Kobo Best of the Month Selection

★ "Twins Storm and Lake, 17, have been tossed from one foster home to the next . . . [Their] stories are told through undelivered letters the two write to each other. Written in true Hopkins style, these verses pack a punch . . . Their captivating voices make it all the more heartbreaking . . . This story is highly accessible and will be devoured by realistic fiction readers."
—*School Library Journal*, **starred review**

"Ellen Hopkins can convey so much in so few words . . . If you came for a stirring page-turner that sparks conversation, *Sync* is definitely a winner." —*Associated Press*

"Storm and Lake share Hopkins's signature lucid free-verse narrative, and while the events are heartrending, terrible, and too frequent, their resilience shows, even when they are at their lowest points . . . Hopkins is a household name in the YA literary world, and her many fans will be eager to get their hands on her latest offering." —*Booklist*

"A gritty, powerful novel in verse . . . poignant, unflinching . . . the narrative doesn't shy away from portraying the harsh realities of a broken foster care system . . . A wrenching and necessary read."
—*Kirkus Reviews*

SYNC

ALSO BY ELLEN HOPKINS

Crank
Burned
Impulse
Glass
Identical
Tricks
Fallout
Perfect
Tilt
Smoke
Traffick
Rumble
The You I've Never Known
People Kill People

FOR YOUNGER READERS

Closer to Nowhere
What About Will

SYNC

Ellen Hopkins

Nancy Paulsen Books

NANCY PAULSEN BOOKS
An imprint of Penguin Random House LLC
1745 Broadway, New York, New York 10019

First published in the United States of America by G. P. Putnam's Sons,
an imprint of Penguin Random House LLC, 2024
First paperback edition published by Nancy Paulsen Books,
an imprint of Penguin Random House LLC, 2025

Copyright © 2024 by Ellen Hopkins

Penguin Random House values and supports copyright. Copyright fuels creativity, encourages diverse voices, promotes free speech, and creates a vibrant culture. Thank you for buying an authorized edition of this book and for complying with copyright laws by not reproducing, scanning, or distributing any part of it in any form without permission. You are supporting writers and allowing Penguin Random House to continue to publish books for every reader. Please note that no part of this book may be used or reproduced in any manner for the purpose of training artificial intelligence technologies or systems.

Nancy Paulsen Books & colophon are trademarks of Penguin Random House LLC.
The Penguin colophon is a registered trademark of Penguin Books Limited.

Visit us online at PenguinRandomHouse.com.

Library of Congress Control Number: 2024937965

Printed in the United States of America

ISBN 9780593463260

1st Printing
BVG

Edited by Stacey Barney
Design by Cindy De la Cruz
Text set in Alkes, Spaghetti And Cheese, and Blackhawk

This book is a work of fiction. Any references to historical events, real people, or real places are used fictitiously. Other names, characters, places, and events are products of the author's imagination, and any resemblance to actual events or places or persons, living or dead, is entirely coincidental.

The publisher does not have any control over and does not assume any responsibility for author or third-party websites or their content.

The authorized representative in the EU for product safety and compliance is Penguin Random House Ireland, Morrison Chambers, 32 Nassau Street, Dublin D02 YH68, Ireland, https://eu-contact.penguin.ie.

This book is dedicated to all those struggling to experience the joy and comfort of "home." My wish for you is safety, shelter, belonging, and love.

STORM
ARE YOU SAFE TONIGHT, LAKE?

It's my job to keep you that way.
I decided that when we were three.
I remember it like it was yesterday,
now almost fourteen years ago.

We were locked in the closet.
Shivering with fear. Every time we heard
Beverly's footsteps outside the door
we'd shrink against the wall.

You got so scared you started
to hiccup. I put my arm around
your shoulder. "I'll protect you," I said.
"It's my job. I'm your big brother."

You whispered we were twins.
That made us the same age.
"No," I argued. "I came out
first. That makes me older."

Sometimes memories like that float
from the depths of my brain,
ascend like buoys before
submerging and sinking again.

It's our birthday eve. We turn
seventeen tomorrow. So of course
you're on my mind. It's the last day
of August. Senior year just started.

I have no clue where you are,
or how long you've been there.
New foster placement? Longtime?
My gut tells me you're not too far away.

I hear from you when our caseworkers

manage to intersect paths, pass on
letters or cards. But I haven't
seen you in five long years.

Well, unless you count that one time
Mom decided we should reunite.
That experiment lasted three weeks.
Honestly, longer than expected.

It was enough time for you
and me to forge our sync again.
Remember how we called it that—
the way our thoughts seemed synchronized?

I wonder which high school you go to.
Do you think, over the years,
we were ever at the same football
game, rooting for opposite teams?

Are you still acing your classes?
Despite all the crap in our childhood,
you vowed to succeed in school,
find a way to live your dreams.

I'm afraid dreaming is a fool's game
I quit, cold turkey, years ago.
Gambling on dreams successfully
requires belief in tomorrow.

I can
barely
hold on
to today.

STRAIGHT UP

I programmed myself
to stop dreaming at night
after the last nightmare.

It was one of those
where you're running
because someone's chasing you.
You don't know who, or why,
only that they want to hurt you.

No place to hide.
No one to turn to.
No help at all.
So you run.
Footsteps behind.
Closing in.
Don't turn to look.
Just get away.

The dream was a rerun.
Only this time
someone catches me
and when I turn,
the grimacing stranger
claims he is my dad.

I've never met my father.
Have no clue who he is.
Occasionally, in deep-of-night
musings, I wonder if he
could be responsible
for the person I've become.

Is there a genetic lean
toward lockup?

I've Been Locked Up Before

And I'm relatively sure
it will happen again.
Don't know when or why.
But it's waiting for me.
I've never expected anything else.

Some people are born marked
by fate, time-stamped
by destinies
beyond their control.

Life never offered
me many choices.
I've been prodded
toward trouble by people
I've known and by total strangers.

My only decisions
seemed to be how low
I was willing to go
and whether to take
someone with me.

So, no. I've never believed
in some fairy-tale future.
But I've always hoped
for happiness.

I've found a small measure
recently, with my current
foster, Jim, who's not only
decent, but he's cool with me
seeing Jaidyn, who lifts the storm
clouds and lets her light in.

But I'll never feel whole
without my sister.

It's like a piece of me
has been excised,
carved out of my heart,
hidden away. If I find
it again someday,
can it be reattached?

When we were little,
we mostly only had each other.
We grew up without many friends.

Who'd want to hang out with us?

They could see it
in our thirdhand clothes,
in our unwashed hair,
in our vacant eyes.

I swear mothers would shoo
their kids across the street
to avoid passing us on the sidewalk.
As if neglect was contagious.

We were untethered.

Until the system anchored
us, "for our own good."

Maybe it was.
Maybe it wasn't.

How would we ever know?

Mom Was Happy

The caseworker took us away.

>I remember Mom leaning
>against the building, relief
>in her slanted smile.

Devin wouldn't let her inside

>while he stuffed our clothes
>in black garbage bags, told us
>to grab our toothbrushes.

We were hurt. Confused.

>Oh, we knew why we were
>being removed, why the school
>counselor called the police.

It wasn't how thin we were.

>No one ever noticed that. No.
>It was the fist prints we wore
>on our skin like tattoos.

But at ten, that was our life.

>Mom went after us from time
>to time, but mostly it was Beverly.
>She didn't like to be called Grandma.

Beverly watched us when Mom worked.

>They traded shifts at the club
>where they "danced." That's what
>they called taking off their clothes.

Yes, our grandmother stripped, too.

> That might seem weird, but she was
> only sixteen when she had Mom,
> who was seventeen when we were born.

Fortyish strippers get day shifts.

> Mom got nights, which was better
> for her bank account, but not
> so great for my sister and me.

Beverly drank at night.

> Sometimes that was good.
> If she passed out in her recliner,
> we could raid the refrigerator.

We were always hungry.

> Other times, something would
> set her off—a dish left on a table,
> a stray sock, a random whim.

She always came for Lake first.

> I was her brother, I swore
> I'd protect her. I managed
> to save her a bruise or two.

Mom pretended she didn't see.

> But she just didn't care enough
> to stop it. So maybe that's why
> she didn't bother to say goodbye.

THAT IS BRANDED INTO MEMORY

Mom stood there, just outside,
under the eaves, dodging
the steady bullets of rain.
She looked down at us
with frosted-glass eyes.

"Mom?"
One three-letter word.
That was my entreaty,
not that it mattered.

      It's for the best, she said.

I turned my back
on my mother,
like she'd turned hers
on my sister and me.

Devin loaded us into
the back seat
of his ugly white car.
"Where are we going?" I asked.

      To my office for now. We're looking
      for someone who can take the two
      of you for a couple of days.

Then we can go home?

      No, Lake. Not for a while.
      But we need to keep you safe
      until we secure a longer placement.

It was the first time
we heard the word *placement.*
It wouldn't be the last.

THE TOYS

In Devin's office were meant
for littler kids, so he put on
a Disney movie while he made
about a hundred phone calls.

Finally, success.
We drove across the city
to a little house with a broken
fence around a potholed yard.

Inside, the place was neat,
but threadbare. The furniture
looked overused, and the carpet
needed to be replaced.

But Kelly, the lady who lived
there, was pretty nice. She held
a baby, and a girl who was
maybe three clung to her pant leg.

> *Come in, come in,* she said.
> *Bet you're hungry, huh?*

It was almost eight by then.
I hoped she meant she'd feed
us and said, "I'm starving."

Lake didn't say anything,
but she ate every chicken
nugget and french fry.

After that, Kelly made us
take showers and brush our teeth,
and then she put us to bed.

> *I'm not really supposed*

> *to let you sleep in the same*
> *room,* she told us. *But since*
> *this is an emergency placement,*
> *I think I can make an exception.*

> What about school?

Lake was always worried
about being late and was
proud of her zero absences.

> *No school for you until*
> *we settle you in somewhere*
> *more permanent, I'm afraid.*

> *Will we go to the same one?*
> *And who will tell my teacher?*

> *I don't know if you'll go to*
> *the same school, but someone*
> *will tell your teacher, okay?*

Nothing would be the same
after that day. Nothing at all.

There were two beds, but once
the lights were out, I pulled
my blanket and pillow over
next to Lake's, slept on the floor.

It was always my job
to keep her safe.

Two Days Later

Lake and I, aged almost eleven,
moved in with Molly and Pete,
their daughter, Alora, and Rex,
the best dog in the universe.

The Whittingtons made us
feel like we belonged
in a storybook family.

>A mom who baked.
>A dad who mowed the grass.
>A big sister who played with us.
>A K9 who aced tricks.

Too bad, like anything too good
to be true, it didn't last longer.
Too bad it was the first step
toward our separation,
not that we knew it then.
I learned a few things there.

>I love amusement parks.
>I prefer dogs to most people I've met.
>Maybe I have a talent or two.
>Including debate, denied me before.

Pete said I should be a lawyer
because I argued so much,
and more than once I actually won.

It was the happiest year
of our lives, or at least
it was for me, right up until
I moved in here with Jim.

Jim's Old Guy Cool

Smart, but not a know-it-all.
Kind of quiet, but funny
as hell when he does talk.

He used to be a reporter
for the *San Francisco Chronicle*,
"back when writing for a newspaper
was a dignified profession."

Started fostering with his wife,
and when Brenda died, he kept
right on caring for hard kids like me.

I try not to get in his face.
In the almost year since I've been
here, we've only gotten into it twice.

I've been working on my temper,
but once in a while I lose it.
Jim doesn't back down, but neither
does he threaten to send me packing.

He's good about handing over
my monthly allowance, and even
gave me a phone, the first foster
who's ever been that generous.

Plus, he's got a dog.
Not a great dog like Rex.
Morley is a cocker mix, more
couch surfer than ball fetcher.
But he's okay to watch TV with.

And the fact that Jim
takes excellent care of Morley
makes me respect him more.

Between the Whittingtons and Jim

Came several years.
Several placements.
Including the one
right after they ripped
Lake and me apart.

What I witnessed there
taught me justice
isn't weighed with a balanced scale.

It was a random placement,
one I knew right away would be
transient. Too many boys—six—
with a single house parent,
a squirrely dude named Russ.

One day I found this guy
Sammy rifling through my stuff.
Wouldn't have minded
much if it was only my clothes.

But he'd opened the envelope
of pics I kept, my only solid reminders
of Lake and Molly, Pete and Rex,
who I missed almost as much
as my sister. Rage mushroomed.

Sammy was bigger, but I lit
into him. I connected a punch
or two, and so did he.
Russ broke us apart, could've left
it there. Instead, he called the cops.

My first lockup was sixty days.
I was officially a "problem kid."

The Problem

With locking up a "problem kid"
is you grow up real fast
in "residential placement,"
also known as juvenile jail.

First-time offenders
with real parents who care
might wind up on probation.
Without them, you'll end up
killing time behind bolted doors
and plexiglass windows,
like animals at the zoo.

And like them, you pace,
think way too much
about all the wrong things,
or seek unhealthy ways
to relieve the boredom.

You could walk on out
of there in better shape
than when you arrived.
But it's likelier you'll tumble
straight down into the repeat-
offender gopher tunnel.

(Some visual, huh?)

Mostly because of the other
stuff you'll learn, if you didn't
already know it.

I hope none of this has touched
my sister. I hope it never will.
It's way too late for me.

AGE THIRTEEN

First time in lockup, I learned
the Five Commandments.

One:
Mind your own fucking business.
Whatever you see.
Whatever you hear.
Look away, plug your ears.

Two:
If trouble knocks, answer the door.
Don't run. Don't hide.
Make no excuses.
Wade straight on in, fists flying.

Three:
It's easier to get by when high.
Scoring meds in lockup requires acting.
Act edgy. Like you can't focus.
Pretend you just might pounce.

Four:
Almost anything can be a weapon.
If it can poke you. Slice you.
Even a book, if it's heavy
enough, can cause severe damage.

Five:
Trust absolutely no one.
Not your fellow detainees.
Not the guards or social workers.
And not the judges who are supposed
to dispense justice with an even hand.

Clue for the clueless: They don't.

Post Detention

Count on a new placement.
It won't be decent.
Not for a problem kid.
Not even if he's only thirteen.

I knew I was in trouble
when my caseworker, Pam,
wouldn't look me in the eye
on our ride to the condo-from-hell.

I got out of her car, eyed
the listing stairs, littered
with cigarette butts and
pigeon shit. What kind of foster
"parent" lived in a place like that?

It's temporary, okay?

"They're all temporary."

I mean, short term. It's difficult—

"Yeah, yeah. I get it."

But I wasn't totally prepared
for a stand-in "father" like Desmond.

He was an ex-Marine
(picture soldier "buff," gone
flabby) surviving on disability
and whatever money
he could make from the state,
taking in hardcore strays.

Boys like me.

I Was the Only One There

All good, since his "apartment"
was more like one big ratty room
with a curtained-off "bedroom,"
and a bathroom the size of a closet.

The fridge, hotplate, and microwave
worked, but the chipped kitchen table
served as Desmond's office. We ate
on TV trays sitting on the sectional
sofa I also slept on.

Social services looked the other way,
if they bothered to open their eyes at all.
Seems doubtful because Desmond
was a scammer, cruising dating sites
targeting hungry older women.

He claimed to be "deployed overseas,"
and the unretouched photo he sent them
was actually him in his uniform, fifty
pounds lighter and twenty years younger.

He played them patiently.
Convinced them a lonely Marine
half their age was crazy about them.
Once they were totally hooked,
he'd reel them in with more lies.
Tell them he took leave
and was on his way to see them.

Except he got rolled.
Lost every damn thing.
If they could just send him
a prepaid Visa, he'd reimburse
them with his next paycheck.
Unbelievably, it worked every time.

I was not supposed to know
that, of course, but for a con,
Desmond wasn't exactly careful.
He'd leave his computer on,
chat windows wide open,
while he took a pee or grabbed a beer.

He was also a little deaf, thanks to
previous proximity to artillery fire.
That made his "private conversations"
a bit louder than he might have preferred.

I didn't care. In fact, I took notes.
Who knew when I might
need a little leverage?

As for the women, I figured anyone
gullible enough to fall for Desmond's
routine deserved what they got.
The idea that they might love him
seemed like a terrible joke.

The only love I'd experienced
was what I felt for Lake.
And maybe something close with Rex.

Sister love.
Dog love.
And look what it got me.
Pain. Tears. Loneliness. Resentment.
No, I never believed
in the power of love.

Until Jaidyn.

LAKE
HAPPY BIRTHDAY TO US

How I wish Storm and I
were blowing out candles
on the same birthday cake
or opening presents together.

Not sure about my brother,
whose current circumstances
I can't even guess, but there will be
no gifts nor special desserts for me.
Not here with Colleen and Jay.

They are uber religious.
Like, the kind who hang Jesus
pictures all over the house,
say grace for twenty minutes,
and insist we go to church every Sunday.

Beyond all that, they believe
the only "birthday"
that should be celebrated
is Christmas. With worship.

They're at Bible study right
now. On Saturday.
Leaving me alone in my room
(where did Parker run off to?)
with a mountain of memories.

I remember when we turned twelve.
Molly and Pete threw a party
for Storm and me, the second
birthday we celebrated there,
in the best foster home ever.

WHEN WE FIRST ARRIVED

We were freaking out.
Storm hid it, but my body shook.

We didn't even know if living
there would be better or worse
than surviving at home.

Our caseworker—can't think
of his name, but he was this
big guy, with skin the color
of milky oatmeal—walked us
through the front door, gave Pete
our stuff, and that was the last
time we ever saw him.

Molly came over, extended
her hand. Storm figured out
we were supposed to shake it.

> *I'm Molly. Welcome to our home.*
> *And now it's your home, too.*

Yeah, right. Who expected strangers
to believe they'd fit right in?
We didn't know what to do
or say, so we just stood there.

> Finally, Pete cleared his throat.
> *Let's take your things to your rooms.*
> *Then you can meet the rest of the family.*

"We can't stay together?"

> *Afraid not,* said Molly. *It's against*
> *foster care regulations for boys and*
> *girls to sleep in the same bedroom.*

> *You'll share a room with our daughter,*
> *Alora. And Storm will have a place*
> *all to himself for the time being.*

We followed Molly and Pete
down a long hallway. Molly pointed
to a bathroom we'd share with Alora.

The white porcelain fixtures
and cream-colored tile were spotless.
Not a hint of mildew or pee or dirt.

Next stop: Storm's room.
It wasn't big, but it had two beds.

> *Pick one,* Molly said.

When Storm chose the one
by the window, Pete dropped
his bag on the opposite bed.

Suddenly, there were scratchy
noises, and in bounded a big fluffy
golden-furred dog, all sniffy
and waggy and happy.

> *Easy, Rex,* said Pete.

The dog ignored me,
but came straight over
and sat on Storm's feet.
He reached down and stroked
the retriever's face.

> *Rex, huh? Good name.*

In That Moment

Rex adopted Storm.

> *Wow,* said Molly. *Do you like dogs?*
> *Because Rex obviously likes you.*

> *I've never been around them much.*

We'd never been around them at all.
I could tell, at first, he made Storm nervous.
But Rex didn't give my brother a choice.
The dog dashed out of the room
and returned thirty seconds later,
slobbering all over his favorite ball.

> *I hope you're good with fetch,* Pete
> said, *because it's Rex's favorite game.*

If Storm hadn't thrown the ball,
maybe the two wouldn't have
connected so quickly. But they did.

Whenever Storm left the house,
Rex was the first one to welcome
him back. And, starting that very
first night, Rex slept beside Storm's bed.

The retriever already knew how to sit
and stay. But within a couple of weeks,
Storm had him climbing ladders,
bringing his (and only his) shoes,
and turning light switches on and off.

> *I knew Rex was smart,* Pete observed.
> *But I had no idea he was so clever.*
> *He was waiting for you to teach him.*

STORM GOT THE DOG

I was rewarded with a close
approximation of a friend.

Alora was a couple of years older
and she treated me like her little sister.
She didn't even mind sharing her closet.
Not that I had very much to put in it.

Our room had dreamy rose-pink
walls, mauve comforters, and white
sheets that smelled like lavender.

It took a couple of weeks to feel
comfortable. I waited for someone
to knock on the door, take us away.
Just in case, I kept my garbage bag
in the bottom drawer of my dresser.

Mostly, I fretted about missing school.
But Molly helped me catch up, and
Alora did, too. She was kinder than
I expected. I mean, it was like Storm
and I stole pieces of her mom and dad.

>Their time.
>Their attention.
>Their . . .

I hesitate to say love, though
they were loving enough. In fact,
we'd never experienced such affection.

We did test them.
But they never reacted
to any of our dares with violence.

THAT SUMMER

For the first time in our lives
we went to Six Flags.

Storm loved the coasters,
I tolerated them,
but just being there
was so . . . normal kiddish.

Pete and Molly
also took us to
        Fisherman's Wharf
        two Giants games
        the Monterey Aquarium

We rode
        cable cars
        ponies
        whale-watching boats
        water slides

We played
        miniature golf
        arcade games
        carnival rip-offs

All of those things
were closer to Beverly's place
than to the Whittingtons'.

They went out of their way
to take us.

To make us believe
we meant something to them.

SIX YEARS AGO

We spent our eleventh
birthday with the Whittingtons.

They threw us a party, the first
we'd ever had with other kids
and presents and cake. I wonder
if Storm remembers that cake.

He wanted chocolate.
I asked for strawberry.
Molly baked a mash-up.
It looked weird but tasted amazing.

We were only two weeks
into a new school year,
but almost our whole class
came. With gifts.

It didn't matter
that they weren't expensive.
Like, Legos for Storm
and craft kits for me.
They were wrapped!
And they belonged to us!

We opened them
                together.
We blew out the candles
                together.
We smashed the piñata
                together.
We celebrated
                together.

WE HAD THE NEXT YEAR TOGETHER

In one place.

One home
        with straightforward
        expectations, fair rules,
        and rewards instead
        of punishments.

One school
        with supportive teachers,
        minimal judgments,
        relatively few upsets,
        and kids who'd play with us.

One Rex
        who mostly loved Storm,
        but would let me throw a ball
        for him. Once in a while
        he'd even bring it back.

One family
        that began to feel like ours.
        More ours, in fact, than
        the approximation of one
        we'd been taken away from.

It was all so normal.

If I've learned
a single thing since,
it's that nothing
that comes easy
is permanent.

TURNING TWELVE

Felt important to me, and maybe
that was prescient because I had
my first period not long after.

I wish it would've happened
with Molly there to counsel
me, but that was not to be.

Three days after our birthday party,
Molly and Pete sat us down.

Rain pelted the kitchen window,
rolling down the glass in thin silver streams.

></br>*We've got some news to share,* Pete
> said, *and I'm afraid it isn't all good.*

Molly couldn't look us in the eye,
but I could sense her regret.
Storm started petting Rex,
who whimpered as if he knew.

> *I got a new job, one I couldn't turn
> down. Unfortunately, it's in Texas.*

"What does that mean?" I asked.

> Storm answered. *They're leaving.
> And we're not going with them.*

"Why not?" I still didn't understand
the way the system worked.

> *California is your custodial state,*
> explained Molly. *We can't take you.*

I Could Barely Breathe

"What happens to us?"

> *A new placement. We're so sorry,
> kids. I wish there was something
> more we could do. But there's not.*

> How long until we go?

> *End of the week.*

"What about school?"

> *Fortunately, we're only a couple
> of weeks into the year.
> The transition should be smooth.*

Molly came over to hug me.
I'd never shrugged one off
before, but that time I ducked.
"I'm going to read."

I went to Alora's room—no longer
half-mine. Lay down on my—no,
the—bed. Closed my eyes,
seeking the comfort of the dark.
But light through the window
made everything gray.

I got up, went over
to the dresser, and found
the garbage bag, still neatly folded.

End of the week
was five days away.
I started packing.

I WRITE THESE VIVID RECOLLECTIONS

In a long, rambling letter to Storm,
trying to regain a small sense of connection.
I ask if there have been other dogs
in any of his placements.

Tell him about Jeffrey, a weird
old poodle at one of mine.
He kind of matched his owner,
Rose, who was a strange old lady,
but not in a super-bad way.

Mostly, she was forgetful.
Like, sometimes she'd be talking
and halfway through a sentence
she'd totally lose track, wander
into a whole different sentence.

And sometimes she'd fix the same
dinner three or four nights in a row.
Then she'd say, "Bet you've never
had that before. It's my special recipe."

As for the poodle, not sure if dogs
can catch forgetfulness from people,
but Jeffrey barked at Melanie and me
every time we came through the door.

Oh. Melanie. I haven't thought about
her in a while. She was the first girl
I got to be really close to.
Like, even closer than Alora . . .

WAY CLOSER

I pause my writing.
Melanie is a private reminiscence,
one I wouldn't want Colleen
and Jay to discover should
they come across this letter.

I was thirteen when I was placed
with Rose and moved into a room
with Melanie. My attraction
to her was immediate.

I wouldn't say confusing, exactly,
though most of my adolescent longing
had been directed toward boys.
Not that I'd acted on any of it.
Not until Melanie.

She was two years older,
and reminded me of a lynx.
Tawny. Green-eyed. Wild.
I fell hard in love with her.
I knew she didn't feel the same.
But it was enough that she wanted
to kiss me. Caress me. Gift me
with a sense of importance.

Of course, that meant losing
someone I cared about when
Rose's daughter arrived,
decided foster was too much
work for her mother.

My Current Bedroom Door Opens

Parker sings her way across the room.
She's always singing in a crisp soprano.
Everything from Julie Andrews to Pink.

> *Happy birthday! Whatcha doin'?*

"Attempting communication."

> *Lost cause. Cool. Anyway, asters*
> *are the official September birthday*
> *flower. This is for you. I love you!*

In her hand is a single small
blue-purple bloom, the only
floral birthday gift I've ever
received. It has no scent.
Its power is in its beauty.

I put the pencil into my desk
drawer, where it joins maybe
fifty more in my obsession,
as Parker calls it. I've collected
pencils over the years, souvenirs
of schools, social workers' offices,
and abundant foster homes.

Parker swivels around in front
of me, pushes the chair away
from the desk, carrying me with it.
Now she straddles my lap.
Lowers her eyes to meet mine.
Her silk lips are slick with gloss
and licorice-flavored spit.

> *The weirdos are gone.*

I sigh. "Are you sure?"
If our fosters catch us, we're cooked.

>*Bible study. We've got two hours*
>*for sure. Think that's enough?*

"My bed or yours?"

>*We could get weird and do it in theirs.*

"Mine, then." We move in
that direction, shedding clothes.

I have always been thin,
narrow, straight up and down.
Parker is all sensuous curves.
I find pleasure in simply tracing
them with my fingers, circling
them with my tongue.

She's been out in the sun.
It perfumes her toasted skin.
I soak it in, secondhand.

In.
Out.
Over.
Under.
There. Yes, there.
More of that.
More, more, more.

We lift each other
out of the realm of ordinary,
and into deliverance.

Outside, Shadows Slant Long

Still, we lie tangled on my bed.

      Parker sighs. *Ever think about aging out?*

At eighteen, we can either stay tethered
to the system for a couple of years
or it will dump us with a small stipend.

"I try not to. Why, do you?"

      Yeah. She animates. *We'll be free.*

"Free to do what? Starve?"

      No. No. We'll get checks every month.

"Only if we go to college or find
some crummy job. And eight hundred
bucks won't go very far. You have
any idea what rent's like in California?"

      She clucks her tongue. *Duh.*
      Colleen has made that pretty clear.

Foster requires Colleen to teach us financial
literacy. Budgeting for fifteen hundred a month
for a little apartment requires mental gymnastics.

"How do you know? You never
pay attention to what she says."

      Hearing and paying attention are two different
      things. Anyway, considering how she always
      complains about not having enough money
      makes me doubt her own financial literacy.

I have to laugh. "Good point."

> *We could move in together. Get jobs.*
> *Pool resources. I know you want to go*
> *to college, but . . .* The thought dissolves.

"See, the 'buts' are why I try not
to think about aging out."

I prop myself up on one elbow.
Sink into the violet blue of her eyes.
Push damp blond strands off her face.

"Hard enough to figure out now."

> *Okay then, let's just pretend we can*
> *do anything we want. Forget about*
> *how we'd pay for it. Close your eyes.*

She pushes me back against the pillow.

> *We'll get a van. Something we can live in.*
> *We'll travel around the country, to music*
> *festivals or something. Hey. Can you sing?*

"No, but I can play the ukulele."

> That stops her cold. *Really?*

"Parker, I've never even seen
a ukulele except in videos."

We both crack up.
The fantasy evaporates.

IT WAS NICE WHILE IT LASTED

But reality intrudes.
"We'd better get dressed.
They might surprise us."

></br>*Parker moans. Yeah. Okay.*
> *Can you imagine Colleen?*
> *Lesbian love! She'd freak!*

I unknot myself, sit up.
"How many times have
I told you—"

> *Yeah, yeah. You don't like the L-word.*
> *Which is weird, since you are one.*

I don't really know what I am.
All I'm certain of is what I feel,
and I'm in desperate lust with Parker.
I kiss her so she won't doubt
that, slip into my jeans.

Parker isn't the first person
I've been with. And that includes
a boy or two. But she's the first
I've let myself even come close
to falling in love with.

It's a mistake. Of course it is.
And not just because Colleen
would lose her shit if she ever caught
Parker and me together.

There's no room in her heart
or mind to accept LGBTQ-ness.
There would be no acceptance.
No understanding.

I lost my brother five years ago
because a caretaker lacked empathy.

It was just a hug.
A small measure of comfort
to ease the pain of our recent
departure from Molly and Pete's.

But our new foster decided
it was something indecent.
There has never been that kind
of love between Storm and me.

But people like Eloise
prefer to believe the worst.
That was the last placement
Storm and I ever shared.

Parker and I must be very careful.
We've made it a game.
One we're likely to lose.

It was a huge lapse of judgment
to fall for her, because nothing lasts.

The bright green of spring
becomes autumn's brown leaves,
raked into piles and tossed or burned.

Love might sprout leaves
today, bud tomorrow,
blossom next week.

But when will it wither?

SOMEONE'S COMING DOWN THE HALL

"I think they're home."
Parker's lying naked on the bed,
eyes fixed blankly on the ceiling.

"Parker!"

I toss her a pair of panties
and the T-shirt she left on the floor.

"Hurry!"

Finally, she sits up, slides
the shirt over her head
just as the doorknob turns.
She pulls the hem down over
her crotch, sits on the undies.

Colleen bombs through the door.
Thank God I'm dressed.

                Still, she's suspicious.
                Uh, what are you two up to?

I cringe. That's what Eloise said
right before she swung
a broom at Storm and me.

Parker stifles a laugh. I shoot her
an STFU glare, answer for both of us.
"I was writing to Storm and
Parker decided to take a nap."

                Colleen turns her focus
                toward Parker. *A nap?*

Yeah. I had a migraine.

Since when do you get migraines?

Cluster headaches, actually.
They come in waves.

First time since you've been here?

Parker nods. Stress causes them.
Probably because of school starting.

Did you take something for it?

Acetaminophen. Had to. Sorry.

You're supposed to ask, you know.
And next time, start with prayer.
"And the Lord will take away from
you all sickness." Deuteronomy 7:15.

Next time I definitely will.

Fine. Well, I could use some help with
the groceries. You okay now, Parker?

Better. And I'm hungry.
Migraines give me an appetite.

Colleen looks confused,
but doesn't argue.

"We'll be right there."
As soon as Parker puts on her shorts.

I Shut the Door Behind Colleen

"That was close, you know."

Parker scoots to the edge
of the bed, spreads her legs,
offering a quite personal view.

>*Exciting, huh?*

"Seriously, don't take chances
like that. Please? For me?"

>She huffs. *Learn to live a little.*

She closes her legs.
Slips them into her undies.
Covers those with sensible shorts.
It strikes me how little I know about her.

I've only been with Colleen
and Jay for six months.
Parker showed up during the summer.
Our attraction was instantaneous.
But acting on it took a while.
Trust doesn't run rampant
in foster care circles.

Even after connecting
skin to skin, sharing personal
information has taken longer.

"Do you really get cluster headaches?"

>*No. But my mom did. They took*
>*her down worse than H, man.*
>*In fact, they almost made me glad*
>*she had easy access to dope.*

I have to admire how quickly
Parker invented that excuse.
Clever. But way too ballsy.

"I'm surprised Colleen
let you off so easily about
the acetaminophen."

We're not supposed to help
ourselves to any medicines,
not even over-the-counter types.

> *Hopefully she doesn't count them.*
> *I had a foster do that before.*
> *Knew exactly how many pills*
> *were in every single container.*

> She laughs. *Busted me with*
> *a bottle of cough syrup one time.*
> *An empty bottle, that is.*

"You drank a whole bottle?"

> *Yeah, baby. I was* (air quotes) *sick.*

"Gross, Parker. That stuff
tastes like absolute crap."

> *Uh, Lake? You don't drink it*
> *for the flavor. And, as you know,*
> *surviving some placements requires*
> *extraordinary measures.*

I do know.
Very well.

STORM
IT WAS UNREASONABLY HOT

The day I met Jaidyn.
That was almost a year ago,
but I remember because it was
October and the weather guys
were freaking out about heat
waves and climate change.

I had to agree that ninety
degrees, closing in on Halloween,
could not be a good thing.

I was eating in the cafeteria,
where the air-conditioning
made things more pleasant.

I'd only recently moved
into this house with Jim,
so I hadn't yet checked out
the hot-lunch scene
at yet another new school.

I was trying to decide
between garlic chicken or veggie
pasta. Guess I took too long because
someone gave me a little nudge.

I spun, expecting to get into
somebody's face. Only it belonged
to a girl, and this is what I saw:

>Auburn hair spiked short
>and tipped bright red.

>Dimples creasing the blush
>of her cheeks.

    Freckles—few, but noticeable—
    spattering her nose.

    Super-long lashes fringing
    eyes the color of topaz.

    Lips, full and soft like heart-
    shaped pillows.

She flashed an incredible smile—
a straight, even row of pearls.

    Take the chicken. It's got
    veggies, too. Plus protein.

I never sputter. But I did right then.
"Uh . . . uh . . . protein's good."

    Jaidyn laughed. *In moderation.*
    You need a balanced diet.

Why was this stunning girl
talking about diets with me?
And what was that luscious
perfume she was wearing?

The kids behind us were getting
impatient. I picked the chicken,
wandered over to a semi-deserted table.

She followed. *Okay if I sit with you?*

But she didn't wait, settling
on the bench beside me,
even as I stuttered, "I g-guess."

Okay, I'd Hooked Up

With a few girls before.
Hit-and-run. Nothing serious.
But this was the first who'd ever
approached so boldly. Why me?

> *I'm Jaidyn.*

I swallowed. "Storm."

> *You're new here.*

"Do you know everyone
at this school?"

> *No. But I'd know if I'd seen you
> before. Are you a senior?*

"Junior."

> *Me too. Maybe we'll have
> a class together.*

I glanced around, trying to
discern a reason for her attention.

"Am I a dare or something?"

> *She chimed a laugh. No.
> What makes you say that?*

"It's just . . . Never mind.
I'm probably not reading
this correctly."

> *Well, what if you are?*

I HAVE NO CLUE

Why Jaidyn decided to take
a chance on me. A problem kid
from the wrong side of the universe?
Seriously, we were galaxies apart.

But some weird gravitational pull
crashed us into each other.
I asked her why she initiated
contact. She said she was drawn
to strays. So maybe it wasn't gravity.

We had three classes together,
including coed PE. Jaidyn was spectacular
in gym shorts and a white T-shirt.
I wasn't the only guy who
couldn't keep his eyes off her.

But her eyes kept coming back to me.
I didn't know what to do with
that. She had to ask me out first.
Luckily, my foster was cool with it.

> *Football games are fine*, said Jim.
> *Movies, too. Just be home before
> midnight. No curfew violations.*

Then he reminded me to treat
Jaidyn like a lady. I didn't need
to be told. And now, eleven
months later, we're still together.
It's mind-blowing, for a couple of reasons.

One, I'm still in Jim's house.
The last time I stayed in a placement
this long was at the Whittingtons'.

And Two

Jaidyn loves me almost as much
as I love her. Not that I tell her
often enough. I'm scared
if I do, poof! She'll vanish.

And if she did, I'd lose
the most amazing girl.
She's like . . .

The crisp inhalation
deep into your lungs,
post–peppermint candy.

The breeze-blown green
perfume of a freshly mown lawn
through an open window.

The little jerk of the chains
on a really big swing, right
before you drop.

The prismatic glimpse
of a double rainbow
in a misty shower of sunshine.

All those things
are so simple, yet perfect,
and in those moments
happiness shivers.

And that's what it's like
when I'm with Jaidyn.

SHE'S PICKING ME UP NOW

Saturday, late morning.
Her parents will be gone all day,
which means we can spend
it together alone at her house.

It's like the best birthday
present ever. Even if my actual
birthday was yesterday.

I pace the sidewalk, anxious
to see her   kiss her   touch her.
Ten minutes feels like thirty.

Finally, her VW Golf pulls to the curb.
When I open the door, she starts
singing "Birthday Cake," by Rihanna.
The song, which isn't about pastry, is hot.

Almost as hot as Jaidyn, in a tight
pink tank, scooped low enough
to reveal some luscious curves.

    "Cake, cake, cake, cake..."

"Hold on. Give me a kiss for now
and we can worry about
that icing in a few minutes."

She humors me, tracing
the outline of my mouth
with the tip of her tongue.

    Okay, birthday boy. Let's party!

It's a Short Drive

Threading city streets, hip-hop
blaring, to an older neighborhood,
shaded by stately trees.

Jaidyn's house was built
almost a hundred years ago,
but has been restored to like new.
She says it's her mom's passion.
One she happens to share.

Inside, the place smells like cocoa
and vanilla. "You been baking?"

>*Wouldn't be much of a birthday
>party without cake, would it?*

"I thought you meant cake
like in the song."

>*We can have both.*

"Starting in the kitchen?"

>*You know better. But first, shoes.*

We leave them by the door.
Socks won't mar the finish
on the polished hardwood.
We take a running start and . . .

She slides way better than me.
Then again, she's had more
practice. None of the places
I've lived had floors like these.

NONE HAVE HAD BEDS

Like Jaidyn's, either.
It's huge, with tall legs and a white
canopy like a frilly umbrella.
I pull back the blanket.

"You know what could
 make this bed better?"

    What?

"You. Come here."

She yanks off that tight tank,
climbs up beside me.
Why, why, why is this so easy?

"You wanna be the cake first?"

    Nah. It's your birthday.

We devour each other
until nothing's left but crumbs.

    That was too fast, she sighs.

"Couldn't help it. Been thinking
about it for days. But give me a few
and we'll go for a slow ride."

    She flops against the pillow.
    I love you, you know.

I close my eyes. Breathe in
the intoxicating scent of our skin.
We're floating, riding a raft
on a lazy stretch of river . . .

Downstream Drift

In this place,

> the current flows gently,
> unhurried, not worried
> by storm or boulders.

In this time,

> the quiet tide is enough,
> ripple teasing ripple,
> wet skin against wet skin.

In this moment,

> her tongue against mine,
> cool mint provocation,
> initiates the torrent.

In this instant,

> no dam could halt us;
> we would find our way over
> or drill straight through.

Unstoppable now,

> wave upon wave
> nothing to halt
> our forward momentum.

Rolling,

> swelling
> cresting
> emptying.

Words Froth Behind My Lips

I hold them back as long
as I can, afraid of their power.
But when Jaidyn sighs and lays
her ear against my chest, they gush.

"I love you."

   She stays quiet. Disappears
   into herself. Finally, she responds.

      Don't say it if it's a lie.

"Jai, there are two people
in the world I'd never lie
to. My sister. And you."

      Why do you only tell me
      you love me once in a while?

I admit, "I'm afraid I'll jinx us."

      You're superstitious?

"Not really. I just know
how life works. My life, anyway.

You're the one exception
to an otherwise totally
fucked-up existence
and I don't deserve you."

      Tough. You're stuck with me.
      Ready to blow out some candles?

NOT ONLY

Did Jaidyn bake me a cake,
she decorated it, too.

With flawless white icing
and purple flowers
all around "Storm."

"Who taught you how
to do this? Your mom?"

>   She laughs. *No way. My mom's
>   excellent with a hammer
>   and saw, but she doesn't bake.*
>
>   *Nah. You can learn just about
>   anything on YouTube. Plus,
>   I like cooking shows on TV.*

I *oof* audibly.

>   *What?*

"Nothing. Just reminded me
of my mom. She was a huge
Hell's Kitchen fan."

>   *She liked to cook?*

"No. She wanted to screw
Gordon Ramsay."

Jaidyn kisses my neck.

>   *No worries*, she whispers
>   into my ear. *Gordon's not
>   my type. I just want to do you.*

I push back from the table.
Pull her into my lap.
Kiss her like I mean it,
and I totally do.

"I love you."

      Little kiss.

"I love you."

      Sweet kiss.

"I love you."

      Sensual kiss.

"I love you."

      Hot kiss.

"Hope that makes up
for a few of the times
I should've said it but didn't."

      Not even close.
      But it's a start.
      And there's plenty
      of time for you
      to make up the rest.

She Lights Seventeen Candles

I extinguish them
in a single mighty blow.

We eat cake and ice cream for lunch.

Have to spend twenty minutes
cleaning up after a cake fight.

I've never had a cake fight before.
Didn't realize how far icing could fly.

I watch Jaidyn bend over
to wipe a few errant drops.

She is something. And she loves me.

Emotions upwell suddenly.
No, damn it.

I can't subscribe to hope.
Let alone happiness.

Those two words have never
belonged to me.

I don't dare try to own them now.

I bite hard on my lip
to keep the tears at bay.

    Jaidyn straightens, stares
    at me. *What's wrong?*

"Nothing. It's just this has been
the greatest birthday ever."

JAIDYN NODS

As if she understands.
Not sure you can really know
what it's like unless you've
walked this particular walk.

> *Your birthday's not over yet.*
> *I've got something for you.*

I never even noticed the shiny
wrapped gift on the counter.

> *I couldn't get you a puppy,*
> *so I got the next best thing.*

It's a T-shirt, with a picture
of Rex and twelve-year-old me
silk-screened on it.

So much for not crying.
"But . . . how . . . ?"

> *Remember that time you showed*
> *me your pictures you keep in*
> *an envelope? And you told me*
> *how much Rex meant to you?*

> *Your foster dad helped me*
> *scan the photo. You're not mad,*
> *are you? We put it right back.*

"Jim helped? When?"

> *That day last summer he sent you*
> *on a bus to Santa Clara to pick*
> *up farmers market peaches . . .*

That Little Outing

Took a half day.
Santa Clara is, like, forty miles,
and forever by bus, away.
I couldn't figure out why
supermarket peaches
weren't good enough for cobbler.

But Jim loves to cook.
Says food, foster kids,
and Morley keep him busy
and out of trouble.

So, if he needed
farm-grown organic
fruit, no problem.
I went with the flow.

Am I mad they went through
my stuff? Not like they were
trying to steal anything.
Besides, Jim had every right to.
It goes with the territory.

> Jim said we could just take
> a pic of Morley for your shirt.
> I told him maybe for some
> Christmas socks. We could
> put a Santa hat on him.

That makes me laugh.
It also makes me happy
for once, thinking
about Christmas.

Holidays

Especially the ones that come
in December, tend to be
problematic for foster kids.

Most of us believe any celebrations
are in spite of us, not because of us.
We're not family. Not even real guests.

Gifts feel like requirements.
Afterthoughts, even.

I remember every Christmas
placement. Good. Bad. Disturbing.
One time at Floyd's (good), this
little kid—Zeke—cried and cried
to spend the day with his mom.

The same mom who decorated
his arms with cigarette burns.

I felt sorry for him, but
after a while I got pissed
and showed him the pocks.
"Look what she did to you!"

> *I know*, he sniveled. *But
> she's sorry. She said so.
> Besides, she's my mommy.*

I couldn't understand
loving his mother so much
that he could forgive her
for branding him
with her own pain.

THE BAD THINGS

My mom did to Lake and me
didn't compare, yet forgiving her
for them has never been in my plans.

I prefer holidays in care.
At least I know I'll be fed
and usually the food's good.

Sometimes I get dragged to church.
I don't believe in God, but I like
the carols, and the Christmas story
seems all about hope.

One time I was placed with
a Jewish family. Hanukkah?
Eight days of candles, games,
and gifts did lift my spirits a little.

That was some heavy lifting,
too, because Lake and I had
just been separated
for the first time in our lives.

Levi and Anna had two kids
of their own, and another
foster, so even without Lake
it was hard to feel lonely.

Levi had an incredible voice,
and when he sang the prayers,
I closed my eyes and this sensation
of peace threaded through me.
I never felt anything quite
like it before, or since.

It Didn't Make Me a Believer

But it did give me a clue as to what
people go looking for in churches
and mosques and synagogues.

A sense that all is well when little is.
Permission to relinquish control,
understanding you're powerless,
looking into the face of the Universe.

It also made me alternately
respect and loathe those
who take advantage of weak minds.

Using misplaced faith to achieve
your goals is admirable in one way.
Encouraging minimum-wage workers
to toss their kids' lunch money
into bottomless offering plates is cruel.

Convincing your followers that the end
of the world allows them, and only
them, safe passage on the freeway
to heaven is totally messed up.

But then I come back to what kind
of idiot sacrifices their last dime
to a guy who flies a private jet
and lives in a thirty-room mansion?
And what's up with this anxiously
awaiting the Apocalypse bullshit?

Some of us still have things
we want to do, places we plan to see.
And amazing girls like Jaidyn
to make love with.

LAKE
TRYING TO FIT IN

At this school is impossible.
The cliques only socialize
within their ranks, which
are mostly organized by
the vehicles in student parking.
From the top down:

        Beamers and Range Rovers
        (Ivy League bound)

        Newer Mustangs and Camaros
        (Cheerleaders and jocks)

        Classic Mustangs and Camaros
        (Quirky, with money)

        Teslas and Audi e-trons
        (Poli-sci majors)

        Bolts and Konas
        (Scholarship winners)

        Kawasakis and Yamahas
        (Bad boys, bad-ass girls)

        Newer economy cars
        (FAFSA seekers)

        Older economy cars
        (After-school workers)

        Bicycles
        (Geeks too young to drive)

Parker and I ride the bus.
Which tells you how we rank.

How many seniors ride the bus?
I started here late last year,
when I was placed with Jay and Colleen.

Before that, I lived with the Hipsters,
who were super cool. (Too cool,
social services finally decided.
Can't have foster kids enjoying life.)

While I was there, I went to a charter.
The curriculum was heavy into theater,
music, even cooking. It was my favorite
school ever, but light on transferable credits.

I had to take summer school
to catch up, and I'm still behind.
To graduate on time, I have to make up
geometry online. Oh, and pass my classes.
That could prove problematic.

I hate this school. I feel like I've got
a red *F* for *Foster* tattooed on my face.
I don't know how they know, but they do.
If I get a smile, it's a sneer, followed
by a snicker. Mostly they turn away.

Maybe it's my clothes. The girls here
are all, like, Nordstrom or Urban Outfitters,
with the occasional Forever 21.

I prefer upcycling thrift store oddities.
Amazing what some people toss.
At the charter, we made it a weekend
game. Who could find excellent stuff
for the cheapest, then dress best on Monday?

Parker likes my weird fashion taste.
No one else here seems to agree.

Including my teachers, except for Ms. Bolton (English), who's into the shabby chic look herself, and Mr. Mason (theater), who enjoys cosplay.

I Only Have One Class

With Parker. Ironically, chemistry.
She's not much into chem.

We're currently sitting next to each
other, last row, but while I'm doing
my best to pay attention to the periodic
table, Parker keeps touching me.
First, with her foot. We're wearing sandals
and her toes thrum against my straps.

When I don't respond, she reaches
across the space between us, slides
her palm over the back of my hand.

"Quit," I finally whisper.

A pair of Newer Mustangs turn to gawk.

>*What the fuck's your problem?*
>Parker growls at them.

One snort-laughs. The other gives
the hugest eye roll I've ever seen.
The exchange ignites the classroom.

"Jesus, Parker, shut up."

She jerks her hand away quite
obviously, and now everyone
understands. Apparently,
that includes Mrs. Pederson.

>*Ahem... this class will prove easier*
>*if you pay attention. So, please keep*
>*your eyes—and hands—to yourselves.*

BARELY THREE WEEKS

Into a new school year and already
on a teacher's shit list. Awesome.

I love Parker, but she's impulsive.
Speaks before she thinks.

I don't need my teachers
to care about me. I just want
them to give me a fair shake.
That won't happen
if they decide I'm trouble.

Maintaining decent grades
when you change schools
way too often is challenging.
But somehow, I've managed it.

I'm not sure why it's important.
College is likely out of reach.
But it always seemed like one
small thing I could succeed at.

More, it was something,
maybe the only thing,
I could control.

Plus, it made my brother
take pride in me, which
probably wouldn't sound
like much to most people.

But it means everything.
He's the only person
who's ever been proud of me.

THE BELL RINGS

Parker grabs her stuff, stalks off,
loudly singing "abcdefu,"
a Gayle song about breaking up.
So now she's pissed at me?

She's always thought
my educational aspirations
are pretty much pointless.
The only classes she finds
worthwhile are chorus and drama.

Chorus = music.
Drama = Parker.
I catch up to her anyway.
"Hey. Why'd you take off?"

    She keeps walking. *Figured being*
    seen with a lesbian might embarrass you.

I put my hand on her arm, tug
her to a stop. "I really don't care
who knows about you and me.
Adding the L-word to my résumé
would probably impress a few."

    A grin stretches cheek to cheek.
    Probably. Especially a couple of guys.

"I have to get to class. See you at—"

    Wait. I don't embarrass you?

"No, girlfriend."

    Prove it.

PARKER BLOCKS MY PATH

The hallway's crowded,
and people are forced
to stream around us.

A few stare.
A few laugh.
A few flip us off.

Whatever.
I know what she wants,
and for me to not be late,
I kiss her.

"There. Now Honors English
awaits. See you at lunch, okay?"

I hustle through the door
just as the tardy bell rings.
Ms. Bolton notices, but I don't think
she marks me late.

We're reading *The Great Gatsby*,
and today's discussion is
the roles of women in the book.

> *Not so long ago, a major glass ceiling*
> *was shattered when we elected a woman*
> *to the office of vice president,* Ms. Bolton
> says.
>
> *What glass ceiling was broken just prior*
> *to Fitzgerald's "Jazz Age"?*

I'm rarely the first to raise my hand,
but when no one else does,
up mine goes. "Women's suffrage."

> *Yes. Thank you. And with the right*
> *to vote, American women changed . . .*

We talk about jazz.
Speakeasies. Cigarettes.
Women's fashion—corsets
to miniskirts.

Marriage. Affairs, and
the reasons for them.

Women in the kitchen.
Women in the workplace.
Women at the polls.

Traditionalism versus modernism.
How *Gatsby*'s three female
protagonists represent one or both.

Women's emerging rights then
versus women's rights now.
How far have we come, really?

It's a great conversation.
That's how it feels, not like
we're being force-fed information.

Honors English.
And my comments are as valued
as everyone else's.

For once I feel like an equal.

THE HIGH SPIKES AFTER CLASS

As I leave, Ms. Bolton stops me.

                     Miss Carpenter?

Damn. She's going to dock me
after all, or at least issue a warning.
I start to apologize but realize
suddenly that's not what she's after.

                    Thanks for diving in and answering
                    my question. I hate when I have
                    to do all the talking. Sometimes I'm not
                    even sure my students are reading.

"But it's an honors class."

                    Exactly. Makes no sense, but that
                    seems to be the case, even in honors.
                    Easier just to skim SparkNotes.

"But how can you get the nuance,
the intent, the language? How can you
hear Fitzgerald if you don't read him?"

                    She smiles. *I knew I liked you.*
                    Go on now. Don't be late for class.

She winks, and I understand
if maybe I'm a minute or two tardy,
I'll probably be okay here.

                    By the way, I love your skirt.
                    It's cute with that vest.

GUESS I WAS RIGHT

I thank her and hurry to
government, still buzzing.
Learning about gerrymandering
blunts the high a little.

But it isn't until lunch
that I'm reminded who I am
will forever eclipse who I might become.

Parker trades the Disciples'
disgusting bologna sandwiches
for a couple of Marlboros, and we head
to the far side of the parking lot.

Yeah, cigarettes are poison.
I never thought I'd touch them.
But then along came Parker.

> *How can we kiss if you don't smoke,
> too? You'll think I taste gross.*

"Maybe you should quit instead."

> *Yeah. But I won't. It relaxes me.*

I resisted but Parker persisted,
and eventually I relented.

I don't like the way they taste.
I don't know if they relax you.
I don't even inhale.

I puff to be amenable.
I puff to be companionable.
I puff in sensory self-defense.

One Small Problem

Neither of us has a lighter.
"Shit. Now what?"

> *Beg, borrow, or steal.*

Clichés aside, I study the parking
lot, looking for someone who can
accommodate one of the three.

> *What about him?*

I see where Parker's pointing.
Kit Beaumont. Leaning against
the hood of his obnoxious pickup,
tempting the stoner crowd
as they exit the buildings for lunch.

I don't know many people here,
but I'm aware of Kit's reputation.

He's only on campus because
it's a condition of his probation.
He's the last human on earth
you want to ask a favor of.

So, of course Parker ambles
over, which means I have to follow.

> *Hey, Kit.* She flashes her unlit
> cigarette. *Can you help us out?*

If his eyes were hands
he'd be groping her.

> *What's in it for me?*

        Parker gives him a flirty
        smile. *What do you want?*

Now his eyes feel *me* up.

             How about a three-way?

"That's an awfully steep price
for a light, don't you think?"

             Kit shrugs. *You might like it.*

"Don't think so."

             Parker winks. *You never know.*

Kit grins, pulls out a Joe Camel lighter.

             Here you go. Hey. You girls in
             the market for a little Vitamin K?
             Goes good with you-know-what.

I'm not above the occasional toke of weed,
but ketamine makes people weird.
And you-know-what with Parker
doesn't require artificial stimulants.

"Sorry. All out of money."

             I've got s—

             Later. Here comes that damn security
             dude. You can find me at Zephyr
             Fun Center most afternoons.

I don't look behind us.
Just start walking. Fast.

PARKER YELLS TO WAIT UP

"Keep up!" I call back over
 the shouting at our rear.
 Can't tell who it's directed to,
 just Kit or Parker and me, too.
"Shit, shit, shit."

 I toss my lit Marlboro
 but don't stop to grind it out.
 Kit's pickup growls to life,
 screeches across the parking lot.

 Smoking isn't as bad
 as purchasing ketamine,
 but cigarettes are contraband
 and could definitely rate
 a three-day suspension.

 Plus, I really would rather
 not be on the school's radar.

 I circle a few parked
 cars before heading back
 toward the main building.

> *Will you please slow the hell down?*

"Is that guy behind us?"

> *No. He turned around when Kit took off.*

"Think he knows Kit's dealing?"

> *Duh.*

THE REAL QUESTION IS

"Think he thinks we were buying?"

        Parker shrugs. *Maybe. But then
        he'd probably still be behind us.*

Guess we're in the clear.
Still, I merge into a crowd swirling
toward the main entrance. I notice
the security guard talking to the vice
principal, but their attention
doesn't turn toward me or Parker.

We also pass Ms. Bolton,
who definitely recognizes me.

I don't know if she actually saw
Parker and me fraternizing
with Kit or noticed us smoking.
I don't know if she cares.
But it's a reminder of how fragile
my place in the world really is.

One stupid decision,
one dumb mistake,
can change everything.

A girl—young, probably
a freshman—wearing upscale
hippie fashion checks
me out as I pass her by.

        She nods appreciatively. *Peace.*

Oh, honey. There is no peace
in my life. None. Not ever.

After the Final Bell

Parker and I take a bus downtown
to spend some of our clothing allowance.
As September withers, we'll need fall shoes.

Parker's good with sneakers,
but I'm hoping to find a decent
pair of boots, and the only place
that's likely to happen for the amount
of cash I have is a thrift store.

There's a discount shoe store
across the street from the bus stop.
We go there first, for Parker's canvas.
Cute styles. Lots of colors. And cheap.
If my thrifting fails me, I'll have to come back.

We head over to Re-Boutique,
one of my favorite secondhand stores.
But I don't see what I'm looking for.
"Let's try Margaret's."

Parker is an expert at hiding
her emotions, but a huge bolt
of apprehension zaps me,
and we're not even touching.

"I know it's a rough part of town,
but I've never had a problem there.
Anyway, it's daytime. As long as
we stick together, we'll be okay."

> *If you say so. But I wish we had
> pepper spray or something.*

IT'S A TEN-MINUTE STROLL

Sidewalks and storefronts
deteriorate the closer we get.

After dark, the area will crawl
with drug dealers and their customers,
but all we see now are a few homeless people.
We hurry by, arm locked in arm,
backpacks tucked between us.

Margaret's vibe is less upscale than
Re-Boutique, and it isn't as organized,
but Parker finds something immediately.

Hey, look. Fits perfectly, too.

It's a brilliant black leather jacket.
Pricey for secondhand, but she claims
she's got money burning holes in her bag.

And, scouring the place top to bottom,
I find a broken-in but not broken pair
of Doc Martens, only a half size too big.

A little polish will make them better
than new, and Margaret is willing to deal
for both boots and leather jacket.
Double score! I've still got five bucks
when we leave, new old boots in my backpack.

The bus stop is several blocks away.
The sidewalk's more crowded,
and it's a sketchy bunch. Kind of
wishing for bear spray myself.

Parker nudges me. *Check her out.*

THE GIRL ISN'T MUCH OLDER

Than we are, and dressed to invite
the attention of men on the prowl.

"Wait. I know her. We shared
a bedroom one time."
Where was it? Placements blur.
It was...

After Rose and her poodle.

Rarely do I indulge in anger,
but when my caseworker
told me I had to leave,
I gorged on it for a while.

Losing a good placement
is always hard.

Losing a first best friend,
who also happens to be your first
crush, not so long after losing
your brother, is impossible.

Melanie and I had no say.
She went one way, I went another.
I have no idea where she ended up.

As for me, I wound up
in a house with three other girls,
all of them fosters.

One of them is standing
over there on that corner,
scamming "clientele."

I'M DRAWN TO SAY HELLO

Maybe because, as I recall,
she was the only one
of those three other girls
who acknowledged my pain.

"Hey! Star!"

Her head jerks sideways
and she squints.

"Come on," I tell Parker.
"I want to say hi."

We approach warily.
An aura of fear surrounds her.
She's probably got a john
nearby, keeping watch.

"It's me. Lake."

        Star nods. *I remember. How you doin'?*

"I've been worse. You?"

        She shrugs. *Surviving.*

"Need anything?"

        Three or four tricks before the night
        is through. Gotta keep my old man happy.

"What happened to college?"
We plotted about it over homework.
She was into school, like I was.

        Best-laid plans, you know?

> *Aging out sucks. No place to live.*
> *Hard to find a job. How would*
> *I manage to pay for college?*

"Grants. FAFSA. You're smart.
Maybe even a full-ride scholarship."

> *Easier said than done. Anyway,*
> *this work isn't hard. Only requires*
> *a few basic skills. She winks.*

Parker and I laugh, but
my stomach's churning.
I don't want to end up here.

> *That's my man waving at me.*
> *Better get back to it. Was good*
> *to see you. Hold on to your dreams,*
> *you hear? Someone has to.*

Star goes back to her corner,
and as Parker and I start
down the sidewalk, a Tesla pulls
up, window rolled down.

Star circles the car and
gets inside. As they drive away,

> Parker tsks. *Too bad.*

"It is."
It really is.

STORM
JAIDYN PICKS ME UP BEFORE SCHOOL

Nice having a chauffeur
who kisses me good morning
like I just got home
from war or something.

"What did I do to deserve that?"

    You wore your Rex shirt.

"Better wear it every day, then."

    She wrinkles her nose.
    Only if you wash it every night.

Jaidyn hits the gas, and we get
to school well before the bell.

We're standing out front,
talking to her friend Delilah,
when Jaidyn's ex walks by.
He bumps me hard and Jaidyn reacts.

    Fuck you, Lance!

        You wish. Can't your loser
        boyfriend get it up?

    Takes him a little longer than you.
    Mostly because he's three times bigger.

        Damn, says Delilah. *Burn.*

A knot of girls hoots.
A couple of dudes snicker.
Jaidyn might have gone too far.

You shut your hole, bitch.

"That's enough, asshole."

I pull myself tall, thrust my chest,
clench my hands. I don't want to hit him.
Don't need this kind of trouble.
But he can't talk shit to Jaidyn.

Whatcha gonna do about it?

Good question. I can't speak
to dick size, but Lance has got
two inches in height and at least
that in reach on me.

I'm calculating my odds
when the bell rings.
A human stampede rushes
the door, pushing Lance forward.

He glances back once, flips us
off, keeps moving with the flow.

Not sure what that was about.
This is a pretty big school,
but it's not like we don't run
into Lance once in a while.

He's never been friendly,
but he hasn't ever seemed
particularly offended by
seeing Jaidyn and me together.
Still, I'm careful to look over
my shoulder the rest of the day.

On the Ride Home

I ask Jaidyn if she knows what's up.

> *I heard his girlfriend broke*
> *it off with him. Frustration?*

Come to think of it, every
time we saw him in the past
he was with a tall, dark-haired girl.

"But why take it out on us?"

> She's quiet for a second.
> *It's football season.*

"I don't get it."

> *When he's playing, he ups his steroids.*
> *Mara was crying in the locker room*
> *last week. Said he pushed her around.*
> *I told her that was probably why.*

Girlfriend broke up with him.
Could be Jaidyn's fault.
It hits me that she and I have never
discussed why she split with Lance.
"Did he ever push you around?"

> *Sort of. He grabbed me a couple*
> *of times. Hard enough to leave bruises.*

> *And when he was mad, there was*
> *something in his eyes that scared me.*

"He never bothered you
after you broke it off?"

He was kind of stalkerish.
Like he'd turn up places where
I was. The mall. The movies.
But that stopped when you and I got
together and he and Mara hooked up.

"Maybe this morning was just
a one-off. But be careful.
And if he does *anything*,
I want to know right away."

The whole episode makes me uneasy.
But nothing else happens.
If Lance is lurking in the shadows,
he doesn't show himself.
My trouble radar quiets.

Jaidyn and I make plans to go
to Friday night's home football game.
Not to watch Lance hold the offensive
line, though that seems appropriate.

We buy tickets.
Decide where to eat
beforehand. Everything's a go.

But Thursday after school
Jim has news.

> *I heard from your sister's*
> *caseworker today. She can*
> *arrange for a short visit.*

"With Lake? Really?"

I Tamp Down Expectation

It's been forever, with no word.

> *Yes, with Lake.*

"When?"

> *Tomorrow evening. She thought*
> *you could have dinner. I'm sorry.*
> *I know you and Jaidyn were—*

"No. No. She'll understand."
Still, when I call to let her know,
I suck in a deep breath, hold it.

> *Oh, I'm so happy for you.*
> *I know it's been a long time.*

I expel all that air from my lungs.
"I'll make the game up to you!
Oh, Jai. I'm so stoked! Hey, have
I told you I loved you lately?"

I do. And I love my sister.
And I get to see her tomorrow.
I can barely eat. Anticipation
flutters in my stomach.

I can barely sleep. Recollections
flicker on and off like old movies.
I only wish they were kinder.

But maybe there's still time.
Maybe Lake and I can create new
memories to carry forward.

SCHOOL IS IMPOSSIBLE THIS MORNING

I keep reading the same
pages over and over,
in English even, and still
they make no sense.

Every class drags,
minute by minute by minute,
until the bell makes me jump,
each one bringing me
a little closer to Lake.

Jaidyn decides to go
to the game without me.
No problem. We'll meet up
tomorrow, hang out, and swap
stories about our Friday nights.

>*Pick you up around noon?*
>she asks when she drops
>me off at home.

"Perfect. Love you. Be good.
Never mind. You're always good."

>*Wait.* She hands me a small
>box, gift wrapped. *I got this*
>*for Lake. It's a bottle of Daisy.*

"Your perfume?"

>*I used to wear it, but switched*
>*to Cloud. I still love Daisy, though,*
>*and hope your sister will, too.*

SHE IS AMAZING

I tell her that, give her a long,
deep kiss for the road.

"Hey, Jim," I call, once inside.
"I'm going to take a shower."

I kind of expect he'll come
tell me tonight's been canceled.

                But he yells, *Okay! We should*
                leave around 4:30. Traffic.

Bay Area roads can be bumper-
to-bumper any time of day.

But late afternoon on Friday
they're total quagmires.

I deposit my backpack in my room.
Search my drawers for clothes.

Grab the nicest pair of jeans I own,
plus my (clean) Rex shirt.

Lake will get a kick out of that.
It will be the perfect icebreaker.

Weird to need one, but four years
apart have made Lake and I strangers.

How can I feel such a deep bond
with someone I no longer know?

Standing Beneath

A rivulet of steaming water,
I think back to the events
that forced us apart.

Eloise fostered for money,
so she took us both in.
We arrived, afraid to be hopeful.
She proved us right.
From the start, our closeness
scratched at her.
That grew into suspicion.

After an awful day at school,
Lake was hugging me.
We were fully clothed.
But Eloise saw us, screamed
incest! and called social services.

Our caseworker, Pam,
believed our denial.
She understood the link
between Lake and me.
But her hands were tied.

It was an ugly scene.
My sister and I had never
been separated before.

I begged to stay.
Eloise insisted no way.
Lake sobbed her own pleas.
But Eloise wanted me gone.
She didn't even mind
losing the stipend.

Pam Did Her Best

To keep Lake and me in touch
for the next year or so.
We exchanged letters.
Scheduled phone calls.
But it wasn't easy.

Levi and Anna, my fosters,
were happy to let us communicate.
Eloise, not so much.

>This was her bullshit excuse.
>*It upsets Lake when she talks*
>*to Storm. Best just leave her alone.*

Pam did manage to arrange
a face-to-face on our thirteenth
birthday. We celebrated with
pizza and ice cream cones.
The day was bittersweet.

Sweet: Precious hours with Lake,
who I hadn't seen in eleven months.

She'd grown two inches.
Her hair had grown five.
Still sapling thin, her cheeks
were hollows. Sadness glittered
in her eyes. She was beautiful.

Bitter: Knowing our fragile
bond would break again.
When we parted, returned
to our separate worlds,
the severing ripped me apart.

I'VE MOSTLY SEWN

Myself back together,
But the stitching is weak.
I hope a visit with Lake can reinforce
it. Maybe now we can stay in touch.

It takes an hour twenty
to drive, like, thirty-five miles.
By the time we pull into
the restaurant parking lot,
I'm shaking. "Hey, Jim? Thanks."

     For what?

"Braving the freeways for me."

     No problem. Ready?

I am. I'm not.
I get out of the car.
Follow Jim inside.
It takes ten seconds to spot her.

Maybe because she scans
every face that walks through
the door and when she sees mine
she jumps up, comes running.

We crash into each other,
but the only pain is what we've held
inside for so very long.
It escapes in two exhaled words.

"Lake."   *Storm.*

By Mutual Silent Agreement

We sit barely touching,
in need of proximity without
raising some weird suspicion.
                          Unthinkable.
We've both brought letters
and cards we couldn't send,
or that came back to us.
                          Undeliverable.
But we leave those for later.
We talk about school.
My girlfriend. Her only friend.
                          Unfamiliar.
We swap stories about
placements. Fosters.
Best of. Worst of.
                          Uncategorized.
Lake explains her fashion
sense, shopping at thrift
stores, vintage versus new.
                          Uninhibited.
I tell her about fistfights,
things learned in lockup.
She looks disappointed.
                          Uncomfortable.
I make a quick diversion.
We discuss dogs. Rex.
Morley. A senile poodle.
                          Unpedigreed.
Eventually we stumble
across information
we should have had by now.
                          Unbelievable.

It's Tossed at Us

By Lake's caseworker, Candace.
She and Jim have been quietly
eating pasta, trying not to interrupt
the conversation across the table.

When we finally quiet,
Candace clears her throat.

> *Sorry to be the bearer*
> *of bad news, and you should*
> *have known this sooner,*
> *but I just found out myself.*

"Sounds ominous," I comment.

> *Your grandmother passed*
> *away six weeks ago.*

The information sinks in
slowly, like through quicksand.
Lake's expression changes
from impassive to morbidly curious.

> *How? Was she murdered?*

I could totally see that.
But that's the kind of thing
Candace would lead off with—
your grandmother was murdered.

> *No. She was hit by a car.*

"Which doesn't completely
rule out murder."

I think it's funny, but

my joke crashes and burns.

>Candace shakes her head.
>*Dark street. Drunk driver.*
>*Camera showed her wobble*
>*off the sidewalk right in front*
>*of the guy. He never saw her.*

That is some serious karma.

>*I thought someone should*
>*tell you both in person, which*
>*is how I was able to arrange*
>*this visit. Thankfully, Colleen,*
>*Jay, and Jim agreed.*

"It's messed up that's what
it took. But thanks anyway."

>*Storm . . .* warns Jim.

>*It's okay,* Candace interjects.
>*I understand and happen to agree.*
>*Let's see if we can do better, okay?*

Did they bury her? asks Lake.

>*I don't know.*

Lake's jaw goes rigid.
I hope they burned her so
she can't ever come back.

Harsh, But I Get It

Jim and Candace, however,
look quite concerned.

I try to lighten the mood.
"Pretty sure burning's for vampires.
Beverly was more of a money
sucker than a bloodsucker."

Only Lake laughs, and even
that is half-ass. Hey, I tried.

    Jim attempts a subject change.
    Anyone want dessert?

    I do, says Lake. *Every good*
    wake requires desserts.

Everyone smiles and orders
something sugary for the death party.

About the time Candace asks
for the check, I decide I should
at least inquire about our mother.
"Do you know what's up with Mom?"

    Sorry, no. I haven't heard
    a word from her since
    we removed you the last time.

Lake and I are given a few
minutes to say goodbye.
She doesn't have a cell, but
her fosters have a landline.
I put the number in my phone.

"It's great we can talk sometimes.

Jim will be cool with it. What about
your people—uh, Colleen and Jay?"

> *Just don't say the Lord's name*
> *in vain if they can hear.*

"That kind, huh? Okay, no problem.
Hey. Should we feel bad about Beverly?"

> *Do you think she cared even*
> *a little about us?*

"No. But did you ever wonder
what made her so damn cold?"

> *Doesn't matter. Everyone has*
> *the choice whether to perpetuate*
> *their terrible childhoods. You and I*
> *grew up without love, but we can*
> *find it now. And pass it on.*

"We loved each other."

> *Still do. But we deserve more.*

I study her for a moment.
"You're tougher than I thought."

> *You're softer than I remember.*
> *Not in a bad way. But that*
> *sharp edge has tempered.*

I take that as a compliment.
And I credit it to Jaidyn.

WHICH REMINDS ME

"Hey. Almost forgot."
The pretty bottle is warm
from my pocket.

        Daisy?

"It's one of Jaidyn's favorites.
She knows how much I like it
and thought maybe you would, too."

Lake opens it carefully.
Dabs a bit on her wrists,
inhales the scent appreciatively.

        It's wonderful, like berries
        in a garden of jasmine. I love it.

"Do you wear perfume?"

        Sometimes. But I could never
        afford something this nice.

It's expensive? I'm clueless.

"You deserve nice things.
Someday I'll make sure
you have lots of them."

        I don't care about things.
        I just want to have you in my life.

"You will. I promise. Every time
you wear Daisy, remember that."

It Takes Under an Hour

To get home. I spend the minutes
going through Lake's notes
and cards. Her handwriting
is impressive. Unlike mine.

I hope she can read what I gave
her, and that it fills in the blanks for her
half as well as she does for me.

We talked about a funny poodle
at dinner. There's more about him
here. Also, something about a girl
Lake got close to. Melanie.
I sense there's more to that story.

When we were little, Lake
and I had this thing. Our sync.
Sort of a psychic connection.
Like, we could finish each other's
sentences, or even say out loud
what the other was thinking.

I have no idea if that kind
of thing fades with time
and distance, or if it's easily
rekindled, but this evening
when Lake was talking about
Parker, I had this feeling
they might be more than friends.

Tone of voice or tenor
of thought, I hope so.

If I deserve love, so does my sister.

I Try Calling Jaidyn

When we get home.
But no luck.
It's a little after nine,
so she's probably still
at the game.

I leave a voicemail.
"Hope you're having fun.
Tonight was awesome.
More tomorrow. See you
at noon. Oh. And I love you."

Jim asks me to watch a movie.
I decline, go to my room, spent.
Happiness is expensive
energy, I guess.

I put Lake's correspondence
on the nightstand. Kick off
my shoes. Toss my jeans
and Rex shirt on the chair, lie
on the bed, close my eyes.

My brain is a kaleidoscope.
Twist, twist.
Memory.
Twist, twist.
Photograph.
Twist, twist.
Paragraph.
Twist, twist.
Dream.

A Shimmer of Sunlight

Rouses me out of a series
of interconnecting dreams.
I was looking for something.
Started in one place. Moved
into another. And another.
In the end, it eluded me.

I wake, frustrated. But I'll see
Jaidyn soon. My spirits lift
and I hum through breakfast.

I'm ready by eleven.
Antsy by eleven thirty.
Anxious at five after twelve.
She isn't that late. But she's never late.
Twelve thirty, I call her.
She doesn't pick up, but if
she's driving she wouldn't.
I redial several times and when
I don't hear anything in an hour,
my stomach starts to knot.

Jim's in his office, writing.
"Can you drive me to Jaidyn's?"

*If you're really that worried,
of course. It's not like her, is it?*

Not at all, and that thought replays
the whole way there, churning my worry.
When we turn down her block,
I can see her car in front of her house.
That should make me feel better.
It doesn't.

LAKE
I OPEN MY EYES

Against the ashen wash
of early morning light.

Window: familiar.
Bed: ditto.
Pillow: same.
But there's something
different. Something new.
It takes a few for it to sink in.

Daisy.
Even hours old,
the fragrance lingers,
as if it has woven itself
into the threads of my sheets.

I think about Storm,
and how happy he looked
when he presented the bottle.

It reminded me of when
we were little and he'd draw
pictures or pick flowers for me.
They were all he could offer,
but more than enough
because they meant he loved me.

He has no idea
how expensive Daisy is.
I only know because I heard
some girls at school talking about it.
But the cost isn't what matters.
What does is every time
I wear it, he'll be with me.

Parker's Jealous

When I came in last night,
she was watching TV with Colleen
and Jay, whose eyes barely strayed
from the screen, even after
I announced, "I'm home!"

But Parker trailed me down the hall.
She watched me set a bundle
of letters and cards on the desk.

>*How did it go?*

"Weird and awesome."

>*Why was it weird, and . . .*
>She sniffed. *What do I smell?*

"Daisy. Like it?"

I put the bottle next to
Storm's correspondence.
She picked it up, opened it roughly.

"Careful. That stuff is pricey."

>*Really? Did he steal it?*

"Why are you such a bitch?"

>*It was just a joke.*

I held out my hand.
"Give it back."

She did.

I FOUGHT THE URGE

To say more.
                Defend.
                Explain.
                Apologize.

And why did I consider that?
Maybe because Parker looked
so hurt, and it was more
than just calling her a bitch.
What I saw in her eyes was envy.

It softened the edge, but didn't
blunt my anger completely.
I picked up one of Storm's letters.
"I need to read some of these."

She retreated to sitcom hell.
I sat, absorbing missing chapters
of my brother's life, for a couple
of hours. When Parker finally
crept back, she was contrite.

        Sorry.

"Me too."

        I'm glad you got to see Storm.

"Me too."

        And I like Daisy.

She went to bed.
I stayed up, reading.

FINALLY CRASHED AROUND MIDNIGHT

Less than six hours ago.
I'd probably still be asleep,
except for the dream.

I hope it was only a dream.
Either that, or my recently
departed grandmother
dropped by to let me know
she's never going away.

Parker's snoring gently.
I listen for movement outside
the door, but the house is asleep.
I tiptoe over, squirm under
Parker's blankets, snuggle against
her. Through the thin fabric of my pj's,
the heat of her unclothed skin
wards off the nightmare's chill.

> She rouses. *Lake? Wha—?*

"Shh. They're still asleep."

> *Hate to point this out, but*
> *I am, too. Was, at least.*

"Okay, fine. I'll leave."

> *Oh, no. Not now, you won't.*

It's a huge gamble
but we make love anyway.
It's sweet. Comforting.
Almost enough to chase the ghosts away.

AFTERWARD, PARKER IS HUNGRY

>*Let's sneak to the kitchen
and make some breakfast.*

"You go. I want to work
on my gov paper."

>*Pancakes sound better.*

"Where you gonna get pancakes?"
Not in Colleen's kitchen.

>*Okay, frozen waffles with fake
maple syrup. That's still yummy.*

Off she stomps. I call after her,
"You're adorable when you're pissy!"

I get dressed, run a brush
through my dream-disturbed hair,
then turn on my school laptop.
My paper's on the Constitutional
Convention and the possibility
of one today. Gov will never be
my favorite class, but this is interesting.

I'm so engaged, I jump when
Colleen's voice falls over my shoulder.

>*What are you doing?*

"Researching a paper for government."

>*Put it away for now. The church
is hosting a community yard sale.
I'll need you and Parker to help.*

"It's due Monday. There's a lot—"

>*Don't worry about it. Government.*
>*History. It's all propaganda anyway.*

"What are you talking about?"

>*Public school. Next thing you know,*
>*they'll tell you it's wrong to be white.*
>*Up to me, you'd go to the right kind of school.*
>*But the state of California disagrees.*

Oh. My. God. Not only a Bible
humper, but a racist Bible humper.
"No worries. I take a daily
anti-brainwashing pill. I'm good."

>*Very funny. Where's Parker?*

"In the kitchen."

>*No, she's not. I was just there.*

I shrug. "No clue, then."
She probably stepped outside
for a smoke. But I'm not sure,
so I'm not really lying.

>*See if you can round her up.*
>*We need to go in a half hour.*

She turns on one heel, exits,
leaving no room for argument.
Today should be fun.

I FIND PARKER

Around the corner, sitting
on the curb, watching cars
drive by, only feet away.
She doesn't see me at first,
or even intuit my presence.

"Hey." No response. "Parker?"

She finally glances up at me.
Her eyes seem kind of spacey.

"You okay?"

>*Yeah, sure. Just zoning out.*

"Got any gum?"

>*You don't chew gum.*

"I know. But you should.
You smell like tobacco, and Colleen
wants us to go to church."

>*Is it Sunday?*

"Parker, you know it's Saturday.
They're having a big yard sale and . . .
Are you *sure* you're okay?"

>*I get this way sometimes. Kind of
>floaty. Like I'm not attached to myself.*

"Like an out-of-body experience?"

>*Sort of. There's a name for it.
>I looked it up. Dissociation.*

"Why didn't you tell me before?"

> *It doesn't really happen when*
> *I'm with you or other people.*
> *Mostly just when I'm by myself.*

"Well, it looks dangerous.
Those cars were passing by
pretty damn close to you."

> *Were they? I didn't notice.*

Concerning. And so are
the cigarette remains that fall off
her lap when she stands.

"Let's get back before Colleen
decides to come looking for us.
Don't forget about the gum."

> *You want some gum?*

"Parker..."

> *Just kidding.*

She seems to be grounded again.
But I'm worried, and worrying
about someone I care for
never leads to anything good.

IN THE CAR

Parker and I sit in back, far apart,
each of us staring out the window.
Before we left, I had a minute
to look up *dissociation*.

I didn't have time to read it all,
but what I got was everyone
experiences it to a small degree,
like when you daydream or get lost
in a movie or a book.

But Parker's thing seemed more
serious, like I had to haul her
back inside the real world.
That kind of dissociation is linked
to trauma, anxiety, and/or depression.

Despite how close we are, I only
know a little about Parker's background.
Her father croaked in jail.
She and her mother lived in a car
for six months until her mom
hooked up with her heroin dealer.

So, yeah, I can imagine a fair
bit of trauma before the state
took control of her life.

I should ask her.
How do I ask her?
Would she want me to ask her?
Or is that place in her life
somewhere she'd rather not revisit?

When We Get to the Church

People are already setting up
tables and tarps, displaying items
they want to shed from their lives.
The parking lot's roped off,
so we park down the street.

> *Get a move on,* says Colleen.
> *The sale starts at ten, on the dot,*
> *and we've got some work to do.*

Jay brought a bunch of stuff
over yesterday, left it in the foyer.
Colleen stakes out a place on the asphalt
while Jay, Parker, and I shuttle clothes,
books, a few porcelain figurines,
some old games and toys.

We hang shirts, skirts, and pants
on a portable rack, arrange
the rest on a couple of card tables.

> *Looks good,* Colleen comments.
> *They're letting people in now. You can*
> *wander around for a while, but check back.*
> *Jay and I might want to scope out*
> *the place and we'll need you to watch*
> *our things. Don't want them to walk off.*

Parker and I look at each other,
trying hard not to laugh.
Like, who'd want to steal this crap?
Especially when you could buy it
for next to nothing? Whatever.

We take off, merge into
the swirling waves of people

perusing secondhand "treasures."
One tarp is covered in toys.

Predictably, it's the kids' favorite
shopping spot. A few seem to have
permission to spend allowances.
A little girl picks up a Jenga game.
Memory strikes. I suck in a deep breath.

> *What is it?*

I start to say nothing, but realize
this could be the way in I need.
"Jenga. The last time I played
it was on Christmas a few years
ago. Storm and I were at Mom's . . ."

We start walking again and I
tell her about our mother's lame
attempt to reunify the family.

When I get to the part about
Mom and Beverly performing
a double lap dance for Mom's
boyfriend, Don, she laughs.

At first.
But then she goes all quiet.

> *Is that why you had to leave?*
> *Go back into the system?*
> *Or was it something worse?*

IT'S ONE OF THOSE THINGS

You push away, out of sight,
out of mind, until it fades into
the shadows. Still, it lurks there.

"There was more. But it
could have been worse."

Mom didn't mind sharing Don
with Beverly, which was sick
enough. But then he turned
his attention my way. At first
it was just inappropriate remarks.

> *If you gained a few pounds,*
> *those curves would fill on out.*
> *Think about cutting your hair.*
> *You'd look like a real woman then.*

They didn't seem all that bad.
Still, they made me nervous.
It was the way he said them,
beads of spit collecting
at the corners of his mouth.

One day Mom was at work.
Don was off somewhere.
Storm had taken the trash
down to the dumpster.

I decided to take a shower
and had shampoo
dripping down over my face
when the bathroom door opened.

"Hey!" I yelled. "I'm in here!"

I can see that.

"Would you please leave
and shut the door?"

I could. But I won't.

"Get out!"

His laughter was like icicles—
frozen and sharp.
The shower curtain ripped back.

He had me cornered.
I couldn't have fought him
off. But I didn't have to.

Leave her alone, you bastard!

Storm smashed into that man
like a bull, headfirst, fists pumping.
Don didn't expect the attack,
so his self-defense was slow.

The second he went down
and I knew Storm had things
under control, I ran for clothes.

By the time I got back, Don
was on the floor, cursing softly.
Storm stood over him, puffing.

*If you so much as look at her again,
I swear I will cut off your balls!*

When I Finish the Story

     Parker nods. *I bet he would've, too.*

"Yeah, but he never got
the chance. Don called the cops."

     Did you tell them what happened?

"Of course."

     But they didn't believe you.

"They did. But Mom decided
she'd rather keep Don than us."

     Cold, man.

"Yep. Well, we should probably
circle back and give the Disciples
time to look around a little."

     She stops me.
     Did you ever have a foster touch you?

"You mean—"

     Yeah. Like that. Ever?

"No."

     You're lucky.

I've heard stories about
sexual assault from other girls
I've spent time in care with.
But nothing like what Parker tells me.

*I was only nine when it started.
I'd been in that house for a little
while, and it was weird because
Scott was always so nice to me.
Like, he'd give me treats and help
me with my homework and stuff.
So, I wasn't afraid of him.*

The guy was well practiced.
She wasn't his first victim.
He took it step-by-step.
Always when his wife was at work.
        Hugs.
        Hair brushing.
        Shoulder rubs.
        Sitting her on his lap.
Progressing to
        Touching him there.
        Touching her there.
        Kissing him there.
        Kissing her there.

*I should've known it was wrong.
But it didn't feel that way. Not until ...*

I wait for the awful thing
I know is coming. It's bad.
But it's not what I expected.

*... the pictures. Scott took pictures.
Sometimes just of me, touching myself.
Sometimes of me touching him.
Sometimes of me with other people.
Mostly other kids. Then, this one time,
this older boy, he ... went too far.*

SHE PAINTS A VIVID PICTURE

I spout the obvious question.
"Why didn't you tell?"

> I did eventually. But at first, Scott swore
> he'd stop giving me my special rewards.
> Then he said I'd never find another
> placement because I'd been spoiled
> like old milk and who'd want a rotten girl?

"What made you tell anyway?"

> When he got another little girl
> and started with her. She was six.

"I'm sorry. Some people are just evil."

> I don't think about it too much
> anymore. But, yeah, he was evil.

Passing a long table, an eight-pack
of sparkly pencils catches my eye.
"Hey, Parker. Have a quarter?"

> What is it with you and pencils?

"When Storm and I lived with Mom,
she never bought school supplies.
Pencils came via our teachers.
Most of them were cool, but in
fourth grade, Mr. Garber yelled
at us to bring our own or take an F.

I decided I'd always have lots
of pencils, no matter what
I had to do to get them."

Parker hands me a quarter.
Then she picks up a package
of note cards, gives the guy
another quarter for them.

    So you can write to Storm.

Church or no church, I chance
giving Parker a thank-you hug.
Pretty sure it looks innocent enough.
As long as people don't hear me whisper,
"Love you more than ice cream."

    Bullshit!

An older couple shakes their heads
in unison. "Parker . . ."

    She chirps loudly. *Who cares?*
    What are they gonna do? Tell?

As much as stuff like that bugs me,
I have to admit I'm a little envious.
It might be nice not to give one single fuck.

Not that I really care what others
think about me. I'd just rather not
draw attention to myself at all.

That's one thing dead
Beverly taught me well.
It's better to tread calm water
than create waves.

FORTUNATELY, THE WITNESSES

To Parker's outburst don't report it.
The tide remains peaceful.

Colleen and Jay have managed to unload
most of the clothes and maybe half
the other crap. Jay pockets the bulk of
whatever was in the cash box, leaving
a little in case Parker and I need to make change.

"Hm. Guess he doesn't trust us,"
I say when he walks away.

> *Don't blame him.*

Parker reaches into the box, extracts
a dollar. But now she notices my grimace.

> *What? They'll never miss it.*

"Maybe he counted. Anyway,
we're better than that."

> *Speak for yourself.*

She scopes out the stuff left
on the tables, picks up a white
ceramic dolphin.

> *Would you take a dollar for this?*

She hands me the bill,
slips the dolphin in her bag.

IRRITATION PRICKLES

Not sure why the relatively
meaningless act bothers me so much.

If the Disciples cared about that dolphin,
it wouldn't have been out for sale.
I doubt they'll even miss it.

They probably wouldn't have
missed the dollar, either.
But that isn't the point.

It has something to do with
dishonesty, I suppose, but
it's not like Parker hasn't ever
swiped something before.
Not like I haven't, either.

Stealing is stealing, but somehow
lifting Twinkies from a convenience
store doesn't seem quite as bad
as ripping off people who take care of you.

Doesn't matter what their motives
are, as long as they treat you decently,
and for the most part Colleen and Jay do.

A little too much Jesus and judgment
are better than making a kiddie porn
star out of you, but I'm not sure
Parker sees it that way.

Maybe it's her indifference.
Borderline callousness.

I get her reasons.

But I've got reasons, too,
and maybe it's even because
of them I maintain at least
a small level of morality.

If I told Parker that, she'd laugh.
Insist I was full of shit.
And hey, I probably am.

I mean, where would I have
learned morals?

Maybe it's just about loyalty.

I would never lie to Parker.
I would never steal from Parker.
I would never cheat on Parker.

I sincerely doubt she feels
half as much devotion toward me.

I'm thinking about that
when a massive shiver
rips through my body.

I don't know
what it means,
but it has nothing
to do with the weather.

STORM
I Ring Jaidyn's Doorbell

Listen for noise inside the house.
An argument, or something
to explain why Jaidyn hasn't called.
But I hear nothing.

Answer the door.
Answer the door.
Come on, Jaidyn.
But it's her mom
who finally comes.

        What's wrong?

"I don't know. Is Jaidyn here?
She was supposed to pick me up
a while ago and I can't reach her."

        She went out for a run earlier.
        I haven't heard her come in, though.

"How long ago was that?"

As she considers, concern
eclipses her face.

        A couple of hours. No. More.

Jaidyn's a decent runner,
but as far as I know she's not
training for a marathon.

"Do you have any idea
which way she went?"

        She likes to run the trails
        at the regional park.

> *It's a few blocks that way.*

"Thanks."

> *Wait! I can—*

I'm not waiting. I jump into Jim's car,
point him in the right direction.

Heart chattering wildly, I scan roads
and sidewalks but see no sign of her.

The park is huge, with a series of dirt
trails intersecting the rolling hills.
Looks like a single path leads to the rest.

"I'll start there," I tell Jim.
"Jaidyn's mom will be along.
Let her know which way I went."

I take off at a decent clip, but slow
to a jog before long, and when I reach
the first Y, I pause to consider.

"Jaidyn!"

> *Jaidyn!* A voice sneaks
> up behind me.

It's her mom. Of course.
We decide to split up.
She goes right. I go left.

I Come Across

A few people, ask if they've seen
a girl with auburn hair,
spiked short, tipped red.

                              A woman points behind her.
                              She's coming this way. I tried
                              to help her, but she wouldn't
                              let me anywhere near her.

Help her?
I take off running.
There, in the distance.
She's limping. Did she fall?

"Jaidyn!"

Adrenaline kicks in.
It's a full-on sprint.
Until she sees me.
Raises both hands.
Backs up a step or two.

I screech to a stop.
Try to comprehend.

Her hair's a mess.
Her face is filthy.
Her shorts are torn.
Her arms and legs
are scratched and bruised.

"Are you okay? What the hell?"

I start toward her.

But She Screams

    Don't touch me!

I've heard this before,
same tone of voice.
    Terrified. Enraged. Anguished.

Different time.
Different place.
Different someone I love.

And suddenly I understand.

"Who?"

She can't meet my eyes.

    Doesn't matter.

"Yes, it does!
Someone you know?"

She trembles visibly,
but when I reach
for her, she stiffens.

"I won't hurt you, Jai.
Not ever. I love you.
But you have to tell me."

She
puddles
like storm water.

    Lance.

I Will Kill Him

That's my first thought,
even before I hear the details.

Jaidyn's quaking legs fail her.
She sits hard on the ground.
Allows me to do the same.

>   *Over there.*

After the game last night,
Jaidyn stopped by an after-party.
Lance happened to be there.
He and Jaidyn sparred.
As she speaks, her tone rises.

I only vaguely notice until I ask
how he knew where to find her.

>   *I don't know! He followed me?*

Stalking her. Did he wait all night?

>   *All I know is he caught me,*
>   *locked his arm around*
>   *my throat, pulled me off*
>   *the trail, into the bushes.*
>   *I couldn't scream.*
>   *Could barely breathe.*
>   *And then ... and then ...*

He tossed her in the dirt.
Shredded her shorts.
Ripped off her panties.

She lies back on the ground.
Stares up at the sky.

> *And he raped me.*

Her voice is rock solid.

Enough for me to say,
"You have to report him."

> *I can't. No witnesses.*
> *No evidence.*

"Jaidyn, there has to be
  evidence. I mean—"

> *He used a condom.*

That son of a bitch.

"Report him anyway.
Maybe someone saw
something. His car.
Him running. Something."

> *The exam. The questions.*
> *I won't put myself through that.*
> *Besides, nothing would happen to him.*

"You don't know that!"

> *Don't you pay attention*
> *to the news? Jocks like Lance*
> *get away with rape all the time.*

I Don't Need the News

To inform me. I've heard
plenty of guys brag about sexual
assaults with no consequences.
Not just jocks, either.

"What if he does it to someone else?"

    Guess that will be her problem.

"Jaidyn. What's—"

What's wrong? Shut the fuck up,
dude! The answer's obvious.
Maybe she'll change her mind.
Maybe her mom can convince her.

"Oh. Your mom's looking for you.
She'll probably send out a search
party if we don't get back soon.
Are you okay to walk now?"

    What choice do I have?

I stand, offer my hand,
pretty sure she won't take it.
But she does, and that gives
a narrow ribbon of hope
that our love is strong
enough to survive this.

Once she's on her feet,
however, she disengages.
It's all I can do not to protest.

WE GO SLOWLY

Cloaked in silence unbroken
by wind or birdcalls or anything
but the sound of our feet.

"I know you're hurt. I can't pretend
to relate to all of it, but I understand
the pain of assault, and the damage
isn't just physical. It can chew
holes in your brain if you let it."

    I think too much anyway.

Bitter humor is also something
I recognize. I'm an expert.

A group of people has gathered
in the parking area. Jim is with
them, and so is Jaidyn's mom.
The search party, I presume.

Before their questions swallow
her, I say, "I love you from the depths
of my heart. Let me help you."

    You can't.

Her mom spots us, comes running.
Like I did, when she sees the state
Jaidyn's in, she brakes.

    What happened?

    Little problem, but I'm okay.

"No. She's not. She—"

       I said I'm fine!

"Jaidyn. Tell your mom."

  She shakes her head so hard
  I think her neck might snap.
"Please. You have to."

             Tell me what?

       Leave me alone! And you . . .
       She aims a vile glare at me.
       You keep your mouth shut.

Jaidyn stomps off.
Her mom gasps, shoots me
a helpless look, hurries after her.
Nothing to do but follow,
I go tell Jim Jaidyn had
an accident on the trail.

"But she *says* she's okay."

Whether it's my tone of voice
or my body language, he knows
it's a lie, but doesn't pursue
the facts. I'm afraid nobody will.

But I know the facts.
I will not forget them.
I will not forgive them.
I will not ignore them.

And I will avenge them.

Exactly How Chews at Me

The rest of the weekend,
gouging deeper and deeper
with every unanswered call.
I've tried a hundred times.
No response. Not even
a voicemail recording.

It's like Jaidyn never existed.

But, oh, she's very alive
in my head. Laughing. Running.
Teasing. Loving. In and out of bed.

Having sex with her makes
me feel worthy, like I've been
blessed with a rare gift.
But I swear I'd refuse it,
if only she'd talk to me.

Sit at my side.
Offer up her pain,
let me shoulder
even a little of it,
though I'd carry it all
if there was a way.

She can't hold it in,
can't keep it secret.
It will consume her
like a cancer.

Because of that sorry
son of a bitch Lance.

Anger Roils All Sunday Night

Come Monday morning I've stewed
in it so long it's affected my thinking.
I stand at the curb, waiting for my ride.

Only it's not coming.
I have to rouse Jim
for an emergency lift.
He's cool and all, but
he does have to wonder.

                    What's up with Jaidyn?

"I'm not sure. She hasn't
returned my calls."

                    You never told me what
                    happened to her Saturday.

"She'll freak out if I tell.
But it was really bad.
Like the worst, for a girl."

He's quiet for a minute.

                    Very sorry to hear that.
                    I hope she's taking care
                    of herself. What about you?
                    How are you feeling?

"A little hurt by Jaidyn.
Pissed at the perpetrator."

                    Please don't take this wrong,
                    but don't do anything rash.

RASH? ME?

Nah. I've been thinking for days.
Lance will expect retaliation.
Might even want confrontation.

He wasn't worried about
provoking me at school
the other day.

It isn't just his size, though
if that were the benchmark,
I wouldn't have a chance.

No, he's not thinking totally
straight, and if he's downing
'roids, that would explain it.

What he doesn't realize
is I've got a dirty trick
or two tucked up my sleeve.

One thing ol' Desmond
taught me was a few Krav
Maga Israeli army moves.

Move in fast, aim for eyes, throat,
balls, keep hitting until your
opponent's totally incapacitated.

I don't have the kind of training
the experts I watched on YouTube
do, but I understand the techniques.

Intensive offense, show no mercy.
I just have to find the right situation.
Meaning one without witnesses.

I Don't Admit

Any of that to Jim.
He calls Morley, who's happy
to hop into the back seat
and ride along, nose against
the window, tail waving.

I've heard dogs intuit
human anxiety, and maybe it's true.

Near the school my nerves start
humming and I'm pretty sure
Morley can hear them.
He leans over the seat,
rests his chin on my shoulder,
whines softly into my ear.

"Don't worry, dude, I'm chill."

Jim turns into the circular
drive and I scan the student
parking lot, but I don't see
Jaidyn's car. Of course not.

I hope she told her mom
the truth. I hope she went
to the cops after all. I hope
she's okay. Solid. Jaidyn.

She's been profoundly wounded.
Body. Mind. Soul.
How does that ever heal?

Morley Slurps

A goodbye kiss all over my face
and I decline Jim's offer of a ride
home, tell him I'll catch the bus.
It'll get me home late, but so what?

I wait just inside the front door,
in case Jaidyn shows after all.
She doesn't. But Delilah does.
I wave to her to step outside,
away from the hallway racket.

"Have you heard from Jaidyn?"

> *Saw her yesterday.*
> *She's pretty messed up.*

"You know what happened?"

> Delilah nods, studies me
> like she's looking for an answer.
> *You haven't seen it, have you?*

"Seen what?"

> *There's a video going around.*
> *It's Jaidyn. In the dirt. Right after . . .*
> *And it shows a lot. Too much.*

My face ignites, white hot.
The pulse in my neck thrums.
I don't need to see it. I hope I never do.
What kind of a monster
rapes a girl, then posts proof?

"But isn't it, like, evidence?"

> She shrugs. *Of what? Lance isn't
> in it, and there's no way to tell
> who uploaded it. Some think
> it might have been you.*

"Me? What the fuck?
I would never! I love her!"

> *The ones who are saying that
> don't know you, obviously.
> Not very many people do.*

True. I don't trust enough
to go looking for friends.
In fact, I've never had one,
male or female. Not until . . .
"What's Jaidyn saying?"

> *Nothing. She told me.
> And you. No one else.
> At least, I don't think so.*

"How about her parents?
They can't be that clueless."

> *Not sure about her dad, but
> her mom isn't stupid. Or blind.*

"Do you think—?"

An obnoxious braying
fires up in the parking lot.

THE NOISE

Belongs to one of two girls
maneuvering past Lance,
who's just exited his Camaro.

Did he say something funny?
Touch something inappropriate?
Show them a pic on his phone?

Another sound.
A low hiss, like a pissed cat.
It amplifies slowly, lifts
into a heated snarl.
It's coming from me.

Lance hears it, too.
His eyes meet mine
and his beast appears,
greets me with a sneer.
Right time, right place,
witnesses be damned,
I sprint full bore across the asphalt.

He tries to dodge, but I'm faster
than he knows and I don't allow
time for decent self-defense.
Roaring now, I rush in low.

Lance comes straight
at me, swinging huge fists.
I feint right, fall to the ground,
away from his blows, hook
his leg with mine, drop
him like dead weight.

He's stunned and I take
full advantage, pummeling

his eyes, throat, nose.
Every blow draws a startled gasp.

But I'm not finished.
Vaguely aware of the crowd
that's gathered to watch
my rash display, I stand over
Lance, who's sprawled spread-eagle.

"This is for Jaidyn."

I kick, shuddering
immense satisfaction
every time my foot
connects with his groin.

Stop. Please. Stop.

"Say it again."

Please...

It's a pitiful whine
like a terrified dog,
and that might make me
quit except now in my head
I hear Jaidyn pleading
with Lance to stop.

He didn't.
And neither do I.

NOT UNTIL SOMEONE

Bear-hugs me from behind.

That's enough!

Yanks me up. Off. Away.

Are you out of your mind?

Officer Banks, the campus cop.
I try to wrestle out of his grasp,
but he tightens his grip, pulls
me back toward the main building.
A howl of defeat escapes me,
despite the fact I didn't lose.

Several people, including
Lance's football coach
and the dean of boys,
hustle to check on him.

He's motionless on the ground.
But he's whimpering,
so I guess he isn't dead.

My initial disappointment
is quickly replaced by relief.
If I killed him I'd be in a world
of trouble. As it is, I'm screwed.

Every single good thing
I've managed to gain
over the last year of my life
is in imminent danger of vanishing.

LAKE
ONCE I LEARNED

About Parker's zoning out,
I spent the weekend stressing.
Saturday night, I kept her rooted
in the moment until she fell asleep.

Ditto Sunday at church.
Not easy. I mean, I disappear
into myself during services,
which aren't exactly riveting.

I'm sure Reverend Houghtaling
(Parker calls him "Rev Hought,"
not that he's hot, and that's the joke)
believes they are. Pretty sure
he rehearses his sermons.

But after you've witnessed his schtick
a few times, you realize he's just
dressing up the same basic talk
with different Bible verses.
So, yeah, usually I slip away,
into a meditative space.

But yesterday I kept watching
Parker, and anytime she'd approach
that place, I gave her a little poke.
After a while she got irritated
and elbowed me in the ribs.

I get I was being ridiculous.
Not a whole lot of traffic
inside a church. Zoning out
there will not get you run over.
I just don't want to be blindsided.

MY NERVES ARE SINGING

Like I'm perched on the edge
of a precipice.
Parker is part of it,
but there's something more.

Maybe it's the clouds,
thick and gray as wet cement,
spitting rain all over
this Monday morning.
Outside, everything's soggy.
Inside, everything's damp.

The bus ride is eventless.
I turn in all my work on time,
including my gov essay.
Classes are fine.
No quizzes. No surprises.

But in between them,
nothing special to focus on,
silent warnings
go off inside my head.

Final bell rings.
Parker and I grab our stuff,
head out the front door.

At the curb, Candace
is standing beside her car,
under an umbrella.
She signals for me to join her.

I want to run.

INSTEAD

I hand my bag to Parker.
"Be right back. I hope."

> She's not taking you, is she?

That was my first thought.
It's every foster kid's first
thought when their caseworker
appears unannounced.

"I have no idea why she would."
Everything seemed fine at dinner
with Storm the other night. Storm...

I shuffle toward Candace.
Needing the information.
Afraid of the information.
Still five feet away, I call,
"Is my brother all right?"

> Her eyes grow wide.
> Get in. Let's talk.

I open the passenger door.
"Parker's waiting. We usually
ride the bus, but we'll miss it."

> I can take both of you home.
> But I need to tell you something.

I slip into the seat. "What is it?"

> I thought you should know
> Storm was arrested today.

ASSAULT AND BATTERY

Storm beat the crap out of a guy
at school. They wheeled the dude
away on a gurney.

"He must've had a good reason."

> *I'm sure he did. But he's not
> talking. Which is actually smart.*

Taking full advantage
of the right to remain silent.

> *Anyway, Storm and you just
> reconnected. I wanted you to know
> in case you don't hear from him.
> He won't be at Jim's for a while.*

"You mean never again."

> *It's a distinct possibility.*

"Can you find out what happens
to him and let me know?"

She promises she will, but I
already know he'll be going away.
Most judges don't care much for
problem kids, and problem foster
kids are easily discarded.

I collect Parker, fill her in.

> *Oh, man. That sucks. Wonder
> what made him go off.*

She gives me a hug and a sweet kiss.

People swirl around us. A few stare.
I don't pay them any attention.

But Candace is waiting
in her car. I doubt she saw.
Hope she didn't. Might lead
to complications, though
the gesture could be excused
as a friend comforting a friend.

    Oh, there goes the bus.

"Candace said she'll drive us home."

I ride up front.
Parker sits behind me.
Candace is quiet most of the way.

    Almost home, though,
    she asks, *How did you know*
    something was going on with Storm?

I shrug. "You told me."

    No. Before that, you asked me
    if he was all right.

    She's psychic.

"Nah. I just know how
the system works."
But that isn't exactly true.

I NEVER TALK ABOUT MY ABILITY

If you want to call it that.
I'm not, like, a seer.

I can't foretell the future.
I can't see into the past.
I can't read palms or minds.
I can't predict which team
will win the Super Bowl
or who'll lose the next election.

After a fair bit of research,
I think what I am is an empath.
I tap into energy streams.

Not like I want to.
Not like I try.

It's scary to feel what someone
else is feeling. No matter if
it's heartache or pleasure.
It's hard enough to carry
the burden of my own emotions.

Doesn't happen with everyone.
Mostly people I become close to.
Storm, of course. Alora. Melanie.
Parker, to some degree.

But it could be a random person.
No tears. No smiles. Our eyes
meet and I know if that person
is happy or pissed or hurting.

Usually it's just a jab. A glimpse.

But sometimes it's a whole view,

almost like an invitation. Believe
me, inside a stranger's head
is no place you want to be.

With Storm, it's a mutual exchange.
Our psyches are linked.

We figured out our sync when
we were little. We could "tell" each
other things without saying a word.
And we could comfort
each other without touching.

When we were forced apart,
the connection remained,
though not nearly as strong
as when we're together.

Seeing him again
the other night
was like tripping breakers—
energy overload.

Every memory,
every confession,
every description,
every explanation
sparked a spectrum
of emotions.

It must have recharged
our long-distance bond.
That's why I've been
on edge all day.

CANDACE DROPS US

The rain has tapered off.
Parker taps me on the shoulder.

> *Bummed a cigarette at school.*
> *Matches, too. Let's take a walk.*

We amble down the puddled sidewalk,
turn the corner, stand with
our backs against a tall stucco wall.

> Parker lights the cig, inhales,
> then asks, *You doing okay?*

I shrug. "Not especially."

> *Here. Take a drag. It'll help.*

Before I can, a car approaches.
"Shit. Here comes Jay."

> *Maybe he won't notice us.*

As if. Parker has just stubbed out
the cigarette when he slows,
pulls over next to the curb.

> He sniffs. *Kind of wet out here.*
> *Need a ride?*

"It's a half block. We can walk it."

> *Okay, then. See you in a minute.*

He goes. But not very fast.

Once Jay Has Rounded the Corner

I take a 360-degree look around.
"Kiss me."

Here? You feeling okay?

Unmoored.   Untethered.   Unleashed.

I push Parker back against the wall.
She gasps, and for once I can read
her easily. She's radiating surprise.
She leans her face hard into mine.
I kiss her longer. Harder. Deeper.

My body responds with an urgent request.
I pull her hand into the V between my thighs.
She might even go there except a car cruises by.

For once it's Parker who reminds me,
Better chill. Sex check, okay?

"Sex check? What's that?"

Like a rain check, but with—

"Sex. I get it. Okay, fine."

What got into you, anyway?
Not like you regularly jump
my bones in public locations.

"I don't know. The rain?
Or maybe hormones. I'm due
to start my period anytime."

Ugh. Ready for the lecture?

THE LECTURE

Comes when our monthly
visitors arrive. We've got to ask
Colleen for feminine hygiene products.

It's another form of control,
and an odd one at that. She claims
she doesn't want us to waste them.

Waste them?
How, exactly?
Use them like Kleenex?

Oh, we're not allowed tampons.
Only pads. See, tampons might
give us "pleasure." Can't have that.

Maybe other kids with regular
moms get similar speeches.
But probably not so reliably.

For them, it might not even be
a churchy thing. But that's where
it starts with Colleen.

Our vaginas, she says, are not
playthings. They are not to be
flaunted, nor taken for granted.

Vaginas are sacred
because they're no less than
God's vessels for procreation.

This has led to more than one
private joke between Parker and me.
Hull size. Swollen seas. Heavenly torpedoes.

I hope Colleen never hears us.
Because there's an obvious
problem with her theory.

If getting pregnant's the only
reason God gave her a vagina, why
doesn't she have kids of her own?

Is she cursed?
Misinformed?
What if she's got it all wrong?

She does everything she thinks God
asks of her. Church. Bible study.
Regular prayer and grace at the table.

Does she clock her cycles?
Breathlessly wait for her temp to rise
and only indulge when it does?

Do she and Jay even have sex?
Are they actively trying for a baby?
Have they ever tried it just for fun?

What. Is. Wrong. With. Me?
Now I've got a disgusting picture
taking up space in my brain.

EVEN WORSE

By the time we walk
through the front door,
I'm feeling a little sorry for Colleen.

Another mistake. Repeated mistake.

Let down your guard, lower
the drawbridge, drop your defenses,
expect to get screwed.
Screwed again. Screwed worse.

Colleen wants to know why
Parker and I were standing
out in the rain. Why we were late.

We weren't late.
The rain had stopped.

I tell her Candace brought us
home. We arrived before the bus
and were talking about my brother.
Arrested again. Disconnected again.

I guess I don't expect real
sympathy. But couldn't she fake
concern? Maybe find it in
her heart to say she's sorry?

Acknowledge I'm wounded.
Temper the pain.

Isn't that
what her Jesus
would tell her to do?

IF HE'S TALKING

She isn't listening.
Instead, she plunges
into a whole different lecture.

> *You have heard that it was said,*
> *"An eye for an eye and a tooth*
> *for a tooth." But I say to you, do not*
> *resist the one who is evil. But if anyone*
> *slaps you on the right cheek, turn to him*
> *the other also. Matthew 5:38–39.*

"What?"

> Parker attempts translation.
> *I think she's saying Storm*
> *should have turned the other cheek.*

I puff up like a riled snake.
"Whatever set Storm off must've
been bad. I've never seen him look
for a fight. Was he supposed to
just stand there and take abuse?"

> *No,* says Colleen. *He's supposed*
> *to let God handle it. Romans 12:19:*
> *Beloved, never avenge yourselves,*
> *but leave it to the wrath of God,*
> *for it is written, "Vengeance is mine;*
> *I will repay," says the Lord.*

I drop my eyes level with hers.
"Maybe tell that to the judge.
Anyway, whatever happened
to 'God is love'? Is love vengeful?"

COLLEEN SPUTTERS

Something unintelligible.
I'd laugh, but nothing is funny.
Not even her inability to respond.

"May I go do my homework?"

>One second. Jay said when he stopped
>to talk to you he thought he smelled
>cigarettes. You weren't smoking, were you?

"Those things are terrible for you."
When a lie is not exactly a lie.

>Jay isn't going for it. *My nose
>works just fine, ladies.*

It wasn't our cigarette, says
Parker. *This guy stopped to ask
for directions. He was smoking.*
When a lie is totally a lie.

>*I didn't see any guy. Only you two.*

Guess you just missed him.

>*Maybe we should look inside
>your backpacks*, says Colleen.

No problem! agrees Parker.

Oh, no. Mine is clean.
But she's sure to have
contraband of some sort.
I hand mine over.

Laptop.

Notebook.
Daisy.
One copy of *The Great Gatsby*.
One copy of *Beloved*.
Three sharpened pencils.
My wallet, which is empty
except for my school ID,
and a photo of Storm and me.

I hold my breath over
the Toni Morrison, but either
Colleen doesn't recognize it
or she's in a hurry to get to Parker's bag.

Laptop.
Notebook.
One pencil stub.
One mostly eaten PB&J.
Gum.
Hairbrush.
Small dolphin statuette.

> Colleen holds up the last.
> *This looks familiar.*

> *I paid for it!* says Parker. *I saw
> it at the yard sale and liked it.*

Colleen looks at me, disbelief
strong in her eyes.

"Well, she did. I saw her."

HARD TO ARGUE

With that, though I can tell
Colleen really wants to.
She snarls one more Bible verse.

> *Nothing is covered up that will
> not be revealed, or hidden that
> will not be known. Luke 12:2.*

Guess we'll see.
And I also guess my righteous
sense of morality only goes so far.
Off the hook for the moment,
Parker and I head back
to our room, stifling giggles.

Once we're out of earshot, I say,
"Phew. That was close. What did
you do with the matches?"

> *I learned a long time ago
> if you're in danger of getting
> busted, keep stuff like matches
> in your pocket where you can
> get rid of them in a hurry.*

"When did you get rid of them?"

> *I didn't. They're still in my pocket.*

Which makes no sense to me,
though apparently it does
to her, and that is so Parker.

> *Hey. Thanks for backing me up.*

"Why wouldn't I?"

       She shrugs. *You hardly ever disagree*
       with Colleen, at least not to her face.
       You don't like confrontation.

"What do you mean? Didn't I
ask her if love is vengeful?"

       Yeah, but that was about Storm.
       You'd take a bullet for your brother.

"I . . ."
My mouth snaps shut.
Because she's correct.
About everything.

I hate confrontation.
I would take a bullet for Storm.
But I doubt I would for Parker.
She didn't say the last one.
But that's what she meant.

No use feeling guilty.
She wouldn't take one for me, either.
And I wouldn't expect her to.

Reality check: the love
Parker and I share
might offer comfort.

But it's like spooning
gravel into a sinkhole—
a shallow fill.

SHE KNOWS IT

I know it. Neither of us
dares say it out loud.

The instant you put thoughts
like that into words,
you give them power.

Instead, I say, "It's been a weird
day. Probably the rain."

    Yeah. Or your hormones.

I unlace my boots, kick out,
happy I took the time to treat
them with vegetable oil.
The puddles barely bothered
them at all, unlike Parker's canvas.

"You should take yours off,
too. Don't need some random
fungus creeping around, you know?"

    She smiles. *Good point.*

No actual homework today,
I pull *Beloved* out of my bag,
plop onto my bed, lean back
against the pillow.

"Glad Colleen didn't recognize
this. She'd probably organize a book
burning at a school board meeting."

    Why? Is it porn?

"Hardly. It won the Pulitzer Prize.

But it does have sex, including
rape and a reference to bestiality."

>She wrinkles her nose. *You mean,
>like people doing it with animals?
>Yeah, that would set Colleen off.
>Bet there's a Bible verse about it, though.*

"The slavery stuff is a lot
harder to deal with, honestly.
Some scenes make me cringe."

>*So why are you reading it?*

"Extra credit in Honors English.
And because it's freaking brilliant."
And maybe, just like 5 percent or so,
because Colleen would despise it.

Parker dives into algebra
while I immerse myself
in Toni Morrison's genius.
Page after page after page.

I've got no idea how long
I've been here in this
masterfully crafted world
when Colleen pushes
through the bedroom door.
I snap the book shut.
But it's too late.

>*Whatcha reading?*

STORM
ARRESTED

Zip-tied, shoved into
the filthy back seat of a patrol car.

My heart beats fury.
My temples pulse fire.
My lungs fight for air.

What the fuck did I just do?
So much noise in the silence.
I struggle to quiet the internal chaos.
Focus on small things.
I study the back of the cop's head.
Black hair, cropped short
and crooked across his neck.

Should I tell him
he could use a decent barber?
I turn my attention
to the stains on the seat.

Blood. Piss. Shit.

"Don't you people ever
clean your upholstery?"

                Cop checks his rearview mirror,
                smiles. *Came back from the detail*
                shop two weeks ago. Those are fresh.

Nice.

                Anyway, where you're going,
                stains won't be the worst of it.

Yeah, I Know

Been here before.
I was in the same facility
the last time I was locked up.

It hasn't changed,
at least not on the outside.

Cop cruises slowly
past the front parking lot,
which is three-quarters full.
Must've been a busy weekend.

He pulls around back,
and like magic the big gate
in the tall chain-link fence
slides open, clanks shut behind us.

He nudges the car clear up
against the chipped cement,
where tall metal portals
allow access to intake.

He parks, circles to let me out.
I can see him tense as he unlocks
the door, and the veins in his neck
look like throbbing ropes.

Let's go.

He pushes me inside
to the desk, where he trades
the zip ties around my wrists
for the cuffs anchored to the counter.

Cop could've cited and released me
with a court date, but in his estimation

the offense was too dire, and the intake
officer knows that, barely glances my way.

       Any identification?

Cop hands her my school ID.
She types my name into her computer.
Now she gives me a hard once-over.

       Back again, Carpenter?
       Why are we here this time?

Cop outlines the deets.

       She gives a low whistle.
       How was he on the ride over?

       Cooperative. No problems.

       Any weapons on him? Drugs?

       Nah. Just this stuff.

He hands over the few personal items
in my possession when he picked me up.
IO (intake officer) logs them:

Eight one-dollar bills.
Another dollar in change.
Wallet, and inside it one picture
of Jaidyn, another of Lake.

       You can leave, Officer.

The Initial Interview

Doesn't take long.
They've got all my basic info.

>Parents: N/A
>Address: N/A
>Siblings: Twin sister, Lake Carpenter
>Age: 17, barely
>Height: 6', almost
>Weight: 162, sopping wet
>Hair: Cola
>Eyes: Lapis
>Scars: Nowhere you can see
>Religion: Hahahahahaha

IO goes down the checklist
of requisite questions.
Point of the exercise: establish rapport.
Played this game before.

>*Sorry to see you back again.*

"Thought you'd be excited. I sure am."

Her expression tells me
to drop the bullshit. Tough.

>*You been drinking or using today?*

Negative. "It's not even noon."

>*Doesn't stop a lot of people.*

"Breakfast of champions?"

>*Breakfast of losers.*

Double negative.
"No booze. No drugs."

> *You still in foster?*

Fake negative.
"Nah. Mother Mary came
to me. Living in heaven."

> *Any health issues we should know?*

Mostly negative.
"Probably a cavity or two.
No cotton candy for me."

> *Any recent thoughts of suicide?*

Negative.
But I say, "Mood swings."
Angling for meds.
Don't attempt lockup without them.

> *You'll have a mental health
> workup, probably tomorrow.*

As expected.
The physical will be today.

> *Any history of sexual assault—
> either as perpetrator or victim?*

Negative.
But I just took care
of a perp. Hope he rots.

Rapport Confirmed

>Who should we call?

I give her Jim's number.
She dials, hands me the phone.
The chains attached to the cuffs
barely let me lift it to my ear.

"Hey, Jim. I'm at juvenile hall.
Guess I was a little rash after all."

I give him the lowdown.
Spare the worst details.

>Except, he already knows.
>*The boy is in surgery, Storm.*
>*You hurt him pretty badly.*

"I don't care!"

>*You might when all is said*
>*and done. Do yourself a favor.*
>*Latch on to a little contrition.*

Did I expect sympathy?
Still, it stings.

"Sure, Jim. I'll work on that."

>*I'm not kidding, son. I know*
>*you believe your actions were*
>*justified. But I doubt a judge*
>*will agree with you.*

He's right. Definitely right.

But if anyone should feel contrite,

it's Lance, not me. Because,
"What about Jaidyn?"

> What about her?

"Doesn't she deserve justice?"

> Sure she does. Just not
> the renegade kind.

I start to say it's the only
kind she's likely to get,
but IO's monitoring
every word, and clearly
growing impatient.

"Will you let Candace know
what happened? I don't want Lake
to think I was abducted by aliens."
My eyes smart.

> Of course. Anything else?

"Reach out to Jaidyn, tell her
I love her, give her my Rex
shirt for safekeeping."
My eyes burn.

His voice is kind
when he promises
to do what he can.

Behind him somewhere,
Morley whines.
My eyes spill.

MISTAKE

Don't bend. Don't bend down.
Don't break. Don't break down.
Don't let them see weakness.
Don't reveal chinks in the armor.

Be cooperative.   Be polite.   Be aware.
No one here is a friend.

Tears don't impress the IO.
She calls a guard to take me
to holding until someone's free
to oversee my shower.

Gotta wash off the street
and delouse the hair
before locking you away.

>*You hungry?* IO asks.

It'll be a while before
I see a regular meal.
"Yeah. I could eat."

First things first,
the guard pats me down.
He knows the cop already
frisked me, emptied my pockets.

>Still, he asks, *Anything stashed*
>*somewhere . . . special?*

"Not that I can think of.
You're welcome to look."

>*I know I am. Maybe later.*

Cavity searches are actually
rare, at least on the juvenile
side. I've never been subjected
to one. There needs to be a damn
good reason. There are laws.

Does that mean stuff gets
sneaked in sometimes?
I've seen contraband in lockup.
Can't say how it got there, though.

The officer unshackles me,
herds me through a door,
down a short corridor,
and into a holding cell.

It's not what you'd call
comfortable—only a cracked
plastic bench to sit on.

Zero to do but stare at the walls,
I plop on the cold cement floor,
which is what my sorry ass deserves,
rest my head on my knees, close my eyes,
and think of my birthday with Jaidyn.

Cake.

    Cake.
Frosting.
    Frosting.
Crumbs.
    Crumbs.

It Takes an Hour

For a sandwich to arrive,
via a probation counselor.
One I'm well acquainted with.
The dude's built to take no shit.

> *Storm. Man, I really hoped*
> *I'd never have to see you again.*

"Yeah, me too, Byron."

He hands me lunch.
I unwrap the hoagie. Salami.
Blech. I take a big bite anyway.

> *When you finish, I'll take you to*
> *shower. Looks like you're checking in.*
> *I talked to the probation officer.*
> *At your detention hearing, the district*
> *attorney will recommend holding you.*
>
> *For now, count yourself lucky to be*
> *assigned to C Unit. Guessing post-*
> *adjudication you'll be moving on up.*

There are seven units here.
Assignments are based on factors
like gender. Age. Emotional health.
Public safety. If you're gay or suicidal,
there's a special unit for you.

Otherwise, the more hardcore
your crime, the more hardcore
your unit mates. Better keep
practicing the ol' Krav Maga.

"Maybe I'll get off?"

> He grins. *Not in front of me,*
> *I hope. And not in front*
> *of any of the other guys, either.*

"Not that kind of get off . . ."
I almost add "asshole,"
but reconsider quickly.

"Maybe the judge will see
there were extenuating
circumstances. Maybe—"

> *Sure, kid. Finish your lunch.*
> *Then we'll get you checked in*
> *to Hotel Extenuating Circumstances.*

I scrunch the sandwich wrapper,
toss it to Byron, wait for him
to buzz us out the door.
He escorts me to the showers.

> *You know the drill.*

My first time in lockup,
I was mortified to strip
and scrub myself
in front of an older dude
watching every move I made.

I shriveled.
Outside.
And in.

It Didn't Take Long

To figure out
there's no privacy
in a place like this.
Humiliation is less
than worthless.

It labels you weak.

So, I let my clothes fall.
Step under the steaming
hot stream of water.

Wince at the smell
of industrial strength
antibacterial soap.

Wash everything,
from my head
to between my toes.

Byron picks up my jeans,
rifles through the pockets
one more time.

He rolls up my clothes,
puts them into a locker,
removes clean county
lockup sweats.
Black pants. Gray shirt.
Plus underwear and socks.

He hands them to me,
and as I slip into them
I say, "You haven't updated."

Nope. And the rules haven't

*changed, either. Still, I'm required
to lay them out for you.*

He does as we head over
to C Unit. They're familiar:

Lights on, six a.m.
Lights out at ten.
Allowed items:
        Court docs.
        Letters.
        Approved photos.
        School assignments.
        Paperback books and magazines.
        One deck of cards.

Three hours of recreation
daily during the week.
Five on non-school days.

No smoking.
No drugs, unless prescribed.
No graffiti.
No spitting.
No gambling.
No gang activity.
No physical contact.

      Any questions?

I shake my head.
Like Byron said,
nothing's changed.

C UNIT

Consists of a big common
area, with tables for games
and a big-screen TV.

It's empty right now,
all the other guys hanging
tough in classrooms.

The bedrooms are on the second
level. Each unit has twenty.
Sometimes you get a bunk
mate. Sometimes it's just you.

I follow Byron to a storage
room. He gives me a clean
mattress, sheets, a comb
and toothbrush, and I haul
them up the metal stairs.

> *Right over here. We'll put*
> *you in a single for now.*

Unbelievably, he opens
the door to the very same
room I was in last time.

"Are you kidding me?"

> *What? Décor not to your taste?*

Cement bed pedestal.
Stainless-steel sink/toilet
combo. No seat for the ass,
which can get interesting.

"Oh, no. Very chic, and still

painted a lovely shade of bile."

> *We aim to please.*

"Not much in the way
of entertainment in here."

> *Make your bed. Pace. Count
> the cinder blocks in the walls.
> Can't let you out among the others
> until after your health screening.*

"Any chance of a magazine?
Paper and writing utensil?"

> *I'll see what I can do. You're
> not contemplating suicide?*

Why does everyone keep
asking me that?

"Suicide? With a magazine?"

> *I guess you could beat yourself
> to death. But I meant like sticking
> a pencil through your eye.*

"It'd have to be a long one to reach
my brain. If you're worried
about it, a crayon would work."

> *I'll see what I can do,* he repeats.

Byron closes my door.
Locks it from the outside.

I Make the Bed, Remembering

The last time I "lived" in this room.
After Desmond, I spent more
than a year rotating through
placements. Revolving doors.
Step in. Random spin.
Step out, into unknown territory.

Spin. Exit: Floyd's.
Big guy. Meant well.
Fostering post-retirement.
But then came the stroke.

Spin. Exit: Kyle and Kerry's.
Ruled us three fosters
like we were unpaid servants.
Which led to rebellion.

Spin. Exit: Cheryl's.
Turned fifteen there, too young
for the present she gave me. Oh,
she never actually touched me.
But, boy, did she put on a show.

Spin. Exit: Paula and Lisa's.
For a while I had two (foster)
moms. They were totally cool.
I blew that majorly.

Met a guy who convinced me to run
drugs at my new (again) high school.
A job with fringe benefits.
Only some of the bennies
increased my anxiety, mood
swings, bad judgment calls.

One Memorable Afternoon

A school resource officer took note
of parking lot activity involving me.
When she tried to interfere
I told her to fuck off.

She invited me to make her.
Two solid punches to her face,
down she went. I kicked her
once for good measure.
I wound up here, detained
until my court date in a detox unit.

Man, I'll never forget being locked
in that concrete box, out of my mind
as I crashed off a regular diet of Xanax
and Prozac, with an occasional Molly dessert.
Once or twice, I thought I seriously might die.

I arrived at the facility
>   sweating
>   shaking
>   coughing
>   puking.

No one gave a shit.

This was early March 2020.
Beyond some punk kid
scrubbing drugs from
his system, others were
>   sweating
>   shaking
>   coughing
>   puking.

A bug seemed to be going around.

By the time I got to court
I was no longer
                    sweating
                    shaking
                    coughing
                    puking.

My public defender argued the attack
was due to a drug-induced psychotic
break and asked for leniency.
The judge sentenced me to six months in juvie.
Ultimately, the joke was on him.

The bug? I might have carried it
to that courtroom. Or to transportation.
Intake. Lockup. Educational services.

Me, or someone else.
Because by April, COVID-19
had hit those places hard.

Not sure if I actually had it,
or whether to totally chalk
up the detention
                    sweating
                    shaking
                    coughing
                    puking
to withdrawal.

I did not develop those symptoms
again in C Unit, where
I was placed in this very cell.

But lots of people did.

We Spent Weeks in Isolation

No recreation.
No community meals.
No visits except virtual.

Not that I had anyone
who wanted to visit me,
with the possible exception
of Lake, who might have, but
probably didn't even know
where I was at that point.

Which made me lucky because
I didn't miss not spending time
with people I cared about.

Didn't miss hearing over Zoom
that my grandma or uncle
or brother died, all alone.

Didn't miss worrying I might
have been the one to infect a friend,
family member, or stranger.

And I sure didn't miss that damn
virus, which managed to catch
up to several people anyway.

I heard one of the guards died
from it. Don't know if that's true,
but he did disappear one day.

Lockup Sucks

Lockup with scant human
contact is debilitating.

Lockup while fighting
a deadly virus is impossible.

The decision was made to let
most of us out early.

We emerged from our concrete
cocoons into a different world.

Summer, but the beaches were closed.
Ditto restaurants, theaters, stores.

Sidewalks were silent, freeways empty.
Church bells and work whistles pealed into a void.

The few people you did see covered
their noses and mouths with masks.

Liberated, and yet I'd gained only
the smallest measure of freedom.

And as I sit here now, it strikes
me that no one's ever really free.

Even love chains you.

LAKE
WHY IS LOVE

Such a desperate desire?
It's what everybody wants.
At least, until they have it.
Then they'd prefer
             different versions
        different rules
different people.

Ask me, love's hurt
waiting to happen.

My "People I've Loved"
list is pretty damn short
and totally tattered.

                Pete
                Molly
                Alora
The hunger of a small
child, starving for family.
Satiated. Purged.

                Melanie.
Adolescent longing,
starbursts of joy,
smashed into memory.

                Parker.
New.
Fresh.
Exciting.
Destined
for the scrap heap.

BEST TO TREASURE

Our time together, however long
it lasts. If any person has taught me
that, it's the one on top of my PIL list.

That's Storm, of course.

The difference between him
and the rest is, no matter what,
no matter where he or I end up,
or why we end up there, we will
always love each other.

Now, it seems, he'll probably spend
a fair amount of time locked up.
He was arrested three days ago. Monday.

On Wednesday, the DA filed
for wardship, and the intake officer
recommended holding him until his trial.

Candace let me know all this,
and also that Storm's public defender
doesn't believe "any judge in his
or her right mind" will let him walk.

Doesn't sound like he'll get much
defending. The only way he might
is if Jaidyn steps up and tells
the truth about what happened.

I only know because of the letter
from Storm Candace brought
with her news today.

NOTHING STORM WRITES

Is truly surprising.
Well, maybe the damage
he inflicted on Jaidyn's ex,
the one who stalked her.
                  Raped her.

Destroying the guy's left
testicle? That is a bit
of a shocker, even if
the asshole deserved it.
                  He won't rape anyone else.

Storm doesn't feel bad
about it. He says the dude
got off easy. Meaning
he didn't outright kill him.
                  Makes me wonder.

Is my brother capable
of taking someone's life?
Is anyone if the circumstances
happen to be right?
                  Would a judge ever think so?

Storm says he tried to tell
his probation officer the assault
was justified. The man asked
if Jaidyn would testify.
                  But she hasn't even told her mom.

Storm wishes she'd come forward.
Not to save him. To save herself.
It's a terrible secret to bottle up inside.
And he's right. It could explode.

I WORRY ABOUT THAT WITH PARKER

She boxes her history,
seals the flaps shut,
pretends the contents
don't matter.

But they are volatile.
Shake them hard enough,
or light the right fuse,
they're liable to blow.

Mostly she manages
things by tuning out.
Zoning. Deep diving
into her fugue state.

But the undercurrent's
a perpetual buzz,
like high power lines
waiting for a windstorm.

I don't see her near breakdown
often, but once in a while
my inner voice murmurs a warning,
and she becomes a stranger.

Most of the time she's bold.
Loud. Forward. Brash.
Prone to wildly
inappropriate behaviors.

Occasionally, she becomes
a little girl. Scared. Confused.
Anxious. And prone to wildly
inappropriate behaviors.

THE COMMON THREAD

Is obvious, but even when it
doesn't go all the way to "too far,"
some variation makes loving her
problematic. Take the thing with
the Toni Morrison book the other day.
When Colleen burst in, asked what
I was reading, I kind of stuttered
under my breath, "B-B-Beloved."

What's that?

She didn't know, and wouldn't
have, either. Except Parker felt
the need to involve herself.

It's a Pulitzer Prize winner.

Instant Colleen suspicion.
Is that so? About what?

"It's about an escaped slave,
after the Civil War, trying
to come to terms with her past."

Slave, huh? Is that assigned?

"No. It's independ—"

Because I don't hold with that
critical race theory garbage. Teaching
kids blacks were mistreated and all.

I WAS TOO BLOWN AWAY

To respond immediately.
But Parker had plenty to say.

>*Jeez, Colleen. It was slavery.*
>*They were starved and beaten and*
>*forced to work hard labor for no pay.*
>*They were sold like animals.*
>*Families were broken apart.*
>*The women were raped—*

>>*Don't say jeez! And that's what*
>>*I mean. All that stuff was bad.*
>>*But it's water under the bridge.*
>>*No use making today's children*
>>*feel terrible about what happened*
>>*so many years ago. We're over it.*

>Who's "we?" You might be
>over it, but you aren't black.

>>*Neither are you. Why do you care?*

>Because I should. And so should you.
>How can we ever do better in the future
>if we don't make up for the past?

I had no idea Parker
felt so passionately about this,
or anything for that matter.
Honestly, I was proud of her.
Maybe even a little bit awed.

Right up until Colleen snatched
the book out of my hands.

SHE REFUSED TO GIVE IT BACK

Plus, she took it into the school,
called for a meeting with the principal,
my English teacher, and myself.

> *What kind of an educator would*
> *hand a child reading material like this?*

Ms. Bolton had to defend the book,
and herself. *I suppose the kind who values*
exceptional stories, superbly written.

> *Do you really think it's appropriate*
> *to upset children with . . . with . . .*

History? Yes. In fact, I'd say it's my job.

> *But th-that . . .* Colleen spit.
> *That isn't real history. It's fiction.*

The novel was inspired by an actual event.
The author read an 1856 newspaper article
about an escaped slave who killed her child
rather than see her returned into slavery.

> *But that's terrible! Why trouble*
> *young people with such ugliness?*

Because it's the truth. You can't hide
from the truth, but you can learn from it.
I see you're wearing a crucifix.

The Bible's filled with horrific stories
of violence. Murder. Infanticide, even.
Its purpose is to teach people to put
away such things in favor of love.

BOOM

Colleen's face flushed purple.
She couldn't manufacture a comeback
because what Ms. Bolton said was true.

I hid my sudden smile behind the back
of my hand. I'd been sitting there,
struggling not to cry, certain Ms. Bolton
would blame me for the trouble.

She didn't. In fact, once Colleen
vacated the building, she apologized.

> *I'm sorry the book dunked*
> *you in hot water. Did you get*
> *the chance to finish it at least?*

"Not quite, and it's amazing!"

> *It will still be in my classroom.*
> *You're welcome to read it at lunch*
> *or for independent reading during class.*

She's just so cool.
Like, if I was looking for a mom,
I'd want her to be like Ms. Bolton.

Some foster kids dream
of being adopted.
I've roomed with a couple
who were obsessed with
the idea of replacement parents.

Not me. The mother I had
made me believe I am
better off all on my own.

I Finish Beloved

At lunch, peruse Ms. Bolton's
classroom bookshelves, ask
to borrow *The Handmaid's Tale*.

> *You sure?*

"I'll read it here if that's
okay. No use rocking the boat."

> *Not in that stormy sea. But you've got
> a deal. By the way, I'm in love
> with your boots. I've always wanted
> some, but couldn't justify the expense.*

"I thrifted these."

> *May I ask where you found them?*

I give her the details on how
to find Margaret's, plus
a couple more shops in the same
general area. "If you want,
I could show you sometime."

> *Maybe we could work that out.
> You could pull buddy duty.*

I grin at the idea
of being a teacher's friend.
Pretty sure Colleen would object.
To this one, anyway.

My pal, Ms. Bolton, and I talk
thrifting until the bell rings.

TODAY IS CHECKUP DAY

After school, Colleen drives Parker and me
to the dentist's office, drops us off,
confirms Jay will pick us up after work.

We check in at the desk, claim two
gray plastic chairs in the waiting room,
weed through the dog-eared magazines.
I find an old copy of *Vogue*, digest
haute couture. I could design better.

A woman in lavender scrubs calls Parker,
who disappears down the hallway.
She's gone for fifteen minutes before
I hear my name. I follow mint-
green scrubs to an empty exam room.

It's all face shields, gloved hands,
miniature shovels, picks, and tooth-
scrubbing tools for way too long.
But the X-rays say I'm cavity-free,
so I guess I need candy to celebrate.

I expect to find Parker waiting for me,
but there's only one person
hanging out in the gray plastic
chairs. He looks up from his phone,
smiles in a creepy way that detracts
from his handsome face.

His vibe is hunger.
For something other than food.

THE RECEPTIONIST INFORMS ME

Parker said she'd meet me outside.
As I exit, I swear I can feel that guy's eyes
crawling all up and down my back.
Too bad my empath ability won't let me
psychically slap the leer off someone's face.

It is, however, shouting that something's
up with Parker. She wouldn't desert me
for no reason. I push through the door.
There. On the corner, on a bus stop bench.
I hustle down the sidewalk. The closer
I get, the harder I'm hit with a feeling of dread.

She's off in the dead zone.
I rest my hand on her shoulder.
She jerks out from under it.

>   *No!*

"Parker. It's me. Lake."

>   *She slips back into now.*
>   *Lake. Holy shit. You scared me.*

"I'm sorry. Didn't mean to.
Why did you leave like that?"
I slide onto the bench beside her.

>   *I ... uh ... did you see a guy*
>   *in the waiting room? Kind of young.*

"Yeah. He creeped me out."

>   *You got that right. He, uh—*

A CAR HORN BLARES

Jay swerves from the second
lane over, barely missing another
car, pulls up in front of the bus stop.

> *Get in.*

> *You could have just gone around
> the block,* Parker complains.

> *I thought maybe you got your signals
> crossed and were going to take a bus
> home. There's one coming behind me.*

I trail Parker into the back seat.
On the sly, I reach for her hand.
But she shakes me off again,
stares out the window, tumbling
back into her colorless space.

I'm dying to know more about
the guy, but that will have to wait.
Jay pulls into a drive-through.
Even with the windows closed,
the smell of hot grease greets my nose.

"Fast food?"

> Jay nods. *Colleen's meeting will
> probably go straight through supper.
> It's burgers or peanut butter.*

Colleen's all into healthy-for-you
stuff, at least if you can buy it cheap.

Jay orders a three-patty monstrosity.

He tells us to get value meals.
I go for broke: cheeseburger
with everything, fries, cola.

Parker tells me to order for her.
I ask if onion rings are okay.
"We can share them and my fries."

She shrugs an okay.
And when our order comes,
she hands the onion rings to me.

Have them. I'm not very hungry.

"Are you sick?"

Something like that.

If Jay notices the exchange,
he says nothing. Too busy wolfing
down his ginormous burger.
Good thing he decided to eat
in the parking lot, or he'd be
wearing more of it than he is.

By the time Jay and I finish,
Parker's only eaten a few bites.
And she's staring out the window.

Something's bothering her, but
I can't quite latch on to it. It's like
she's hung a curtain between us.

COLLEEN'S MEETING

Is at the house. Maybe fifteen women
are in the living room, sipping tea
and snacking potluck style.
Guess we weren't invited.

Parker goes back to our room,
but I hang out, mostly because I hear
Colleen mention Ms. Bolton.

>   *That woman should not be allowed*
>   *to teach our children,* she tells eager ears.
>   *First the books. Then we'll take care of her.*

Damn. I thought she'd dropped
this garbage. But no. She's organizing
a protest. That sucks so bad.

When I said she'd probably take
Beloved up with the school board,
I was kidding. But that's exactly
what she's doing, plus recruiting
an army of church busybodies
to offer backup. Unbelievable.

>   *Here's a list of books provided by*
>   *the Scrub the Shelves organization.*
>   *Step one is to identify them in our schools.*
>   *Encourage your children to look for them.*

Turn your kids into spies.
Excellent parenting. I try
to escape, but Colleen spots me.

>   *Lake! Please pass out the flyers.*

I scowl quite obviously,

look every biddy straight
in the eye when I hand them
the propaganda sheets.

Nineteen women, with not
a whole lot better to do than dictate
what others can read.

When the last flyer's distributed,
I ask, "Anything else?"
Under my breath, I mutter,
"Bonfire, perhaps?"

     No, I think I've got it covered.

I collect my backpack, retreat
before she changes her mind.

"You wouldn't believe the crap
Colleen's saying," I tell Parker,
closing the bedroom door behind me.

Silence. Except for heavy breathing.
She's sunk deep into Dreamland.
Maybe she really is sick.

I let her sleep and spend
the evening writing a paper
on *Gatsby*. Guessing Colleen
wouldn't mind scrubbing the shelves
of this one, too. If she'd ever read it.

I HIT MY OWN BED EARLY

Have no trouble falling asleep,
though as I drift off, I wonder
vaguely if Parker's contagious.

I wake, blanketed by obsidian
night, to hot skin and a soft voice.

> *Lake?*

"Parker? What's wrong?"

> *Will you hold me?*

I open my arms to her body,
which wears a shimmer of sweat
and nothing more. "Tell me."

> *That guy? The one at the dentist?*

It takes a minute to extract
the reference from the darkness.

"The creepy one?"

> *Uh-huh. Remember the pictures I told
> you about? And that time a boy went
> too far? It was him. I'm sure of it.
> And . . . yeah . . . it hurt so bad.*

"Oh, Parker. I'm so sorry."
That's inadequate, but I don't
know what more I can say.

> *I don't think he recognized me.
> But I could never forget him.*

*Just seeing his face... It was
like I was right back there.*

I kiss her gently, offering
sympathy. But when she kisses
me back, I understand she wants
me to make him disappear.

I do my very best.

I've never made love
like this before. Completely
caught up in each other.

There's no one else
in this—or any—world.
Just the two of us robed
by black velvet night.

All I can see of her is a pale
silhouette, edged in darkness.

But her muted moans sound
like wind chimes in a slight breeze.

The pungent scent of sex
hangs in the air, and the sharp
taste of woman lingers on my tongue.

It's a sensual feast.
Impossible to hurry through.

I gorge.
Retreat from the table.
Return for dessert.

BUT BEYOND THE PHYSICAL

There's something more.
Something bigger.
Carrying more weight.

It's like Parker threw open a door
inside her, one she's kept bolted.

I could never see past it,
and only rarely tap into the energy
beyond, but the other side flows
into clear view now.

What's hiding there, cowering
behind a façade of bravado,
is a perfectly created spirit
stained by deception,
scarred by brutality.

We might not be genetic
twins, but we share this soul-
deep reality in much the way
Storm and I do.

I'm struck
by a sudden upwelling.
A huge emotional surge.

Uninvited.
Unexpected.
Unreal.

For once, I won't question it.
I'll embrace it.
Who turns their back on love?

WE LIE

Smooshed together,
the crown of Parker's head
just beneath my chin,
inhaling the complex
perfume of love.

Love.
It's like an essential oil,
soaking into our skin.

I know I can't chase away
her demons forever,
but maybe I can make
them step back for a while.

Who knows?

With time
        distance
                devotion
                        healing

would they retreat
even farther?

Contentment
surrounds Parker
like an aura, shimmering
in a cool bronze.

        Her voice is syrupy
        when she sighs.
        I'm almost happy.

ALMOST

The word echoes inside my head
as Parker floats toward dreams.

Almost.
Happy.

At first I think that makes me sad.
But I reconsider. Understand.

I'm not sure
I've ever been happy.
Not even when I've felt good
about grades or a new outfit
or seeing Storm again
after too much time.

Because the little voice
residing in my brain
reminds me none
of those things
truly belong to me.

They can vanish
snap
on a whim.

To experience
true happiness
would require
a sense of permanence.

As sleep swallows me,
I resign myself
to *almost*.

I'M JERKED AWAKE

By an ear-shattering screech.

> *What are you doing?*

Colleen rips back my blankets.
Discovers a naked Parker scrambling
to un-attach herself from a naked me.

> *I knew it! Perverts!*

She grabs Parker by the hair,
pulls her onto the floor.

> *Bitch!* screams Parker.
> *That's child abuse, you know.*

> *Your word against mine.*
> *Who are they going to believe?*

"Two of us on this side of the story."

> *Obviously. But not for long.*
> *Your disgusting games are over.*

She storms out of the room,
leaves the door open.

"Care to watch?" I call, knowing
it will only exacerbate the problem
but unable to stop myself.

Holy shit.
There goes *almost*.

STORM
Four Days Waiting

To plead my case in front
of a judge, knowing it's useless
without Jaidyn's cooperation.
I asked Jim to see if she'll come.
Meanwhile, more screenings.

Physical health. Check.
A bit on the lean side.
Vaccinations up to date.
No allergies.

Dental health. Check.
Could use some work.

Sexual health. Check.
No STDs.
Not an assault victim.
Not an assault perp.
Does not present LGBTQ.

Mental health. Check.
The counselor asks if I feel
I need meds to stave off anxiety
and/or aggressive behaviors.

I understand the game.
"What makes you think
I might become combative?"

Ms. Wilson is fortyish, black,
with bleached hair that circles
her face like a platinum cloud.
Her eyes are so emerald green
I wonder if it's the color of her contacts.

        This game belongs to her.

> Oh, I don't know. Something about
> your history of violent assaults?

"All totally righteous."

She opens a folder, runs
her finger down a page inside it.

> Totally righteous. Uh-huh.
> Thirteen years old, you beat
> the crap out of a kid because
> he looked at some photos.

"*My* photos. Could've asked
to see them. And, by the way,
he beat the crap out of *me*."

> Mutual crap beating. Noted.

"Yeah, well, he was bigger.
What was I supposed to do?
Not defend myself?"

> Sounds like you started it.
> So, he was defending himself.

I hate logic. I don't respond.

> She moves on. *Two years later.*
> *Wow. You escalated, didn't you?*

I figured lockup was my calling.
Why not play hard and fast
for whatever time I had on the outside?

But What I Say Is

"It wasn't all my fault."

>She actually laughs. Laughs.
>*That seems to be your theme song.*

My pissed response triggers.
"What's so damn funny?"

>*Nothing in this folder is funny.*

"True. It's also not all my fault.
Maybe start with my mother..."

>*Okay. When did you last see your mom?*

"Mother. I mean, I called her Mom,
but she was more like an incubator."

>*Understood. So, when was the last
>time you saw your incubator?*

"Three years ago, at Christmas.
She wanted Lake and me for the holidays."

>*And how did that go?*

"We figured out there was no Santa."
I say it with a straight face,
and I think she actually believes
me for about two seconds.

>She grins. *Why was that?*

"Where do I start?"

The Living Situation Was Impossible

Mom had moved in with one
of her strip club customers, a wiry
little son of a bitch named Don.

Their apartment had a single
bedroom, and they shared it.
I insisted Lake take the couch,
which meant I slept on the floor.

"Mom and Don fought about work.
About money. About whose turn
it was to shop, to cook, to clean.
About Mom's part-time stripping."

He didn't like her stripping?

"No, he was fine with it, but
he wanted her to put in more hours.
She said kids needed supervision.
We were her excuse to stay home.
Not that we noticed her
worrying about us."

No one else could watch you?

I shake my head.
"Our grandmother did when
we were little, but she was
mostly out of the picture,
though she did drop by once or twice."

She always left buzzed on booze.
Beverly hadn't changed at all.

One of Those Times

Happened to be Christmas.
Mom claimed to want us home
specifically on that day, but never
bothered with a tree or lights or tinsel.

Lake and I scrounged cardboard
from beside the apartment dumpsters.
We cut it into Christmas tree patterns,
like we did in school once, only bigger.

Then we glued on pebbles, buttons,
bottle caps, and whatever else
interesting we could find.
It was crude, but better than nothing.

We finished it on Christmas Eve.
The end product at least added
sparkle to the plain living room.
"Santa would like it," I said.

       Lake agreed. *Doesn't even matter*
       there aren't any presents to put
       underneath it, she added.

       Who says? asked Mom.
       Beverly's bringing them.

Later I overheard Mom in
her room, on the phone.

       Just get something, Mother.
       I swear I'll pay you back.
       Pause. Thirteen. Remember?

No presents. No surprise, and neither
was Beverly forgetting our age.

Lake and I laughed about it.
We were immune to hurt by then.
All that mattered was being together again.
We found ways to feel happy.
Until everything turned to complete shit.

Christmas morning, the yelling
started before Mom and Don
even opened the bedroom door.

> *They're your damn kids.*
> *Why do I have to get up?*

> *It's almost eleven. My mother*
> *will be here anytime.*

Beverly showed up maybe
an hour later. When I opened
the door, she bolted into the room.

> *Merry Christmas! Ho. Ho. Ho.*
> Each "ho" was a gin-scented huff.

Presents? Yeah, she had them.
One for Lake. One for me.
Wrapped in newspaper.
Plus a big bottle of cheap booze,
already open and missing a little,
which she gave to Mom and Don.

> *Caught Santa at the liquor*
> *store. He said to bring you this.*

Booze for Breakfast

Tends to set the tone for the day.
By the time Lake and I sat
on the floor to open our gifts,
the three so-called adults
were downing gin and tonics.

"You go first," I told Lake.
We didn't expect much,
and that's what we got.

Memory for Lake.
Jenga for me.

> *I didn't know what you'd like,*
> *but when your mom was a kid,*
> *she used to play those games.*

> *Thanks, Beverly*, said Lake.

Honestly, considering how
few things we had to entertain
ourselves with, we were grateful.
We moved off into one corner
and I set up the Jenga.

Mom went into the kitchen
to work on dinner—turkey
lasagna, as it turned out.

Don and Beverly sat on the sofa
and watched Don's favorite
"Christmas" movie, *Die Hard*.
Lake creamed me at Jenga.
I beat her at Memory.

After *Die Hard*, Don found

*an NFL game. Football on
Christmas! There is a Santa Claus!*

*Told you I saw him at the liquor
store. Speaking of which...*

Beverly stumbled into the kitchen
to refill her glass.

No clue what triggered it,
but on her return she started to dance.
Not like the waltz.
More like what she did at work.

I mean, she kept her clothes
on, but the way she wriggled
her body in front of Don
was totally meant to turn him on.

Isn't this better than football?

I figured Don would yell
for her to get out of the way.
I figured Mom would get pissed
and tell Beverly to cool it.
But Don and Mom started dancing, too.

"It's a sandwich," I whispered.
"Beverly and Mom are the bread.
Don's the meat."

Gross.

It was.

Ms. Wilson's Face

Remains totally blank
as I relate the experience.
"You don't think that's funny?"

> *I don't find child abuse amusing.*

"Child... That wasn't abuse."

> *Oh, but it was.*

"Not compared to..."

> *What?*

"Doesn't matter. Long time
ago." And the bitch is dead.

> *It does matter. But we can
> talk about that another time.
> Okay, so what about school?*
>
> *Assuming you'll be with us
> for a while, are you going
> to participate willingly?*

"Guess so. Why wouldn't I?"

> *She shrugs. Some people don't.
> What about vocational aspirations?*

"Like, what do I want to be
when I grow up?"

> *Yes, exactly like that.*

"What makes you think

I'm going to grow up?"

> *You told me you're not suicidal.*

"That shit's not up to me."

I might have her stumped.
She sits there gawking
for a decent length of time.

> *Let's say you do grow up.*
> *What would you like to do?*

"Ms. Wilson, no one decent
is going to hire me. I'll never go
to college. I'll probably flip burgers."

> *Humor me here. If you could go*
> *to college, what career path*
> *would you want to choose?*

I've never really thought
much about it. Not since . . .

Something Molly once said to me
surfaces. Rex messed with bees
and one day he got stung on the nose.
He let me put baking soda paste on it.

> *You're so good with him,* she told
> me. *You should think about being a . . .*

"I guess a veterinarian."

That Seems to Impress Her

> *That's a fine ambition.*
> *You like animals, I take it?*

"I like dogs. Never been
around other animals unless
you count the human kind."

> *You don't much like that*
> *kind, though, do you?*

"I like the few I can count on.
Jim. My sister. My girlfriend . . ."

Except, where is she? Move on.
"And I like you."

> *You are a player.* She grins.
> *Of course. But tell me about*
> *your girlfriend. What's her name?*

"Her name's Jaidyn. And, yes,
I'm in love with her. And, yes,
that complicates everything."

> *At least you're honest.*

"Believe it or not, I have no
reason to lie. Truth matters."

> *Okay, then. Is Jaidyn possibly*
> *responsible for why you're here?*

I bring my eyes level
with hers. "In every way."

She expects me to give her

the details, but I hold on to them.

> *You going to make me guess?*

I hate betraying Jaidyn's confidence.
I hate that it might make a judge go easier.
I hate that Jaidyn's put me in this position.

"I promised I wouldn't tell.
Figure it out. You're a woman."

> She nods. *I get it. I'm sorry.
> No chance she'll change her mind?*

I shrug. "Either way, that son
of a bitch won't be hurting
anyone else for a long time."

> *I wouldn't be feeling too
> noble about that, Storm.*

"Noble? Hardly. Satisfied?
A little, though he should be
the one talking to the judge
tomorrow, and I don't mean
as a witness against me."

> *I doubt he'd risk that unless
> he knows about your deal
> with Jaidyn. Or he's stupid.*

"He's a successful predator.
He's anything but stupid."

LANCE IS NOT STUPID ENOUGH

To make an appearance.
My public defender, who isn't much
interested in defending me, informs
me of this first thing.

We meet ahead of my hearing,
in a windowless puke-green room.
A fluorescent bulb's buzzing overhead.
He doesn't shake my hand.

Picture a five-foot-five packrat
in a cheap suit, and you've got
Peter Maxwell. Scraggly whiskers
and dark eye circles make ol' Pete
look like he's been on the job too long.

> *The DA's filed a petition*
> *to keep you detained.*
> *The charge is felony assault.*

I nod. Basic information.

> *This is your detention hearing.*
> *The DA will present the basic*
> *information about your case.*
> *You can contest the petition*
> *if you believe what he says is false.*

"He isn't prone to lying, is he?"

> *I'd stow the attitude if I were*
> *you. Are you saying you're guilty?*

"Why would I make something
 up? There were witnesses.
 Also extenuating circumstances."

And what might those be?

"The guy assaulted someone first.
  Someone I care about."

*I see. Well, that person can
testify at your jurisdiction
hearing, which will be within
fifteen business days.*

*Meanwhile, since you have
no parent here on your behalf,
the judge will order continued
detention until that time.*

"What about Jim?"

*He consults his notes. Oh.
Your foster father. I'm afraid
the system won't allow it.
Not with the impending charge.
You could be a danger to him.*

"Serious question. What do
you think will happen
at my jurisdiction hearing?"

A long pause, punctuated
by that damn humming light.

*Three assaults in four years,
each more vicious than the last.
Even with your extenuating
circumstances, you'll do time.
The only question is, how long?*

BLUNT

But that's better than bullshit.
Guess only pricey personal lawyers
tell you everything will be fine.
No worry, just sign the check.
While the walls of your carefully
constructed domain crash down.

"Extenuating circumstances
are a reason to plead not guilty,
right?" Don't want to appear
too eager to be locked up.

Allow me to do my job, please.

Maybe I want one of those
expensive lawyers after all.

Peter Maxwell exits the cubicle
before I do. I wait for a guard
to escort me to the courtroom.
It's mostly deserted.

Juvenile detention hearings
aren't generally newsworthy,
and underage defendants
require some anonymity.

Jim is here, though, dressed
like he's going to a funeral.
I've never seen him in a suit.
But I'm elated to see him now.

He's here, so he hasn't turned
his back on me completely.
He nods a silent hello.

I Shuffle Across Polished Floors

Sit in a polished wood chair.
At a polished wood table.
Stare at the ceiling, try to avoid
the fluorescent glare off all that polish.

All rise.

The Honorable Judge Clayborn waddles
out from chambers. If ol' Pete is a packrat,
the judge is a walrus, all odd tufts of hair
and a wide mustache that looks like it
would get in the way of a sandwich.
He settles into his cushioned chair.

You may be seated.

He consults his notes. Looks up.
Cuts me in half with a scathing scowl.
As expected, Judge Clayborn detains me
until my jurisdiction hearing.
Three weeks, give or take, to reel
in witnesses for the packrat to call.

I only have a moment to speak to Jim,
who hasn't managed to contact Jaidyn
but promises to give it another try.

Morley surely misses you.
Afternoons, he waits by the door
for you to get home from school.
I miss your company, too.

Back to lockup, eyes smarting.
Still in C Unit until my sentence
becomes set in cinder block.

One Day Bleeds into the Next

I start juvie school.
None of the core classes they offer
promises a future in vet science.

I don't talk much. No use making
connections when I'll likely move
into a different unit with tougher dudes.

I do utilize the gym. I lift. Run.
Practice martial arts moves that
might come in handy before long.

When I'm not doing those things,
I'm confined to my room. I study.
Read. Write. Think.

About Jim. Wonder.
        If he's replaced me yet.
        If Morley still waits by the door.

About Lake. Wonder.
        If she's disappointed
        in the me she's discovered.

About Lance. Wonder.
        If he's working on single-
        testicle sexual assault.

About Jaidyn. Wonder.
        If she's still in denial.
        If she's healing.
        If she's wondering about me.
        If she even remembers who I am.

For Whatever Reason

I maintain a slim hope
that Jaidyn will decide she loves
me enough to come to my defense.

I came to hers. And then I put
everything on the line to exact
the revenge she'd never
even seek for herself.
I love her that much.

I know the psychological
fallout of abuse, assault.
I live with it every day.

But I've never been raped,
and can only guess
how my brain would
process the aftermath.

   Something happened.
     What happened?
   Think about what happened.
     Can't remember what happened.
   So nothing happened.
  Don't tell me it happened.

   Too
     much.
       Shut
        down.

But at some point the synapses
must reboot, fire up again.
The problem is time.

LAKE
WISHING

I hadn't listened to Parker.

> *Don't worry*, she said.
> *We'll be fine*, she said.
> *We can make it on our own.*

Here we are, two weeks
after stuffing our pitiful
belongings in our backpacks,

swiping sixty bucks
out of Colleen's purse,
and running off into
the teeth-cracking cold
fog-draped morning.

We had no idea where to go,
only that we were going together.

> *Don't worry. We'll be fine.*
> *We can make it on our own.*

At first, I said no way.
"I'm scared."

> *Of what?*

"Where we're going."

> *More scared of that than where we've been?*

"At least they feed us here.
At least we have warm beds."

> *Don't you get it? Colleen*
> *won't let us stay here anymore.*

Echoes of Eloise.
Only instead of letting
one of us stay, Colleen
would send us both away.

She wasn't about to let
queer girls sully her house.

I might have played
wait and see, but Colleen
was yelling into the phone
that whoever was on the other
end had better come get us.

> *Don't worry. We'll be fine.*
> *We can make it on our own.*

Honestly, when we first tore
out the front door it was exhilarating.

Parker grabbed my hand.
We started to run.
She started singing
Pharrell Williams's "Freedom."

> *"Hold on to me. Don't let me go . . ."*

We hit the city center,
jumped on the first bus.

> *Don't worry. We'll be fine.*
> *We can make it on our own.*

Reality Set In Quickly

Let's start with this: Freedom
isn't free. It isn't even cheap.

I knew we couldn't find
an apartment for sixty bucks,
but had no clue one night
in an iffy motel could cost that much.
I've never stayed in a motel.

"What about a shelter?"

>You need an ID to get into one,
>and there are long waiting lists.

Neither of us has an ID,
except for our school ones.
School. Forgot about that, too.

>Besides, pretty sure we've been
>reported as runaways by now.
>Shelters are supposed to screen people.

Parker knows more about those
things than I do, since she and
her mom were homeless for a while.
I've never been homeless.

Until now.

That first day we wandered
unfamiliar roadways in alien
neighborhoods, searching for
a suitable place to crash until
we figured something out.

We spent that night nestled
beneath a palm tree in the side yard
of a Catholic cathedral. Next morning
Parker said an angel must have visited
because she had come up with a plan.

> *Let's look for an abandoned car.*

I would've never thought of that.
It took most of the day, but eventually
we found an ancient rusting sedan,
left to rot on a quiet street.

It wasn't locked. Thank you, angel.
One problem was obvious right away.
"Where we gonna pee?"

> *If you get desperate, in the trunk.*

She laughed at my expression.

> *Kidding. We'll use public restrooms.*
> *Parks. Libraries. Fast-food places.*
> *Convenience stores. As long as you*
> *buy something, they can't say no.*

"Then we'd better scope out
the closest place to buy candy."

> *You mean water. Your body needs it*
> *and it fills you up better than candy.*

Water. Candy. Jerky. Nuts.
Buy one. Lift two.
It's become our motto.

THE DAYS SMUDGE INTO EACH OTHER

Sleep comes hard at night,
not knowing who or what
might wander by. A single
drop of Daisy brings me closer
to Storm, and is my reward
for surviving another day.

Parker and I wake up
when we feel like it or when
a blast of exhaust belches by
or when the car seats become
impossible to stay curled into.

Sometimes it's still dark
when I'm jolted awake
by Parker fighting nightmares
or singing in her sleep.

For a couple breathless seconds
I don't know where I am.
What closet is this,
clothes hanging like ghosts?

Then the smell hits.
Old motor oil. Old leather.
Old sweat. Old cigarettes.
I remember then.

One more night
in an abandoned sedan,
spare clothing curtaining
the windows from curious eyes.

One more morning hoping
freedom is worth the struggle.

THAT MISPLACED SENSE

Of morality I once clung
to has deteriorated,
and any droplet of shame
I used to possess has evaporated.

I haven't used the trunk.
But a couple of desperate times
in the gray of predawn I hurried
down the sidewalk to a litter-strewn
lot, peed in the dirt, and air-dried.

Mostly, we rely on public
restrooms for our most
personal necessities.
Using the toilet.
Brushing our teeth.
Washing off grime and stink.

If you don't think that's awful,
try shampooing your hair
in a cold-water-only sink
and drying it with industrial-
strength paper towels.

After "laundering" your two
spare pairs of panties with soap
that smells like kerosene.

All while someone waits outside
the door and, when you exit,
hair and underwear dripping,
quite obviously considers calling
either the manager or the cops.

WE'VE BEEN SUPER CAREFUL

With those sixty dollars,
but have to spend a little
almost every day, the price tag
for flushing our poo.

The money won't last forever,
so we've been looking for jobs.
A lot of places are hiring.
Problem is, you need more
than just an ID to get one.

We learn this the hard
way when Parker fills out
an application at McDonald's.

> *It's asking for my Social Security
> number. I don't know mine.*

I shrug. "Make one up."

She writes 35826 and when
she hands the paper to the manager,
he looks confused.

> *You forgot four numbers.*

I did? Oh, 7549.

> *So, 358-26-7549?*

I guess. Is that right?

His glare says she's either off
her rocker or being purposely obtuse.

He says he'll call if she gets the job.

Only, no phone. No address.
Not that her fake responses
on the application indicate
either. So many complications.

We splurge on a two-dollar
chicken sandwich to share,
use the toilet (paid for), grab
cups of water, and exit, giggling.

> Next time I'll remember nine numbers.

But we both know it's next to
impossible to score regular jobs.
We're undocumented workers.

"Maybe we should hitchhike
to Salinas or something."

Parker gets my reference.

> *If I must toil for next to nothing,*
> *picking produce will be a last resort.*
> *Mostly because I'm a total wuss.*

We sit at a table outside,
with a spectacular view
of the drive-through line,
and feed each other bites
of a mediocre chicken sandwich
like it's a gourmet meal.

It kind of is.

WE DECIDE

To go to the public library
and use a computer to check for
under-the-table work like maybe
babysitting or dog walking or something.

Luckily, our bus passes are good
for a while. We plop into a rear
seat, dare to share a long kiss.

It's a twenty-minute ride.
Parker sings the whole way.
This older woman with silver-
streaked hair turns, squinting.

> *You've got a beautiful voice.*
> *I bet you could sing for a living.*

Parker literally beams.
Think so? Well, thank you.

"Maybe we should find a busy
street corner, put out a hat,
and you could sing for dollars."

> *More like pennies. But in a pinch...*
> *Anyway, people might misunderstand*
> *why I'm on that street corner.*

I think about Star, who left foster
care, only to land on a sidewalk
in a sketchy part of town,
waving down customers.

For the thousandth time,
I pray we didn't make a major mistake.

At the Library

We discover we made a minor mistake.
All the computers are in use.
You have to reserve them ahead
of time, with your library card.

We've never been here before,
so we spend time checking out
the gorgeous artwork displays
before perusing the magazines.

Parker picks *People* and *Rolling Stone*.
I peruse *Vogue* and *Harper's Bazaar*,
checking out clothes I'll never afford.
Then I dig a notebook out of my bag,
sketch my own brand of fashion.

We don't find jobs, but we do
take comfort in spending an afternoon
reading and drawing in plush chairs,
almost like regular people.

Then we get on a bus for the return
trip to our borrowed rusting car.

No dinner.
No movies.
No shower.

No heat except each other.
We rely on that to thwart the chill.
But, more, to conquer the fractured
certainty of tomorrow with tangible
human-to-human connection today.

IN THIS MOMENT

Tomorrow doesn't exist.
The only thing that matters
is the intricate weave
of our bodies. Here. Now.

We know the pattern well.
And yet, there are surprises.
The perfume of library
somehow clinging to her hair.

Goosebumps lifting into
the cool evening air
with the feather stroke
of my fingers against
the thrum in her throat.

The way she heats my skin
with no more than the brush
of her lips as she whisper-moans
a love song into my ear.

Discovering joy in the listing
back seat of an old sedan
unworthy of ownership.
Sort of like Parker and me.

All I have is her.
All she has is me.
And we celebrate that
with lustful abandon.

Wild.
Wicked.
Wonderful.

TOTALLY IMMERSED

In the magic, the *tap-tap-tap*
on the window doesn't register.
But now it becomes *knock-knock-knock*.

                        A man's voice. *Hey, girls.*
                        Whatcha doin' in there?

Parker scrambles to make
sure the doors are locked.
I always make sure they are.

        What if it's a cop?

I don't want to move
our makeshift curtains, so
I yell, "Who wants to know?"

                        Just me. Teddy. Been watching
                        you for a couple of days now.
                        You two all alone in the world?

        Don't say anything, Parker
        urges. *Maybe he'll go away.*

"Seriously? If he's been
watching us, he's a creep,
and creeps don't just go away."

        So, what do we do?

"Two of us. One of him.
We could probably take
him. First, let's try playing nice."

I PEEK PAST

The sweatshirt covering the window.
Teddy is a little guy, pushing sixty,
with short but unkempt hair.
Probably doesn't smell great
from the looks of his clothes.

"We're fine," I call to him.
"Just down on our luck is all."

You need anything? Food? Money?

"No, thanks. We're all set."

*One of you has a pretty voice.
I sit out here listening at night...*

Goosebumps climb up my back.
But when he speaks again,
his energy stream is gentle.

*My wife sang like that. I miss her.
If you sing for me, I'll leave a couple
of bucks under the windshield wiper.*

Parker gives me a "should I?"
look. I answer with a shrug.

What song?

*Do you know "Over the Rainbow"?
I love that song. Did you ever
see that movie? The Wizard of Oz?
That was my wife's favorite.*

He sounds sincere.

Parker must think so, too.
Her soprano lifts toward
that rainbow, and all the way
up over it. Part Judy Garland.
Part Israel Kamakawiwoʻole,
that famous Hawaiian singer.

She even fades into "What
a Wonderful World" for a few.
I kind of wish I could play
the ukulele for real.

When Parker finishes, Teddy
and I reward her with applause.

Thank you. Have a good night.

The clunk of a wiper
against the windshield
implies Teddy's kept his word.
I move the sweatshirt enough
to see him fade into the night.
A ripple of paranoia remains.

"Think it's okay to check
if he actually left money?"

We'd better. Someone else might take it.

I open the door cautiously.
There's no one around,
so I take a chance and exit.
There, as promised,
is a wilted five-dollar bill.

IT'S A SURPRISE

I wouldn't have thought the guy
had an extra five bucks to spare.
But apparently he has an income
source, because he returns the next night.

And the next.

Five nights in a row, as darkness
falls, with different song requests
every time. Two per visit.

Most are from musicals.
Carousel.
Fiddler on the Roof.
The Sound of Music.

I asked Parker how
she knows those songs.

> *Mom sang them all the time.*
> *When she was young, before she met*
> *Dad, she was all into musical theater.*

Reminding me again
how little I'm acquainted
with Parker's background.

Night five, however,
she blows me away.

Teddy's request: "Ave Maria."
I've never heard anything
quite as beautiful. Parker
really should sing for a living.

Teddy must have his ear

right up against the window
because his sobbing is obvious.

>*You're an angel*, he says
>when Parker finishes.

We hear the wiper lift.

>*No seconds tonight?* calls Parker.

>>*Not after that. I want to
>>hold on to it for a while.*

He leaves. We collect payment.
Five nights. Twenty-five dollars.

"How long can this last?"

>*Until he runs out of musicals
>or money? Anyway, don't jinx us.*

"How do you know 'Ave
Maria'? That isn't from a show."

>She shakes her head. *My mom
>sang in the church choir, too.
>It was the only reason I liked Mass.*

"Wait. You're Catholic?
And you used to go to church?
Why didn't you ever tell me?"

>*Never seemed important.
>It's not who I am anymore.*

MY TURN

To sleep up front, I stuff my feet
under the steering wheel, tuck
my cheek against the cracked
vinyl seat, bury my face into the fold
of my elbow where it's relatively warm.

It's not who I am anymore.
The sentence ricochets inside my head.
I'm not who I was only a couple of weeks ago.
Circumstance has changed me.

I'm a child of the street.
Wild, if not truly free.
Is that better or worse
than being safely caged?

I miss regular meals. A warm bed.
School. Especially school.

I love Parker more fiercely
than ever before.

I'd only seen a pale outline.
Never realized her inner strength.
It hasn't faltered.
Since we've been here,
she hasn't zoned out once.
I worried about that.
But, unlike me, she hasn't wavered.

"Hey, Parker. You asleep?"

Not quite. What is it?

"You seem happy. Are you?"

Yes.

"How? Things aren't easy."

*One time on this TV show—America's
Got Talent—a girl named Nightbirde
sang this song she wrote—"It's OK."
A line was "It's alright to be lost sometimes."*

*Turned out she was dying of cancer.
When the judges asked how she could
sing about such a hard thing, she said,
"You can't wait until life isn't hard
anymore before you decide to be happy."*

I've decided almost happy isn't enough.

"I love you."

*Love you, too. Now, sleep.
I think it's starting to rain.*

Fat drops *plink-plink-plink*
against metal and glass,
sparking a reverie. Again,
Parker's depth surprises me.

It's like I was treading
shallow water, but once
I dove down, the treasures
I discovered made me
content to drown
rather than risk losing
them in favor of nothing but air.

THE NEED TO PEE

Rouses me, forces a tough
decision. It's early. Both Parker
and the neighborhood are still asleep.
The dirt lot isn't far. But it's raining.

"Hey, Parker?" I say, loud enough
to wake her. "I've really got to go,
and don't want to squat in the mud.
You want to come with?"

    Seriously?

"Please? We can splurge.
Get some breakfast. But hurry."

    Fine.

We don't have jackets, so we slip
into sweatshirts, slide the hoods
up over our sleep-mussed hair,
grab our backpacks, and run.

    Where to? shouts Parker,
    sky tears dripping.

Sky tears.
Where did that come from?

Closest bathroom's a mini market.
We duck inside. The guy behind
the counter's familiar with our tactics.
Luckily, he's pretty cool.
He hands me the restroom key.

Parker and I take care
of business. I go first

and while I wait for her
I think about that phrase.

Sky tears.

It hits me.
It was the day
the state first took
Storm and me away.

It was spitting rain
when the caseworker
walked us past Mom.
Puffing on a cigarette,
she looked down at us
like we were strangers.

    Mom? whined Storm.

        Her voice was flat when
        she answered, *It's for the best*.

    Storm turned his face
    up toward the clouds.
    At least the sky has tears.

Now he's on my mind.
Guessing he'll be locked
up for a while. But once
he gets out, how will I find him?

Will I ever see my brother again?

PARKER AND I SPEND THE MORNING

Trying to stay dry.
We decide to invest a little cash
in staving off starvation.

Two orders of pancakes.
A side of bacon to share.
Coffee. Coffee. Coffee.

Cheap feasting feeds
my body if not my soul.
But I must admit the gooey
sweet fake maple syrup
gives me a shot of happiness.

Parker and I crack stupid jokes,
make inane comments about people,
draw stick figures in the smears
left on our plates.

We hang on to the table
until the waitress starts
wandering by regularly,
glancing down at the bill.

Probably wondering if her tip
will be worth putting up
with our obnoxiousness.

"I think she wants us to go."

    Drop a few bills. Give her a decent tip.

"I don't have any money.
I thought you brought it.
It was under the back seat."

Shit! Realization strikes us
simultaneously. We left
our cash stash in the car.
"What do we do?"

  Dine and dash. Act like you're going
  to the bathroom. I'll stay here until
  I see you leave, then I'll do the same.

I've never played this game before,
but if there's a better option,
I don't see it. I stand.
"Better pee. Coffee is a diuretic."

Parker rolls her eyes at my obviousness.
But no one else notices. Not even the waitress.

I walk past the restroom, out the door,
wait beyond view of the windows
until Parker comes running.
I join her and we sprint down the block,
around a couple of corners.

Out of breath, we pause
for air. "Where to?" I ask.

  The car. And our money.

It's fine, I tell myself. No one knows
it's there. But when we turn down
the familiar street, our money
is disappearing.

And so is the car,
on the hook of a tow truck.

STORM
THE DAY BEFORE MY HEARING

A letter from Jaidyn arrives.

> *I love you, Storm. I know my silence*
> *says otherwise, but what it can't tell*
> *you is I'm terrified. Of Lance. Of school.*
> *Of opening the door and going outside.*
>
> *The bruises are gone, and so is the grit.*
> *It took days to pick it all out of my knees*
> *and hands. Soap and water hardly*
> *even touched the black beneath my skin.*
>
> *I finally told Mom. She knew anyway.*
> *She wants me to press charges, but*
> *there was no evidence. The minute*
> *I got home, I douched it down the drain.*
>
> *I decided to homeschool the rest of the year.*
> *Maybe next year, too. I can barely show*
> *my face in public. Not after that video.*
> *I'm such a goddamn coward.*
>
> *I can't testify for you. I'm sorry.*
> *But I gave a written statement to Jim.*
> *He said he'd pass it on to your lawyer.*
> *I hope it makes a difference.*
>
> *I wish I wouldn't have gone running.*
> *I wish you'd never found me that way.*
> *I wish you'd never seen Lance that day.*
> *But wishing is a waste of time, isn't it?*

THE BRUISES ARE GONE

And so is the grit.

And so is the girl
I fell in love with.

Her passion.
Her courage.
Her humor.
Her joy.

Gone.

All that's left
is a shell.

Beautiful.
Scarred.
Hollow.

I lie on the thin
cell mattress,
tomorrow's likely
court outcome
fast approaching,
conjure her face
in the darkness.

Allow myself to cry.

I don't waste time
with wishes.

On the Hook

Held to account for an act
I most certainly committed.

The system claims it's criminal.
I call it righteous.
But I'm not in charge.

The man who is sits
in his cushy chair above me,
elevated to remind whoever
comes into his courtroom
that his decision is the only
one that matters.

Lucky me.
It's Judge Walrus.

> *I'm familiar with your case.*
> *Is there anything you'd like*
> *to say in your defense?*

I glance at the packrat,
who's holding Jaidyn's statement.

> *My client would like this*
> *to be read into the record*
> *and hopes it will influence*
> *your decision for leniency.*

It's a straightforward narrative
of the day I found Jaidyn
stumbling away from the scene
of her violent rape.

Judge Walrus pretends to listen,
but doesn't look convinced.

Why didn't she testify in person?

I wait, but the packrat
doesn't explain. So I do.

"She says she's terrified
to even leave her house.
He-e-e did that to her."

I extend the "he" so the judge
understands exactly who
I'm talking about.
He considers the information
for longer than I expected.
But the outcome isn't a surprise.

*I'm sorry for the young lady.
But we mustn't rely on
vigilantism to extract justice.*

The packrat attempts
a lame defense. *Your honor,
I'd ask you to remember
the defendant's age.*

*I haven't forgotten that.
Seventeen, and capable
of mayhem. Regardless
of extenuating circumstances,
he must be held accountable.*

Two Years in County Lockup

>Consider yourself fortunate.
>If you were another year older...

He'd send me to prison.

>Use the stretch to turn
>your life around.

He doesn't say how I'm supposed
to accomplish that, treading time
with dudes as bad as I am.
But then he opens a door.

>I'll allow a six-month review.
>Keep your nose clean and you'll
>have the chance to enter the Youth
>Offender Treatment Program.

Successful completion might
mean early release.

>But one more hint of trouble,
>there'll be no second chance.
>Judge Walrus sits, glaring.

>Thank you, Your Honor.
>I'm sure... uh...

The packrat consults his paperwork.

>...Storm here will take
>your advice to heart.

Holy shit. He forgot my name?

The Packrat Offers

Three words of heartfelt advice.

> *Don't fuck up.*

Too damn late. I fucked up good.
Let emotion trump logic.

Two years. Who will I be?
Who will be left for me?
Lake will never desert me.
But all that remains of Jaidyn
are memories. They haunt me.
I hope they don't desert me.

> A careless sweep of auburn hair
> not quite hiding one topaz eye.
>
> Those incredible lips, kissing
> every inch of my body.
>
> Satin skin. Dancing tongue.
> Rain between her thighs.

Remembering
> makes me shiver
> makes me hungry
> makes me hard.

Remembering
> stabs me
> shreds me
> rips me in two.

But I'd rather weather the pain
than have nothing left of her at all.

THE MORNING'S WEIGHT

Presses down hard. Every foot
back to Housing feels like a mile.
Silver raindrops pelt the windows.
Figures. Gloom means doom.

As predicted, I'm no longer in C Unit,
with the mostly sane guys. No,
I'm moving to E, with hardcore dudes
into big-time shit like jacking
cars and rolling old ladies.

At gunpoint.

I have to wait while Officer Harris
goes through my stuff, searching
for contraband, though stashing
cell-crafted weapons is a bigger
problem on E. Where I'll soon be.

Can't call it living.

They claim the routine—up by six,
breakfast six thirty, half-hour to brush
and crap, classes, lunch, cell time,
gym, dinner, an hour of "recreation"—
is to prepare you for workaday
life beyond your release.

That's a lie.

It's designed to break you down
psychologically, batter you with
boredom. Unfortunately, guys
my age are hardwired for physical
and mental stimulation.

Case in Point

As we enter E Unit, a few guys
are hanging out in the commons.
They all stare as Officer Harris
and I walk by. Sizing me up.

I acknowledge them with a flick
of my head but don't meet
any of their eyes directly.
Challenges can be subtle.
Non-challenges can be misperceived.

The new guy on the block
should proceed carefully.
No looking for trouble.
No courting friends.
No trying to be entertainment.

But a skinhead type pokes
the tattooed guy across from him.

> *Hey, Ripley. That dude*
> *could be your brother.*
> *Your mama mess around*
> *when they sent up your dad?*

Ripley utters a low growl,
and in two seconds flat, he's over
the table, cartwheeling swings.

Skinhead, who has thirty pounds
and three inches of reach on the guy,
is forced to defend himself.

The others hoot encouragement
as he connects with Ripley's nose.

Stay out of this! Harris yells
at me, moving toward
the fray. *Break it up!*

Cameras have caught the action.
Another guard comes sprinting.

Ripley puffs hard, out of breath.
His attack loses power.
Skinhead, barely affected, laughs.

Harris curses. *Goddamn it,
Baxter. What's wrong with you?*

Me? Ripley started it.

*Shut the hell up! Isolation
calling your name or what?*

Aw, c'mon, sir, fake-pleads
Skinhead, aka Baxter.
*It was just a little romp.
No serious harm done.*

Harris and his coworker
look at each other. Shrug,
almost in tandem. We all
know what that means.

Who wants to do paperwork?

If the Guards

Wanted to go by the book,
the outcome of the event
would be very different.

But everyone agrees,
for whatever reasons,
that Ripley blowing off
a little steam isn't worth
the time and stress involved
to isolate him and Baxter.

I'm a little relieved
myself, to have remained
on the periphery.

Still, even as an offhand
joke, Baxter chose
to involve me.

He's someone to watch out for.
I don't think I can avoid him.

Every unit has a hierarchy.
Baxter's at the top
of the food chain,
though I suspect
he's more hyena than lion.

I don't need to be his friend.

But I don't want
to become his enemy.

BLOODBATH AVERTED

Harris leads me upstairs
to a double room.
Neither bed, however,
is currently occupied.

"Roommate?"

>　*Not at the moment.
>　Lucky you. Put your stuff
>　on the desk and we'll head
>　down to the storage room.*

I get a new (used) mattress,
pillow, sheets, and blanket.
As I haul them to my room,
Harris repeats the rules.
Only he emphasizes a couple of things.

>　*We work real hard over
>　here to mitigate gang
>　interaction. You see anything
>　like that, run the other way.
>　Participation means prolonged
>　isolation. You don't want that.*

"I have no affiliation."

>　*White power guys will try
>　to recruit you. Just say no.*

"Guys like Baxter?"

>　*He shrugs. Ripley, too.
>　As far as I know, just since
>　he's been incarcerated here.*

Both Safety and Danger

Come with connection.
I want no part of it.

And I definitely do not
want to spend protracted
time in hardcore isolation,
which is basically
solitary confinement.

> *You start school tomorrow.*
> *Take it seriously. Do well, your PO*
> *could recommend you start*
> *the transitional program*
> *ahead of schedule. Got it?*

"Yeah."

> *You have a hundred dollars*
> *in your commissary account—*

"How?" I didn't put any
money in there. I don't
have any money.

> *Beats me. Someone must*
> *care about you. Surprised?*

Shocked. "Must've been
Jim. My foster dad."

> *Could be, I guess. Whoever*
> *it was left a stack of letters*
> *and cards, too. Once we go*
> *through them, you'll get them.*

Mail can't contain dirty

pictures or gang mentions
or anything that might
provoke problematic behavior.

Those must be my letters
from Lake. At least I'll have
something to keep me
close to her, in spirit
if not sitting next to me.

Phone calls from here
are expensive, but since
I have money in my account,
maybe I'll use some to hear
her voice. If I still have
the number, and if her fosters
will accept a call from juvie.

Another question surfaces:
Would Jaidyn take my call?

The morning's business
made me miss lunch.

Harris says he'll bring
me a sandwich to eat
in my cell. Er, room.

They want us to feel
right at home here.
Ha ha ha ha ha ha.

But it isn't Harris who
returns with a food tray
and a stack of mail.

IT'S BYRON

        Well, shit, Carpenter. Sorry
        to see you're back.

"You and me both."

        I've set up an assessment meeting
        with Educational Services.
        We want you to graduate on schedule.
        I heard you met Baxter and Ripley.
        I'll repeat Harris's advice. Steer clear.

"Any idea how to do that?
It's pretty tight quarters."

        You're a clever guy.

"If I was I wouldn't be stuck here."

        See that? You already learned something.

I like Byron. He takes no shit,
but he's not hard-nosed, either.

        Here's your mail. The letter
        on top is from Jim. You should
        probably read it right away.

"Something bad?"

        Not good, he agrees. *But not all*
        bad, either. I'll be back for you
        a little before three.

His look of sympathy makes me hesitate.
But curiosity takes full advantage of me.

Jim's Letter

Is written in a shaky hand.
He apologizes for not making
my disposition hearing.
Says he's under the weather,
which means he's pretty sick.

Oh shit. Candace called to let
him know Lake and Parker
ran away a couple of weeks ago.
That Colleen person caught them
in a "compromising situation."

Shades of Eloise, except they made
things a whole lot worse by stealing
money and jewelry. Why, Lake?
That does not sound like you.

I let that sit for a minute, then
continue reading.

> On a slightly brighter note, I have
> a proposal. I know the probation officer
> asked for a two-year sentence.
> I'm hopeful the judge was a bit more
> lenient, but even if you're there for half that,
> you'll be eighteen when you leave.
>
> The system wouldn't let you stay with me,
> but you'll have aged out by then. If you need
> a place, my door will be open for you.
> Oh, I dropped a little cash in your commissary
> account. Everyone needs candy bars.
>
> Keep in touch, Jim

I Reread

The letter several times.
I dismantle it line by line,
inserting personal commentary
I'd like to send in a letter to Lake.
Only she's not currently
receiving mail.

> Lake and Parker ran away.

Really, Lake? After all
you've been through,
this made you run away?

> . . . caught them in a compromising situation.

Okay, maybe I figured
you and Parker had a thing
going on, but I would never
have believed you'd let it
take you down.

> . . . no idea where they might have gone.

Where are you?
How are you living?
I'd just started to feel
like you were safe.
Two weeks on the street?
Who will protect you there?

Okay, not like I could do
much protecting in lockup.
We both fucked up, huh?

Only it's worse for you.

I never really believed
there'd be anything else
for me. But you?

What about school?
What about books?
What about fashion?

    ... they stole money and a piece of jewelry ...

What got into you?
Stealing was never your gig.
It complicates everything.

    The woman wants to press charges ...

Holy shit.
Lake could wind up here.

This cell has no windows.
It's a soundless cement box.
I can't see drizzle or hear
tapping against the roof.

But I'm one thousand percent
certain it's still raining.

LAKE
THIS RAIN

Feels like God is pissing on us.
I mean, as if a universal intelligence existed.
But if it did, it would be pissing on us.

Parker and I stand, helplessly
watching the crumbs of our lives
disappear on the hook of a tow truck.

All our money. Gone.
Most of our clothes. Gone.
Water. Candy. Jerky. Nuts. Gone.

Well, that's fucked up.

"Why are you so calm?
What are we going to do?"

She clutches my shoulders,
looks me straight in the eye.

Start over.

"Start over? That's all we ever do!"

Parker laughs and, for the first
time ever, I want to laugh
when there's nothing to laugh about.

"We need drugs."

Plural?

"Okay, maybe just one, as long
as it can make me feel better."

A. You don't do drugs.

> B. *If you did, buying them requires money.*
> C. *We don't have any money.*
> D. *First we'd better figure out a new place to stay.*

Things are upside down
when Parker's the one dealing logic.

We start back toward town,
don't get far before we spot
a familiar form limping our way.
This is the closest we've been to Teddy
without metal and glass in between us.

> *Saw them towing the car. You okay?*

"Wait. How? I mean—"

> *Told you I'm keeping an eye out for you.*

I didn't think he meant all the time.

> *Sure, we're okay,* says Parker.
> *Broke. Wet. No place to sleep.*
> *But we did have a good breakfast.*

> *Right way to start the day,* quips Teddy.
> *Anyhoo, figured maybe I could show*
> *you a couple of things.*

"Like . . . ?"

> *Like a place you'd maybe want to stay.*
> *And somewhere decent to find dinner.*

WE HESITATE

              Teddy tries to assuage our worry.
              Lots of people where we're going.

He could be lying, but our choices
are few and what I read from
him is sincere concern.

We follow Teddy toward the freeway.
He keeps on walking until we approach
a big dirt area, dotted with tents,
beat-up trailers, and cardboard huts.
We stop under a wide oak tree,
survey the encampment.

              Once upon a time, this was a park.
              It used to have flush toilets and
              running water, but once our little
              village sprang up, the county closed
              those down, hoping we'd all leave.

The remains of what were restrooms
are visible, beneath graffiti, gum,
and substances I'd rather not guess at.

              They did bring in outhouses for us.
              Most of us use them.

"They let you stay here?
No problems with the law?"

              Lots of homeless. They'd rather keep
              us here, out of sight, than camping where
              "the right kind of people" shop and see movies.
              There've been rumblings about purging
              the place, but so far it's just gossip.

So are you saying we could live here?
Parker sounds intrigued.

        Probably not a long-term solution
        to whatever it is you're running from.
        And there are a couple of folks
        you need to watch out for.

        But it's better than crashing behind
        a dumpster in an alley. Trust me.
        That's no place for young ladies.

Trust him. Okay. And yet it strikes
me that I trust this homeless stranger
more than I do my own mother.
"We don't have a tent or anything."

        Just need a tarp, some boxes, and duct tape.
        Kind of late today to begin construction—

We're all out of money, Parker
complains. *It was in the car.*

        I still have a little nest egg tucked away
        from my disability. It's not much,
        but I can front you the money.
        For a song or two. How's that?

"I don't get it. Why are you
so nice? You don't even know us."

        Long story. Tell you some of it over dinner.
        Have you discovered St. Vincent's?
        Decent food. Bit of a hike, so we'll have
        to leave before too long. The line forms early.

St. Vincent's Soup Kitchen

Opens for dinner at four, and by the time
we arrive at three thirty, the line's down
the sidewalk, around the corner.

It's mostly men, with some women
in the weave. Parker and I are by far
the youngest, but not everyone's ancient.
You might expect the majority to be gaunt.
Hollow-eyed, life-weary street people.
Some, yes, but others are rotund. Labor built.

Food uncertainty—modern buzzwords
for *hunger*—strikes without prejudice.
It also seems to create a sense of camaraderie.
Overall, the mood is light.
It's like anticipating a satisfied belly
encourages humor. People joke. Laugh.

> Parker's mind is elsewhere.
> *They won't ask for ID, will they?*

>> *The people in there are volunteers, and way
>> too busy to worry about who they're serving.
>> If someone needs help, though, like a doctor
>> or to make a phone call, they just have to ask.*

"It doesn't cost anything?"

> *Nope. Not a red cent.*

> And you can eat every day?

>> *A lot of these people do. Some earn small
>> paychecks and only eat here when the money
>> runs out, at the end of the week or month.*

"So, not everyone's homeless?"

> Teddy shakes his head. *But most are.*
> *It's a problem with the mild climate.*

It's raining, you know.

> *Yeah, but it's not snowing.*

Teddy's "glass is half full."

The huge dining hall's brimming.
It takes forty-five minutes to get inside,
another fifteen to load our trays
with pasta, green salad, fruit, and bread.

Not fancy, but balanced, and our
second free meal today.
One meant to be that way.

We find three places near
the end of a very long table.

The noise of silverware clacking
against several hundred plates
is not exactly conducive to conversation.

Still, Teddy's determined to try.
He says he's not asking for sympathy,
only wants us to know why
he took an interest in helping us.

THIS IS HIS STORY

> I started working at seventeen.
> Apprenticed for a plumber,
> learned the trade. Honest work.
> Never felt bad about not going
> to college or getting rich.
>
> Love didn't find me until I met
> my Millie. I was almost thirty
> and had given up on it.
> She was a music teacher
> and filled my life with singing.

He takes a swallow of coffee.

> We got married. Bought a house.
> And when Millie got pregnant,
> we named our daughter Melody.
> She was the light of our lives.

He addresses Parker.

> I told you your singing brought Millie to mind.

Now he looks at me.

> You remind me of Melody.

Tears fill his eyes.

> I adored my daughter, but she and Millie
> were tight. They did everything together.
> Until the cancer got Melody.

*She fought, that girl did. But two years
of chemo and radiation couldn't stop
that vile disease. Melody was twenty-two,
when we laid her in the ground.*

*I'd worked all those years. Saved a penny
or two, but I never had insurance.
We lost our savings. Lost our house, too.
It was all too much for Millie.
One day she put a bullet in her head.*

*The day I buried her next to Melody
was the day I gave up. Stuffed the cash
I had left in my pocket and settled
on life in the streets.*

Or in a Tent City

The sky has mostly cleared
by the time we leave St. Vincent's.
Just a stray cloud to tease the moon.

As we walk, I respond to Teddy's revelation.
"I'm sorry about your family.
It's hard to lose people you love."

> *Thank you, uh . . . I don't believe
> you've told me your names.*

At this point he might as well know.
"I'm Lake. And this is Parker."

> *Good names. Thank you, Lake.
> I imagine you've lost people, too.*

"Only one I care about.
My brother. He's in juvie."

> *What about your parents?*

"Never knew my father.
Our mom dumped Storm
and me when we were little."

> Teddy tsks. *Too bad. Not everyone's
> cut out to be a parent. God should've had
> a better vetting process in place.*

> *You believe in God?* asks Parker.
> *After everything?*

> *I was pretty damn mad at him, for sure.
> Sometimes I still get that way.
> But if there's a heaven, and I think there is,*

> Millie and Melody will be there waiting for me.
> So I have to figure ways to be worthy.

"Like looking out for a couple
of strange girls who might be
just a little desperate?"

Teddy laughs.
It's the first time I've heard him
laugh, I think, at least like that.

> Maybe that exactly. And while
> we're on the subject, you ladies
> may share my tent tonight.

Parker grunts. I gasp.

> No, no. I meant just the two
> of you. I have a place I can go.

He winks, and we get
his meaning. "Girlfriend?"

> Nothing serious if you catch my drift.
> He glances skyward.
> But I don't lie to her, don't cheat
> on her. We're an exclusive friendship
> with benefits, and she knows it.

The look we both shoot
him is semi-shocked.

> Hey. I ain't dead yet.

TEDDY'S REVELATION

Isn't totally surprising.
And it's also sort of endearing.

I just keep waiting
for a different side of him
to finally appear.

Label me suspicious.
But I've never met
anyone who didn't
have ulterior motives.
Sometimes it takes longer
for them to surface,
yet they always do.

But I can usually sense
them, and can't with Teddy.
Every vibe he emits
dismisses the notion
of underlying evil intent.

And he's giving us
a dry space to sleep
tonight, plus the promise
to help us construct
our own shelter
tomorrow.

Besides,
I know how to take
care of myself.

TEDDY'S TENT

Is a blue "four-person"
that would probably fit two
comfortably. On the outside,
it isn't too shabby.

It sits in a cluster of four, set up
around a ring of large granite
rocks surrounding the charred
remains of scrap wood.

I've only been camping once,
way back when, with Molly and Pete.
But I know what this is.
"You get away with campfires?"

> *We keep them small, and only light*
> *them if it's really cold. But not*
> *when it rains. Too smoky.*

Movement inside the tent
to the right of Teddy's.
Soft rock on the radio.
The other two look empty,
at least at the moment.

There's other activity, however.
A woman wheels a shopping cart
up to a listing old trailer, starts
to unload some bags.

Another sweeps a canvas "welcome"
mat in front of a cardboard lean-to.
She's either rapping or babbling to herself.

PARKER MOTIONS

For us to move a short distance away.

>*What about your neighbors?* she asks
>Teddy. *You said we should be careful.*

>>*You don't have to worry about
>>the folks in my little 'hood.
>>Barb—she's the one next door
>>playing music—will talk your ear off,
>>but some of what she says is pretty interesting.*

>>*Now, Howie, who's directly behind
>>me, is a bit strange, but harmless.
>>He's a vet who saw action in Iraq.
>>Killing was not his thing, but
>>the Army didn't give him a choice.*

>>*The last of our bunch is Jackson.
>>He's not much older than you.
>>A couple of years. His parents
>>kicked him out because he's queer.
>>Can you believe it? In this day and age?*

Parker and I exchange a silent look.
"Oh, yeah, we can believe it."
But Parker can't quite let it go.

>*So, you're okay with gay?*

>>Teddy shrugs. *No skin off my nose.
>>I don't lean that way, and even if I did,
>>I'm way too old for the likes of Jackson.
>>He's a nice kid. That's good enough.*

"Then who should we be
worried about? And why?"

Some people rely on substances to cope.
Alcohol, mostly, and you know I'm not
above taking an occasional snort or two.
But some fall back on harder shit,
opioids or that goddamn meth.

"Meth? Why meth?"

Keeps them up and moving to stay warm
at night or fend off assaults. Plus, it's cheap.
But it's a plague, and once you're sick,
you'll do anything to ride that high.
Lost a friend to it last year. His old heart
just couldn't take the good times, you know?

"But I thought homeless people
were broke. How do they pay for drugs?"

Panhandle. Sell their bodies. Deal to
cover their own costs. Burglarize or rob.
That's why I buddied up. Safety in numbers.

I can't tell you ladies how to manage
your lives, but if I can convince you
of one thing, it would be to steer wide
around that soul-crushing bullshit.

Will you point out the bad guys?

Of course. But they're pretty damn
easy to spot. Whatever you do, don't leave
your stuff unattended. Keep it on you.

GOOD PLAN

One I most definitely will adhere to.
Oh, why did we leave anything
in that car? We have to be more
conscientious about hanging on to
our money. If we ever get any.

We're okay for a day or two,
but we'll need cash at some point.
That fact is underlined when Parker
declares she needs to use the outhouse.

>*If you gotta do number two, take TP*
>*with you. They don't supply that.*

"You realize girls use it for
number one, too, right?"

>*That stuff's scarce around here.*
>*Best learn to drip dry.*

Like we haven't already.

>*I don't even have a Kleenex.*
>*Spare burger wrapper, anyone?*

Teddy ducks inside his tent, returns
with a folded wad of toilet paper.

>*Pay me back when you can.*
>*Not a good thing to run out of.*

Hope I win the lottery. We're in debt to you
big-time. Here, she says to me, *hold this.*
She hands me her backpack, runs.

Teddy invites me to look inside the tent.

There's a thin mattress off to one side,
covered by a sleeping bag.
His folded clothes are neatly
stacked in a far corner.

Essentials, including the toilet paper,
I assume, are in a big plastic tub.
A small crate serves as a table for a lantern
and a book. *All the Light We Cannot See.*
I skim the cover. It's a World War II novel.

> *You can borrow it when I'm done.*
> *If you want to sit, my neighbors*
> *and I share some camping chairs.*
> *But mostly we use them outside.*

"Are our bags okay inside?"

> *Long as you stay close, or ask one of us*
> *to watch them. Come on. I'll introduce*
> *you to Barb. Oh, and I see Jackson coming, too.*

I've cycled through placements
for seven years. And only once
before, back at the very beginning,
have I ever felt even close
to this sense of welcome.

I'll get hurt in the end, no doubt
sooner rather than later.
But for one small moment in time . . .

I'LL TAKE IT

Teddy goes to get Barb.
The filmy nylon tent fabric does little
to conceal either dialogue or giggling.
Guess I know where Teddy's spending the night.

By the time they quit fooling around,
Jackson has reached his little abode,
carrying a pallet. He puts it down
just as Teddy pulls Barb into the evening.

>*Hey, Jackson!* he calls. *Come meet
>our new friends. Hey, Lake.
>Where's Songbird?*

"I was just wondering that.
Maybe I should see if she's okay?"

>*Nah*, says Barb. *Here she comes.
>At least I think that must be her.*

Parker's moving slower on the return.
I go meet her. "Everything okay?"

>*Not exactly. Tell you later. Looks
>like everyone's waiting for us.*

Teddy makes the introductions,
explains our plan to construct
some kind of shelter tomorrow.

>*There are more pallets near the tracks
>where I found that one,* Jackson says.
>*And there was a big wooden crate,
>too. Think they fell off a train.*

"The crate was empty?"

Jackson nods. *I doubt it was when it
fell, but whatever was inside was long gone.*

*There are people who travel the tracks,
looking for stuff,* Teddy explains.
*If the crate's there tomorrow, we'll bring
it back. Better than cardboard, for sure.*

I'll help, says Jackson. *If you want.*

"Of course. That would be great."

Barb's somewhere in her fifties,
and diminutive. She wears her long
brown hair tied back off her ruddy face.

Jackson's well over six feet,
and good-looking, with jet-black
hair over dark skin.

And you're the singer? Barb asks
Parker. *I'm a little jealous of you.
Can't carry a tune to save my neck.*

You sound pretty good with the radio,
gushes Teddy. *Top forty with me!*

Anyway, says Barb, *thank you,
girls, for giving Teddy here the excuse
to hang out with me tonight. All night.*

She winks and we all laugh.

Gonna start a fire, Teddy says.
Who's up for campfire singing tonight?

WE ALL AGREE WE ARE

But curiosity gnaws at me.
I coax Parker inside the tent.
I keep my voice low.
"So, what's not okay?"

She starts digging through
her backpack.

> *Guess what showed its bloody*
> *head early this month?*

Great timing. "Oh, wonderful.
Did you have enough tissue to—"

> *Barely. Luckily, I thought*
> *to borrow some pads from Colleen.*
> She air quotes the "borrow."
> *They're in here somewhere.*

"Well, at least you won't have
to sit through the lecture."

> *I'll have to change my clothes,*
> *though, and will need to wash*
> *these out somewhere.*

> *There's no running water*
> *at those outhouses, by the way.*
> *And they freaking stink.*

"We'll have to scope out
some closer convenience stores."
And get our hands on some cash.

She yanks, and out comes a handful

of sanitary pads. But there's something
else threaded around them.

"What's that?"

It's hard to make out in the fading
light, but I think it's jewelry.
I reach for it, but she jerks it away.

"Let me see!"

She lays it across her hand.
It's a necklace, and it looks expensive.
Like real diamonds and rubies.
And it's somehow familiar.

"Is that Colleen's?"

> *No. It's mine now.*

"Parker!"

> *What? It was on her dresser.*
> *Next to her wallet.*
> *When I grabbed the sixty dollars,*
> *the necklace just kind of came along.*

"But why?"

We needed the money
to eat for a few days.
The necklace feels personal.

> *Because she deserved it.*

Parker's Vindictiveness

Does not serve her—or us—well.
The necklace was one of Colleen's favorites.
She wore it to church regularly.
Petty theft is one thing.
This is something else.
Nothing I can do about it, though.

"Why don't you get cleaned up?
Teddy's building a campfire.
I'll go see if I can help."

He's already stacked the wood
inside the not-quite-circular
rock enclosure. "What can I do?"

> *Pretty much got it covered. You can*
> *set up the chairs if you like.*

He points me toward five folding
canvas chairs, says Barb has another
in her tent, should Howie participate.

> *He's shy of strangers, so he might*
> *not come out of his cocoon.*
> *I let him know he's invited, though.*

I arrange the chairs.
Teddy lights the fire.
Jackson carries an armload
of wood to add as we need it.

The pulsing flames mesmerize,
carry me back to my first and only
camping trip with Molly and Pete,
Alora and Storm. And Rex, of course.

WE ROASTED HOT DOGS ON STICKS

Gorged on gooey s'mores.
Played Yahtzee and poker.
No betting allowed.

Alora, Storm, and I shared a tent.
It was cold outside, but our sleeping
bags were warm, and we talked about
nothing most of the night.

It's such a happy memory.
I'm completely lost in it
when Teddy interrupts.

> *Where's our nightingale?*

Parker. Yes, where is she?
"I'll go check on her."

It's completely dark inside the tent,
except for a low campfire glow
through the nylon. Parker's sitting,
staring into the pewter. "Parker?"

I touch her shoulder. She jumps.

> *Lake! What's the matter with you?*

"What's the matter with *me*?
You're the one who's zoned out."

> Her voice is creamy. *I am?*
> Wow. Guess maybe I was.
> Sometimes that happens when
> I start my period. Hormones.

WORRY GNAWS

And it's not just because
I found her contemplating the void
again. There's something else.
Something subtle I'm picking up on.

But I let it go. "Teddy's waiting
for a song. We kind of owe him."

Song requests circle the campfire.
Eventually even Howie joins us.
It's weird, finding camaraderie
here, of all places. But we do.

I have no clue what time it is when
Parker and I finally crawl under
Teddy's sleeping bag, but it feels
like it's been a very long day.

We lie for a while, absorbing
each other's warmth and inhaling
the not entirely unpleasant smells
of campfire smoke and gentle BO.

I'm floating toward sleep
when Parker decides to talk.

> *So I've been thinking. About drugs.*

"We don't do drugs. Remember?"

> *You don't have to do them to sell them.*
> *And you don't need an ID.*
> *We could make some serious bank.*
> *Enough to get our own place.*

"But you have to buy them

to sell them. You need money.
And a supplier. And who
would we sell them *to*?"

> *We could start here. Teddy said*
> *some people here use. We can pawn*
> *the necklace. Probably won't get much,*
> *but I bet enough. And we know a dealer.*

"Who?"

> *Kit Beaumont.*

"How are we going to find *him*?"

> *Zephyr Fun Center. Most afternoons.*

"I don't know, Parker."

> *Well, we've got to do something.*
> *And selling drugs would be better*
> *than selling our bodies. Right?*

I don't want to sell either one.
Storm would be pissed if he ever
found out. Oh. Storm.

I reach inside my backpack
for a daub of Daisy. Wait.
Where's the bottle?
My frantic search nets nothing.
Last time I used it was . . .
in the rusting sedan.

STORM
EIGHT WEEKS

The unrelenting routine
is driving me crazy.
But, hey, only ninety-six
more weeks to go!

I trudge through school.
The classes are useless.
Directed toward guys with even
less ambition than I possess.

It's not that they're stupid.
But it's obvious school
was never a priority.
One or two can't even read.

So, while the teachers focus
on remedial bullshit, those
of us who've mastered fractions
tap pencils and spit paper wads.

I'd rather be learning.
I'd rather be keeping
my brain tuned up.
I'd rather be working it out.

Still, I try not to take it
too far. I don't want to lose
privileges. TV. Cards. Books.
Small things distract from boredom.

But some of these guys
are willing to risk isolation
for a solitary moment
of feeling in control.

Precisely Why

They segregate the units.

So the hardcore creeps—
guilty of egregious crimes
including rape, armed robbery,
and manslaughter—can't enjoy
tormenting losers whose offenses
lean more toward burglary
and small-time drug dealing.

The worst are in units F and G,
the softest in A and B, which puts us
E Unit dudes in the upper middle.

Skinhead Baxter has positioned
himself as unofficial head of this space,
with Ripley claiming the sidekick role.
No one else—currently sixteen
of us—seems to mind.

I've heard Baxter's here for kicking
the crap out of his girlfriend.
Maybe so, but she visits him once
a week, toddler in tow. Must be his.
Like the world needs a Baxter Jr.

Not that I'd say that to Senior's face.
He actually seems proud of the daddy deed.
Claims he'll set things right once he's out.
Like Baxter Jr. needs that kind of dad.

Some people shouldn't be parents.
I know from experience.
And so does this kid named Clay.

I TRY

To remember my own advice:
Don't make friends,
don't make enemies.
I mostly accomplish that.
But sometimes it's hard
not to make connections.

For whatever reason,
I've connected with Clay.
He's like the little brother
I never knew I had.

First day he arrived, I watched
him shuffle in, looking like a scrawny
mutt in need of a kind hand, but one
who'd turn on the person offering it.

Fear biters, they call those dogs.
And I could see it in how his wary
eyes darted this way, that way.
Looking for the source of the blows
he felt sure were coming.

It didn't take long for the verbal
punches to fall, courtesy of Baxter.

> *Hey, Ripley. Check out the new*
> *guy. At least, I think it's a guy.*

Clay winced, but held his tongue,
sizing up the threat level.

> *Yeah,* answered Ripley.
> *He looks kind of gay, huh?*

There are generally two reactions

to that test. One, you start swinging.
Or, two, you slink away.
Clay did neither. He turned and smiled.

> *I am! In fact, I'm about*
> *the happiest guy you'll*
> *ever meet in a place like this.*

Then he proceeded to dance.
I mean, I guess you could call it
dancing. It was like an Irish jig
or something, meant to be terrible
because that made it funny.

The entire commons cracked up.
And then a couple other guys
started dancing, too, while the rest
of us clapped a beat. It was amazing.

Brilliant, really.
Because even though
it was a giant fuck you
to Baxter and Ripley,
had they done anything
but snicker, the slim respect
they own would've narrowed.

I can't speak for the others,
but I suspect, like me, they figured
Clay's response was rooted in abuse.

Make your abuser laugh,
you just might escape
the apex of his (or her) wrath.

CLAY'S A CLOWN

One of those guys who makes
you laugh with nothing more
than a facial expression or pretending
a broom is his dance partner.

At first, I thought it was an act,
but I've learned it's a product
of ADHD and a hint of bipolar
disorder. Plus, the meds
that keep those kind of in check.

But every now and then you see
a flash of the Clay who was arrested
for assault with a deadly weapon.

"Why are you in here?"
I asked a few days after
his noteworthy arrival.

>   *Speared my stepdad
>   with a screwdriver.
>   Got the mofo good, too.*

"How come?"

>   Clay shrugged. *He went after
>   my sister. Slapped her so hard
>   I heard it in the other room.*

"The judge sent you up
for protecting your sister?"

>   *Wasn't the first time I stabbed
>   someone. Sometimes my temper
>   gets away from me.*

I Can Relate

Probably a good thing
I didn't have a weapon
when I went after Lance
or I just might be facing
life in prison instead
of a couple of years here.

Would I have felt bad
if I'd killed him? No.

I can't honestly say
I would have, and that
should probably concern me.

But maybe what I did to him
is worse, considering
his brain resides in his balls.

Oh, man. I lobotomized him.

The thought makes me laugh
into my milk, sending droplets
flying across the table.

A big-ass dude looks
up from his chili.

Watch it, asshole.

That's not very nice, says Clay,
who's sitting next to me.

*What are you going
to do about it, jerkoff?*

Aw, Shit, Here We Go

Clay's itching for a fight.

"Hey," I say. "Don't worry about it."
Then, to the other guy, "Sorry, man.
Didn't mean to blow milk at you."

I don't mean to do this, either.

He picks up a plate of salad,
tosses it in my direction.
I duck and the dish hits a dude
walking behind me square
on the side of his face.
He howls, throws his entire tray.

Fortunately for me,
it goes over my head.

Fortunately for the first
guy, it misses him, too.

Unfortunately for the kid
next to him, he finds
himself wearing chili.

Now the entire mess hall erupts
with an impressive food fight.
Clay and I take cover under the table.

Guards arrive within minutes,
breaking up the melee before
the room's totally wasted.

Cameras caught the action.
All except for a few drops of milk spit

across from where I was sitting.

Fortunately for me.

Between trays clunking,
feet slapping, catcalls, and
regular conversation among
dozens of guys, the comments
that drew the original toss
are completely lost in the din.

Fortunately for Clay.

But upon studying the video
record, the salad that missed
me and the tray that caught
the guy beside the guy
who should've caught it
were perfectly clear.

Unfortunately for the salad
thrower and the tray tosser,
who are both rewarded
with a few hours in isolation.

Unfortunately for Clay and me,
because now we both have two
new someones to watch out for.

Just my luck.
When making a friend
means making an enemy.

On the Plus Side

Neither salad thrower
nor tray tosser dwells
in this unit. Which means
we only have to be on alert
at meals, classes, or in the gym.

That's where I'm headed
now. At least I won't have
to worry about an ambush
while shooting hoops today.

Not with those guys killing
time in isolation. Hell,
maybe by the time they get
out of there they'll have
forgotten what I look like.

As if.

    Storm? Hang on a minute!

Byron's expression shouts
something major is wrong.

"What is it?"

    He shakes his head.
    Just come with me, please.

Our footsteps echo loudly
in the empty corridor.
He buzzes us out one door,
in another, leads me to
the counselor's office.

THERE'S SOMEONE

With Ms. Wilson.
He hasn't visited me since
I went to court.
And today isn't visiting day.

"Jim? What are you doing here?"

    Ms. Wilson answers first.

    Sit down, Storm. He's brought
    bad news, I'm afraid. We debated
    whether to tell you, but ultimately
    decided you have the right to know.

"Lake?"

    I haven't heard anything
    about your sister, says Jim.

"Then... my mother?"

Like I care if something
bad happened to her.

    No, Storm. Not your mom.
    It's... He hesitates. *Jaidyn.*

"Tell me!"

    She... she... He can't finish.

    So Ms. Wilson does.
    She took her own life.

I CAN'T

My brain is a cement
mixer, churning concrete.
"What do you mean?"

Took her own . . .

My face freezes.
My hands turn to ice.
"She's dead? How?"

    Pills.

No.
No.
No.

    I'm so sorry, Storm.
    Jim's crying.

No.
No.
No.

It's a mistake.
It's a lie.
Why would they lie like this?

"You're lying!"

Jim sucks a ragged breath.

    I would never . . .

    I know this is hard to
    accept, says Ms. Wilson.

"You don't know *anything*!
Accept? She and Lake were all
I ever had. Now one's dead,
and for all I know,
the other might be, too!"

No.
No.
No.

"You want me to accept
this? No way! Fuck you!"

I jump to my feet,
but my legs buckle.
I fall to my knees.

No.
No.
No.

She can't be gone.
Not, like, forever gone.

Why, Jaidyn, why?

You
let
him
win.

I Vow to Change That

Only problem is, I say it out loud.
"I will not let him win."

Lobotomizing him
wasn't good enough.
When I get out of here . . .

> This isn't the boy's fault.
> Ms. Wilson's voice is a low
> buzz, like an electric wire.

"Seriously? Seriously?"

> It's okay to be angry.

"Glad I have your permission."

I push myself up, back
into the chair.

Jim's face is the color of milk.
His hands tremble against his knees.

Even through the soul-searing
grief, I notice he's lost a lot
of weight in just a few weeks.
He looks like he's aged twenty years.

It hits me.
I was wrong.
Jaidyn and Lake
weren't the only
people I ever had.
Or the only ones I've lost.

My Heart Implodes

In the space of seconds
I go from wanting to kill
someone to wanting to die.

If I did, would Jaidyn be waiting
for me on the other side?
Or would Beverly?

I push the thought away,
reach out to Jim.

"Are you sick?"

> *I've been better,* he admits.
> *But I'll be fine. What about you?*

The rage pulses
through me like fire.

"I have to be fine, don't I?"

Jaidyn.
No.
Why?

"Did she leave a note?"

> Jim nods. *She said not to cry*
> *for her. That sleep was her*
> *only escape from the nightmare.*
>
> *And she asked . . .* He chokes up.
> *To be buried in your Rex shirt.*
> *She was wearing it when . . .*

A God-Awful Sound

Spews from my mouth—
half growl, half wail.
"N-n-no m-more! Stop!
Can I go back to my room?"

> *I thought maybe a little time
> in B Unit, says Ms. Wilson.
> Plus, pharmaceutical care
> for two or three days.*

B Unit is where they put you
to keep a watchful eye on you.
Offing myself isn't in my plans,
but pills sound like a great idea.

"Wait. When I told you I needed
meds, you said that was bullshit."

> *Extenuating circumstances.*

Ms. Wilson hands me a little cup
with a yellow tablet. Xanax, it says.
I gulp it down without water.

> *One last thing, says Jim.
> Jaidyn's mom wanted me to
> thank you for the happiness
> you gave her daughter.
> And for trying to protect her.*

"Please tell her I'll always love
Jaidyn. She was the best
thing that ever happened to me."

Byron Comes to Collect Me

Before we go, Ms. Wilson grants
permission for Jim to give me a hug.

Apparently, there's a rule
against physical contact.
One I never knew about,
because out of all the times
I've been locked up, no one
has ever asked to hug me.

To be real, except for those
I shared with Lake and Jaidyn,
my life's been mostly embrace-free.

Oh, maybe once or twice
Pete hugged me, but he's for
sure the only man I can
even pretend to remember.

This is definitely the first
between Jim and me.
It feels simultaneously
comforting, necessary,
and like I wish
I could've avoided it.

Because as much as it assuages
a bit of my pain, it also underlines
the fact that Jim isn't well.

His spindly arms tremble
even as they draw me in.
And my ear against his chest
listens to a struggling heart.

I Realize

Our first hug might very well
be our last, so I don't cut it short.

Is this what it's like to have a real dad?
Do real dads actually hug their kids?
I wish I'd had the chance to find out.

"Hey, Jim. Love you."
Where the hell did that come from?

> *Hey, Storm. Ditto.*

And where the fuck did that come from?

> *And I'm heartbroken about Jaidyn.*

Byron clears his throat.
I step back, lose connection.
Turn away.
Helpless.
Hopeless.
Empty.

Byron stays quiet
most of the way to B Unit.
Finally, he sputters.

> *Sorry about your girlfriend.
> I lost someone close to me
> last year, and it's been hard.
> Something her mom told me
> resonated and it's helped a little.*
>
> *She said think of the reasons
> you loved the person who's gone,
> then try to be those things.*

The Xanax is kicking into high
gear, which drops me real, real low.

The yellow ones must be extra strong
because conjuring an image of Jaidyn
doesn't hurt as much as it should.

"She was pretty. And hot.
I probably shouldn't try to be
those things around here."

> *You could work on being the good
> things you found inside of her.*

He opens the door to a small
room, not much different from mine,
other than the (lack of) trimmings.

"No blanket?"

> *You cold? They keep it
> pretty warm in B Unit.*

"Freezing."

> *Normally we don't provide
> blankets or sheets here.*

No possible instruments of suicide.

HE SAYS HE'LL SEE

What he can do.
At least he lets me keep
my clothes. I've heard
if they're super worried
you might try to off yourself,
they take everything
but your underwear.

Nothing to do but lie
on the comfortless cot,
staring at the padded walls,
I settle and let the little yellow pill
work its spell around freeze-frame
shots of my beautiful Jaidyn.

Sunshine streaming
over her hair as she runs.

Pouring hot cocoa over
a half cup of marshmallows.

Holding my hand
in a dark movie theater.

In her kitchen,
baking a birthday cake.

Singing hip-hop
as we cruised to the beach.

Dressed in my Rex shirt
lying still on her bed.

SLEEP ROLLS OVER ME

Like San Francisco fog.
I stay lost in the mist
for a while. I'm not sure
exactly how long until
I'm allowed to return
to my regular room.

Two whole days
in the haze.
Even as it starts to lift,
I'm a zombie.

I follow Byron back to E Unit,
wondering what the annoying
buzz is echoing in the corridor.

The source becomes clear
when he opens the door
to the commons.

Guys talking.
I've been mired in
silence for a few days.

I'm not sure if B Unit
itself was mostly soundless
or if that was just the space
inside my head.

Byron stops me before
I can go on up to my quarters.

>   *Almost forgot to tell you.*
>   *You have a roommate.*

Kit Beaumont

Is an unpleasant surprise.

Tall.
Spindly.
Long, scraggly hair.
Pockmarked face.
And the son of a bitch
is going through my stuff.

Not that there's anything
valuable. Except my photos.
It's déjà vu of the worst kind.
"What the fuck are you doing?"

> Oh, hey, man. Sorry. Was just figur-
> ing out where to put
> my shit and came across these.
> This is weird. You know this girl?

He holds out a picture of Lake.

I don't answer him.
Instead, I say, "I assume
you know her somehow?"

> I know her girlfriend
> better. Parker?

The residual Xanax buzz vanishes,
leaves behind a throbbing headache.
"What about her?"

> She's actually why I'm here.
> Little bitch got me busted.

"For what?"

> *Meth. Wasn't really my gig,*
> *but she insisted I score it.*
> *Worked out for a little while.*

"Meth? I don't know about
Parker, but Lake doesn't use."

> *He shrugs. Mostly it was a way*
> *for them to make money.*
> *But we smoked it together.*
> *Lowered the ol' inhibition, too.*
> *Hey. You ever been with two girls?*

My jaw stiffens.
My shoulders go rigid.
My fists clench into knots.

Don't do it.
Fuck that.
Don't do it.
Fuck that.
Don't do i—

I snatch Lake's photo
out of his slimy grasp.

> *Wha—*

My left hand grabs his throat.
My right draws back.
Maybe he's lying.
Maybe not.
I don't care either way.

LAKE
IMPLOSION

Bulldozers scoop up
every tent, every crate,
every cardboard dwelling.

What little is left of my stuff
is in my backpack. And in Parker's,
which is in my possession.

I have no clue where she is,
or has been for the last . . . three days.
It's hard to keep track anymore.
I keep waiting for her to come
back from her last drug run,
which is why I'm watching
the city reclaim the park.

Teddy warned it could happen.
Once the notice posted,
he and Barb decided to make
themselves an official couple
and find a new place to crash.

> *Two tents are better than one,*
> he said. *I wish I could help*
> *you ladies more, but we're not*
> *even sure where we'll end up.*

He slipped me a twenty,
which will mostly go to paying
down Parker's debt with Kit,
if I ever see her again.
My intuition says he's the reason
she hasn't returned.
But what do I do now?

ALONE ON THE STREET

Is not a good place to be.
Especially not with winter leering.
The fog rolls in every night, cold
and wet and dreary. Mornings dawn
the same way. Gray and teeth chattering.

The mist starts to lift around midday,
which is probably now, since
the sun's trying to peek through.

How long do I wait?
I'm hungry. Haven't eaten
in a couple of days.
Didn't want to leave
in case she stumbled "home."

A couple of cop cars swing
into view and park, deciding
for me it's time to move on.
"Parker," I whisper. "I'm sorry."

I understand the odds of ever
seeing her again are long.
But I've got no choice.

I turn away, trudge toward
downtown. Screw it. I'll spend
a few bucks on cheap fast food.

People avoid me on the sidewalk.
I must look—and smell—awful.
I need more than a restaurant
bathroom cleanup.
But I'll start there.

WHO'S THAT IN THE MIRROR?

Oh my God! No wonder
people walked wide around me.
I look like an orphan kid
in a war movie.
My face is filthy.
My hair hangs in limp tangles.
My shirt is torn, stained.
And my eyes . . . are empty.

I can't believe I'm thinking
this way, but I could use a bump.
Yeah, meth is what dropped
Parker and me down into
the pit. But right now I'd kill
for the way a little makes me feel—
like I'm on top of the world.

No wonder so many street
people fall under its spell.
It makes your spirit dance.
Until it cuts you off at the knees.
It's a vicious cycle. The problem
is the apex makes the crash worthwhile.

But I don't have any.
So I'll settle for a weak substitute.
I can smell the coffee from here,
now that I've washed away my stink.

My face is scrubbed.
My hand soap–shampooed hair
is brushed straight.
My shirt's changed.
But my eyes are still empty.

I Order

A burger, fries, and coffee.
Carry it to a table by a window
in a far corner of the place.
I'm starving, but I eat super
slowly, savoring both the mediocre
food and warm place to sit.

I watch people walk by,
fantasize about following
one or two of them home,
and asking for somewhere
to shower and maybe sleep.

Where are you, Parker?
God, I miss her.

Her laughter.
Her songs.
Her kisses.

Yes, she had pulled away.

Toward Kit.
Toward drugs.
Toward money.

We had a little money.
But it went to drugs
before anything else.
Another vicious cycle.
Doesn't matter.

I don't know where to go.
I don't know what to do.
I don't know how to be on my own.

TIME IS WATERY

But it's been more than two months
since Parker and I hit the streets.
On the way out the door, I grabbed
one of my school notebooks.

I call it my Storm journal, and decide
to write in it now. Not sure why.
He'll probably never read it.
I'll probably never see him again.

But if something bad happens to me,
maybe this will make its way to him.
It's got his name inside. And also the phone
number of his foster dad, Jim.

I've already written about why we ran.
Filled him in on how we lived right up
until Parker decided dealing drugs
for Kit Beaumont would solve everything.

I open the lined notebook, dig for a sparkly
pencil. I brought my collection along.
Continue:

> Parker insisted it had to be meth,
> because some of the tent people use it.
> Problem is, if you deal it, you use it.
> I tried it. I liked it. But not enough
> to let it take control. Parker loved it.

> She said it made her feel "right."
> What she meant was, it evened out
> some roller coaster stuff in her brain.
> It also made her agree to do those
> things with Kit. Sex, you know?

I DEBATE

Exactly how much to confess.
But Storm would never judge
me, and the truth is too
powerful to hold inside.

> *Meth annihilates dignity. I'll never touch*
> *it again. I can't believe the things I did*
> *for crystal or money when we owed*
> *Kit more than we could pay.*
>
> *Parker left with him a few days ago*
> *and never came back. I'm alone, Storm.*
> *Scared. I wish you were here to keep me safe.*

But he's not. I tuck the notebook
away, finish my lunch, drink two
cups of water, and wander aimlessly,
a backpack over each shoulder.
Eventually I see signs for a city park,
and follow the arrows until I find it.

I sit on a dry patch of grass, prop
myself against the backpacks, soak
up the weak sunshine, watch
moms and dads push their children
in swings, catch their children.

I've never known anything like
that. The closest I've come is Molly
and Pete, next to the merry-go-round
Storm and I were riding, giant smiles
plastered across their faces.

Pretend parents.   Pretend caring.   Pretend love.

NOT FOR THE FIRST TIME

I wonder if dragging myself, one slow day
at a time, toward dying is all I've got.
Would a quick death be preferable?

If you're checking off your list of goals,
aglow with achievement, or have love waiting
for you at the end of those lingering days,
maybe the journey is worth the struggle.
I'm mostly hanging on for Storm.

The sun arcs low and the wind riles up.
I reach into my backpack for my sweatshirt.
Touch something soft, leather.

Oops. This is Parker's bag, and this
is the jacket from the thrift store.
Margaret's. Margaret! Something
she said once floats into my head.

> *You've got an eye for fashion, not to*
> *mention bargains. If you ever need a job...*

Would she hire me without ID?
Pay me under the table, if I work cheap?
Could I trade labor for a place to sleep?

Okay, probably none of that,
but what do I have to lose
by dropping in and asking?

Anyway, it will give me a goal
I can check off my list.
Gotta start somewhere.

IT TAKES THREE BUSES

And a long span of time to even
come close to Margaret's, and then
I have to walk for fifteen minutes.
By the time I reach it, the store's
been closed for over an hour. Oh, well.
Guess I'll be first in line in the morning.

This neighborhood is sketch by day,
and now it's getting downright volatile
with people looking for some kind of good time.

I don't see Star on that street corner,
but three different working girls vie
for paid attention, encouraged by their "manager"
from his vantage point across the street.

He eyes me suspiciously, no doubt
wondering if I'm trying to take
advantage of his customer base.
That's not the work I'm looking for.
All I want now is a place to spend the night.

I settle against the locked door
of a boarded-up storefront,
hoping I'm out of the light
enough so as not to invite solicitation.

I've lost track of time, but think it
must be Friday or Saturday
night because traffic, both auto
and cruising on foot, is super heavy.

In the alleys, people smoke weed.
Pop pills. I see needles, too.
And living, breathing corpses.

Alcohol flows, mostly between
lips and down throats. California
isn't an open container state,
but that's not stopping anyone.
The cops are busy elsewhere.

On the corners, taunts and catcalls
are tossed in all directions.

>*Hey, baby, let's see what you've got.*

>*Ain't hard to see what you've got.*

>*Whatcha shopping for, honey?*

>*Depends on the price tag.*
>*You discount?*

>*Does your wife know you're here?*

>*Does your mama know you are?*

The collective energy
is raucous. Raw. Raunchy.

I struggle not to tap into individual flows.
I don't want to know why they're here
tonight. Still, I catch snippets.

>*. . . need a reminder of how it feels to be*
>*loved.*

But you can't equate sex to love.
Sex without love is physical release.
Love without sex is still love.

One Energy Stream

Keeps flowing by me.
Around me.
Bumping into me.

It's disturbing because I know
it conducts harm.

It seethes. Roils. Rages.
Magma, famished for release.

It belongs to someone
prowling the sidewalk.
Circling the block.

Acknowledging it
carries risk, engaging
it would be insanity.

I'm not that crazy yet.
I pull the collar of Parker's
jacket up over my nose.

Breathe in the scent
of leather, cigarettes.
A faint hint of Daisy.

Chase away the bad
vibes with a few
bittersweet memories.

Jenga.
Six Flags.
"Ave Maria."

I SWIM UP

Into the cold emptiness.
Guess I fell asleep.

The street's quieter, if not
completely still, so it must be
edging toward morning.

One girl remains on the sidewalk,
frantically waving at the few cars
cruising by. If one slows, she lifts
her thigh-high skirt, leaving no doubt
what the game is. She must have come
up short on her quota tonight.

I'm desperate to pee.
Nothing will be open nearby,
so I'll have to find a place
in the closest alley, which
happens to be behind Margaret's.

I creak to my feet.
Grab my stuff.
Hurry around the corner.
It's eerily silent, but I scout it
cautiously anyway, see no
possible witnesses.

Lucky me.
There's still some TP
in my backpack,
plus a dumpster to go
behind and dispose
of the used paper.

POST SQUATTING

I'm standing and starting to pull
up my jeans when that evil
energy slams into me.

> *Oh, now why'd you have to go*
> *and piss on my sleeping spot?*

The voice matches the power
flow, and so does its owner.
The guy's built like a Rottweiler—
barrel chested and thick necked,
and even in the semi-dark,
his arms look like sledgehammers.

"S-s-sorry. I didn't know—"

> *Now, don't bother with those*
> *pants. You won't need 'em*
> *for what I've got in mind.*

I keep tugging anyway.
"There's still a lady out
there on the sidewalk."

> *Ah, I don't like to pay for it.*
> *Anyway, you're prettier.*

I back away, look for an escape.
Can't go past him. Can't run backward.
But if I turn, I can't see him.
"You don't want to do this.
I'm just a kid, man."

> *Exactly.*

I PLUNGE MY HAND

Into my backpack, pray for a weapon.
I come away with one of my pencils,
thankfully very sharp, as he pounces.

I toss both bags and run.
For such a big man, he's fast,
and on me immediately.

He drops me facedown
and my forehead opens
as it scrapes the cracked asphalt.

He yanks at the waistband of my still-
unzipped jeans. They start to slide.

Told you we don't need these.

"No!" I scream, flipping over and
stabbing the pencil toward his face.

He clamps one hand over my mouth.
The other grabs the pitiful weapon.

Whatcha going to do with that?
Poke my eye out? Think again, bitch!

I try to kick, but his knees pin
my legs. My left ear rings
as the ball of his right thumb connects.

His left hand moves
from my mouth to my throat.
Squeezes, cutting

off air and voice.

CAN'T YELL

Can't fight.
Can't move.
Ripping.
Thrusting.
Gushing.

And he is laughing.

Pain.
Pain.
Pain.

I slip into Parker's zone.

Empty.
Numb.
Silence.

I think
I might
die here.

Maybe
I'm already dead.

Parker.
I love you.

Storm.
I need you.

But you're
not here
to keep me safe.

I'M NOT DEAD

Not unless death
is a stinking alley
spattered with piss
and blood. My blood.

I climb out of the zone
into the first light of morning.
I'm alone. Thank God.
No one's come along to find me,
lying battered and half naked.

He took everything.
Money. Backpacks.
What little remained of my pride.

At least he left my pants.
My arms shake as I pull them
into the proper place.
My hands fumble the zipper.

My head pounds.
My jaw might be broken.
My throat's on fire.

Crawling is the best I can do.
Like a baby testing its body,
I make my way to Margaret's back step.
Lean against the door. Wait.

For what, I'm not sure.
Who'd want to help me?
If I looked like a war orphan
before, now I must look like a casualty.

I understand why Parker's
drawn to her gray zone.

It might not be safe here.
But it feels that way.
I wander in and out.

In: Pain recedes.
Out: Everything throbs.
Including my brain.

I fold myself
into the shadows.
Wait.

As the light strengthens,
cars rev and honk.
People scurry and shout.
Somewhere a garbage truck
is doing its thing.

A woman hustles up the alley.
Something's familiar. I know her.
When she draws even, I croak
her name. "Ms. Bolton?"

She stops. Studies me.
Her eyes light with recognition.
And, I think, compassion.

Lake? What happened to you?

"Long story. Will you help me?
I need you to call my caseworker."

STORM
Damn Long Odds

That's what I'd call winding
up in a cell with someone
who knows my sister.
Especially in the way
Kit Beaumont claims to know her.

As usual, I play it all wrong.
Let my emotions take control.
Fury. Frustration. Marrow-deep pain.
Beaumont curls into a ball.
Pussy won't even defend himself.

By the time a guard pulls me off
the bastard, I've only blackened
one of his eyes and maybe
loosened a tooth.

> *What the fuck's wrong with*
> *you, dude?* snarls Beaumont.

> *Excellent question*, says the guard,
> who happens to be Hardass Harris.
> *Hungry for time in isolation?*

"No. He . . . that sonofabitch
turned my sister on to meth!"

> *She's your* sister? *Well,*
> *ain't that a slap in the face?*

I fight Harris's grip.

> *I don't give a shit what he did.*
> *Let it go*, Harris cautions.
> *And come with me.*

Damn it.
Damn it.
Damn it.

Why didn't I try to find
out more about Lake?

Obviously, she's alive.
But if she's out on the streets,
she must be alone.

That is, if Parker
got arrested when Kit did.

"Hold on, Officer."

Then, to Beaumont, "What
happened to Parker? How did
she get you busted? And do you
know where my sister is?"

His smile's hideous.
That tooth I loosened
seems to be missing.

Wouldn't you like to know?
Too bad you didn't ask nicely.

Damn it.
Damn it.
Damn it.

Isolation Sucks

It isn't just that the room
is spare—concrete cot
and lidless, seatless toilet.

It's that the door stays
closed and locked
at all times. Your only
connection to what's on
the other side is a little
window, and even that
has a metal shade.

Too much time alone
in a room like this
will mess with your head.

They try to limit
how long you're punished
with isolation.
Usually, it's measured
in hours, not days.

But if you're judged
a danger to others,
exceptions are made.
I believe I now qualify.

Unfortunately,
I'm Xanax-free.
Well, unless you count
the hangover, and that
is a definite bitch.

I'm vaguely nauseous.
Bad enough to feel

breakfast churning,
but not quite enough
to puke it out.

The headache is
a hammering
against my skull.

Each blow nails
in one word.

        Stupid.
                Stupid.
                        Stupid.

Wonder how many
times coincidence
has led to consequence.
Good or terrible.

I sit on the cement
floor, cocoon myself
in the tight corner
between the bed
and the adjacent wall.

I'm a worm
without hope
of wings.

VIOLENCE BEGETS VIOLENCE

Who said that?
Martin Luther King?
I don't remember.
But I suspect it's true.

The sad thing is, I vowed
I'd do better, be better
than how I was raised.

But I'm no different
from Beverly or Mom,
or the men who cycled
through their lives.
Including my father, I bet.

Someone hurts you. Lash out.
Something pisses you off.
Ditto. Only harder.

I'm not good enough, not strong
enough to fight my nature.
Might as well embrace it.

      Stupid.
           Stupid.
                Stupid.

I should've finished
Lance off. Rid the world
of toxic waste. Sealed my fate.

No chance for redemption.
I'm destined to spend
my life behind bars.

Thinking Too Much

Exacerbates the hangover.
Maybe I can sweat it out.
Push-ups. Sit-ups. Planks.
Lunges. Leg raises. Hip swings.

At first, my head complains,
but working my body feels good.

I walk the circumference
of the cell, cooling down.
And when I sit again,
the headache has retreated.
If only it was that easy
to discipline my brain.

I'm not sure the genius
who thought up isolation
considered the consequences
of leaving someone like me alone
with nothing but his own meditations.

Guilt
swells into
shame.

Regret
billows into
self-loathing.

Resentment
surges into
hatred.

This is how
monsters are built.

That's What Emerges

After three days in this lair.
Something starved.
Something primed.
Something anxious.

I have no desire to shackle it.
I want to feed it.
But it will have to stay
hungry for a while.

I doubt they'll put me
back on E Unit. Not with
Beaumont there.

So, when Harris opens
the door, I expect to land
on F. Instead, he silently
pushes me down a set
of three corridors,
to Ms. Wilson's office.

She's all business today.

Come on in and sit.

Harris nudges me forward.
I plant myself across from her.
He hovers close behind me.

"So . . . am I in trouble?"

Aren't you always?

RHETORICAL QUESTIONS REQUIRE NO RESPONSE

> I've been over your file again.
> There's always a good excuse
> for your escalating behaviors.
> I get you're not looking for trouble.
> But just because it seems to come
> searching for you doesn't mean
> we can condone the outcomes.

Harris is so close, his breath's
threatening on the back of my neck.
But I've got no desire to hurt Ms. Wilson.

> In a different time or place, you'd serve
> out your sentence in isolation. Society
> has little use for someone who deals
> with life's ugly incidents tit-for-tat.

> But when negative patterns keep
> repeating themselves, at some point
> the only way forward is to try something new.

She pauses. Studies me.
Assessing my non-reaction.

> I've consulted with your probation
> officer, and we've decided it's best
> you don't remain here. We still believe
> rehabilitation's possible, but moving you
> to F or G Units would be counterproductive.

"Afraid I'll teach those bad
 boys some new tricks?"

> Ms. Wilson offers a wry smile.
> Exactly that. Rather than risk it,

> we're going to relocate you.

"Shit—sorry. Where?"

> A few years ago, it would've
> been state detention, but
> those facilities were deemed
> unfit for juvenile populations.
>
> *Lucky you,* comments Harris.

Ms. Wilson shoots him
a withering look.

> *Actually, I'd say you are lucky.
> Many states aren't quite as
> forward thinking as California,
> and continue to lock young men
> like you in long-term isolation.*

"Young men like me?"

> *You know. Delinquents.*
> Harris smacks my shoulder.

> Ms. Wilson scowls. *Would
> you please step outside for
> a few minutes? I'll be fine
> alone with him. Right, Storm?*

"Absolutely!"

Harris Grunts, Annoyed

Ms. Wilson waits until the door
clicks all the way closed.

> *I've done this job for more
> than twenty years, and in that
> time, I've seen three kinds of boys
> walk through these doors.*
>
> *One: kids who do stupid things
> and get caught. Usually, we send
> them home fairly quickly to repent.*

Repent.
Interesting word choice.

> *Two: kids who, nature, nurture,
> or both, start off bad and keep
> getting worse and worse.*

Met a few of those.
Something lacking.
Like a soul.

> *Three: kids like you, who are
> circumstantially screwed.
> Ruled and often overruled by
> emotion. A tendency toward
> violence. And yet, who possess
> a slender filament of decency.*

Thanks for that, I guess.

> *Frankly, without solid intervention
> and your sincere determination
> to turn things around, your odds of lifelong
> incarceration are excellent.*

"You got me there."

> *Is that what you want?*

"I'm not sure I have a choice."

> *We're giving you one. A last chance,*
> *if you will. The county maintains*
> *a facility designed specifically for kids*
> *like you. It's a ranch so far up*
> *in the hills even rattlesnakes avoid*
> *it. The focus is work. Lots of work.*

"What kind of work?"

> *School. Sports. Facility upkeep.*
> *The boys cook their own meals.*
> *Clean their own toilets. Sweep—*

"Okay, I get it."

> *In fire season, we coordinate with*
> *the state's youth conservation corps.*
> *When you turn eighteen, you can move*
> *into fire suppression if it interests you.*
> *While you're still a minor, it's clearing*
> *fire breaks and defensible spaces.*

"When's fire season?"

> *Generally May through August.*

SOUNDS... HOT

But I don't think participation
is voluntary. Whatever.
Can't be worse than being
stuck inside this place.

"When do I leave?"

>   About twenty minutes.
>   Use the bathroom and collect
>   your personal belongings.
>
>   And, Storm? Utilize your time wisely.
>   We're offering an opportunity
>   to disembark the sinking ship.
>   You may not get another chance.

Drowning might be preferable,
but I thank her anyway. With luck,
I'll never see her again, and at least she tried.

>   I'm on my way out when she adds,
>   I want you to know I listened.

Harris doesn't give me the time
to ask her what she means.

He lets me pee.
Tells me my stuff
is already on the bus.
Handcuffs me, mostly
to let me know he's still
in charge. For the moment.

THE BUS

Is an eight-seater van.
Driver in one front seat.
Guard, not Harris, in shotgun.
Me, on the front bench.
One other person, afforded
this "privilege," beside me.

"Clay?"

I'm not surprised.
He's definitely a type-three kid.
But he seems to feel differently about me.

> *What the fuck? Seriously?*
> *I figured you'd be killing*
> *time in San Quentin by now.*

"They were afraid I'd be killing
something other than time, so here I am."

> *Ha ha. Very funny. Wait.*
> *You're kidding, right?*

"Pretty sure they don't send killers
where we're going. Right, guys?"

> Shotgun offers an awkward
> grin. *You never know. Now,*
> *you're not planning on yapping*
> *the whole way, are you?*

"Would you rather I sing?"

> *I'd rather you shut the hell up.*
> *We've got a long way to go.*

Freeway to Highway

To narrow paved road to a well-kept
stretch of hard-packed base, which
looks like rain could turn into mud.
"Ms. Wilson said rattlesnakes
avoid it up here. I see why."

        Highly inaccurate, Shotgun says.
        I guarantee you'll run into them.

Really? Clay's worried.

        Yeah, though not this time of year.
        They're in their holes until spring.

What else dangerous is up here?

        Coyotes. Bears. Bobcats. Cougars.
        Black widows and scorpions, too.

"They're just trying to scare us."

        I'd suggest checking your sheets,
        and I wouldn't take late-night strolls.

"Are those even an option?"

        Ms. Wilson didn't give you
        the details about the facility?

"Not really."

        Well, I won't spoil the fun. All I'll say
        is you'll have a surprising amount of
        freedom up here. You'll be tempted
        to take advantage of that. Don't.

I UNDERSTAND WHAT HE MEANS

About freedom when we pull
up to a wide aluminum gate,
big enough to let trucks through,
but relatively insubstantial.

The fencing, at least what
I can see of it, is nothing more
than four-foot-tall chain link.

No razor wire.
No electricity.
No other deterrents.

Unless it's patrolled
by rattlesnakes, scorpions,
or black widows.

The main building's a long,
single-story wooden structure.
Flagpole out front.
Housing, I assume,
is somewhere in back.

    Boy Scout camp! Clay exclaims.

        Close, says Shotgun. *This used
        to be a church camp but the county
        claimed it, like, fifteen years back.*

"You've been to Boy Scout camp?"
I try to picture Clay in a khaki uniform.

    Long time ago.

We get out of the van, stand

around waiting until a very tall
man with longish silver hair
comes toward us.

> *New arrivals. Excellent.*
> *Storm? Clay? I'm the guy*
> *in charge, Officer Dunn.*
> *But you can call me Michael.*

He sticks out his hand
with so much energy
I'm a little afraid
to shake it. I do anyway.

The officers go inside.
I expect we'll follow.
Instead, Michael leads us
off to one side of the building,
where maybe a dozen animals
are munching whatever's growing.

"Goats?"

> Michael nods. *Weed control.*

And geese.

> *Snake control, believe it*
> *or not. A couple will try to bully*
> *you, too. Run, they'll chase you.*
> *Back away slowly instead.*

Michael Gestures Wide

> *This property is fifty acres.*
> *Behind it is wilderness.*
> *Not much out there, including*
> *water. Avoid getting lost.*

If I was going to run, I'd run
toward the city, follow the roads
back the way we came.
But I've got nothing there to
run to except more trouble.

Which is the point of this exercise.

I look out at the nothingness,
absorb weak afternoon sun,
listen to birds singing.
It's a hell of a lot better
than cement and clanking doors.

Suddenly, the quiet's
broken by raucous barking.

> *Guard dogs?*

I'm not sure if Clay's joking.

> But Michael seems to be
> when he says, *You've got it.*
> *Mean mofos, too. We try*
> *to keep them a little hungry.*
> *Makes 'em anxious, you know?*

"Pretty sure he's kidding, Clay."

> *Yeah. I am. Come on inside*
> *and I'll tell you about the dogs.*

Turns out the ranch is running
a pilot program, one used
successfully in several prisons.
It's called Last Chance K9s.

> We pair our residents with rescue
> dogs who might end up euthanized
> without the training we provide.
>
> The dogs live in your rooms.
> You feed them, care for them,
> and work with them until
> they become adoptable.
>
> A few talented animals can even
> become service dogs. Almost
> all of them arrive here either
> hyper or skittish due to prior
> abuse and/or neglect.

"Sort of like us."

> Exactly, Storm. You can opt out.
> We have other programs
> you may participate in instead.
> But this is a unique opportunity,
> one your detention counselor
> believed would work for you both.

Ms. Wilson. Right.
Sounds like she really did listen.

LAKE
SOME COINCIDENCES

Seem like they must be part
of a Grand Plan. Not that any plan
with my name on it is likely to be grand.

But maybe there *is* a Goddess.
One who loves fashion and books
and who sent Ms. Bolton on a Saturday-
morning mission to Margaret's.

When I asked for help, I didn't expect
her to wrap my shivering, bloodied
body in her coat, put her arms around
me, and guide me inside my favorite
thrift store, where it's safe and warm.

Margaret doesn't invite me to take
up residence in her back room,
but she does allow me to sit here
while she brings hot coffee.

I float in the gray space inside
the zone, too timid to crawl out,
though I understand I must.
It's like waking up mid-nightmare,
knowing it's safer outside the dream,
but unsure how to exit.

Finally, the questions come.

> *Where have you been?*
> *Why did you run?*
> *Where's Parker now?*
> *What happened in the alley?*

My voice hitches, but I answer
each truthfully, including the last one,

though my brain freezes and I have
to start and stop, start and stop again.

> *You must file a police report,*
> insists Ms. Bolton.

"No way!"

> *Marina is right,* Margaret says.
> *He's roaming this very neighborhood.*

Her words sink in slowly,
like through quicksand.
One settles solidly.
Ms. Bolton's name is so pretty.

"Can I call you Marina?
Since you're not my teacher now?"

> *If you like. Now, what's your*
> *caseworker's name? I'll try to have*
> *her meet us at the ER.*

"Emergency? What for?"

> *Honey, that SOB did a number on you.*
> *We need to make sure you're okay.*

She called me honey.
My eyes sting.
Water.
Spill.

I AGREE TO GO TO THE ER

Every inch of me throbs.
I might have broken bones.
I might have damaged organs.
I might need a stitch or two.

The bleeding's stopped,
but there's a nasty gash
across my forehead.
Marina says it will leave a scar.
A forever reminder.

When I ask if I should wash up
before we go, Margaret and
Marina say an emphatic *NO!*

*They'll want to check for evidence
pretty much everywhere,* says Marina.

*Including your clothes. I'll get
you something you can change
into after the exam is finished.*

Evidence of assault.
Sexual assault.
Rape.
They'll want to look for his hairs.
Skin, under my fingernails.
Semen.
Fucking awesome.
What if he infected me
with some disgusting disease?

What if I'm pregnant?
Seriously fucking awesome.

I HAVE TO SCAN

My confused memory banks
to come up with Candace's personal
number, which she gave me many
months ago, in case of emergency.
Guessing this more than qualifies.

Marina manages to connect
with her, and she agrees to meet us
at the hospital, even though it's Saturday
and she should be having
a fun day off with her family.

A social worker's job is 24-7,
Candace told me once.
My kids understand that.
My husband, not so much,
though he tries to be supportive.

A girl like me will never
have a family like that.
I came close once,
with Molly and Pete.
But standing on the brink
makes tumbling into the pit
hurt exponentially worse.

Since then, I just keep sinking.
If there's a bottom to this swamp,
my toes are touching it.
Maybe I should go ahead and drown.

Why reach for air?
Why swim toward the light?
There's nothing for me up there.

NO STORM

                    Lake?
No Parker.
                    Lake?
Not even Teddy.
                    Lake! I'll get my car. You wait here.

                    Margaret drapes a blanket
                    around my shoulders.
                    Here's that change of clothes.

Jeans. My size.
Soft flannel shirt.
Lavender, my favorite color.
No undies, not a thrift store thing.
She puts the rest in a plastic bag,
along with a pair of shoes.

"I don't have any money.
He took it. But I'll pay you back."

                    No, you won't. I want you to have
                    them. Come shopping when you can.

"Maybe you can give me a job?"

                    Margaret smiles. *Maybe.*

                    Marina reappears. *All set?*
                    I'm illegally parked. We should go.

I thank Margaret, trail Marina
through the store. The few people
here can't help but stare. I think
I'll avoid mirrors for a while.

Her car's in the alley.

I freeze. What if he's there?
Hiding.   Waiting.   Watching.

"I can't."

>*Take my hand. You'll be okay.*

"What if—"

>*He's gone, hon.*

"How do you know
what I'm thinking?"

>*Because I've been there.*

I don't ask for details.
Take Marina's hand.
We walk to her car. I jump in.
Lock the doors. Safe and sound.

Still,
my head swivels
my eyes pivot
my stomach lurches
my brain insists he's nearby.

"Does it ever get easier?"

>*It consumed me for a long while.*
>*Years. But then I decided*
>*fear would not control me.*

"I've never not been afraid."

THAT DROPS US INTO SILENCE

She cruises slowly up the alley.
I stare out the window, looking for . . .
The sun glints off something
shiny. Sparkly. Familiar.

"Wait! Stop, please."
I open the door cautiously,
scan 360 degrees, see no sign
of anything human. And now
I home in on the glittery thing.

It's one of my pencils. And it's broken.

I put it in my pocket.
Look for others, almost desperate.
Like, maybe he left a pencil trail
leading to my backpack
and the tatters of my life.

My photos.   My letters.   My Storm journal.

One hint of Parker, clinging
to three pairs of panties,
a broken-strapped bra,
a pair of jeans, two T-shirts,
and my sweatshirt.
Five wilted dollar bills.
A handful of change.

But no.

Just this one broken pencil
shedding glitter
in my pocket.

IT'S ALL THAT REMAINS

Of who I was before.
I wasn't much then.
Now I am nothing.
But maybe that's good.
Being nothing makes it easier
to fade into the shadows.

Nothing doesn't worry
about the pitiless stares
of strangers in the ER foyer.

Marina takes charge at the desk,
explains what happened,
informs the receptionist
that my caseworker is on the way.

> *We have a SANE—sexual assault*
> *nurse examiner—on staff, but it*
> *might take her a while to get to you.*
> *Have a seat. Fill this out while you wait.*
> She hands me a clipboard.

"Will you stay with me, Marina?"

> *Of course. I wouldn't leave you alone.*

Nothing doesn't care that filling
out the ream of paperwork's impossible.

No address.
No phone number.
No known insurance.
No preexisting conditions.
Only my name.

I show page three to Marina.

It asks about sexual history
and recent activity.
"Why do they want this?"

> *To eliminate other evidence*
> *they might find. Something*
> *not belonging to the perpetrator.*

What does "recent" mean?
It's been days since I've been
with Parker, and when we were with
that prick, Kit, or one of the others,
we made them use condoms.

Doubtful any of that would show up.
I go ahead and write "none."
Turn to page four.

Nothing grits her teeth, outlines
the assault in as much detail as possible.
She describes what she can
remember about the guy.
Tells how he approached her.
Attacked like a rabid dog.

How she tried to defend
herself with a very sharp pencil.
At that, she has to swallow a laugh.

Only a nothing
would do something
so stupid.

WE'RE STILL WAITING

For the SANE when Candace
breezes through the sliding door.
Like, all fluttery, and yay,
see how I'm here?

But then she takes one solid
look at me, and my nothingness
registers. She shakes her head,
tsks something like a hello.

>*I'm sorry, Lake, but I'm glad to see
>you're still with us. You had me worried.
>We can discuss the particulars later.*

The particulars. Ha.
I show her the clipboard.
"I don't know some of this
stuff. Do I have insurance?"

>*You're covered by Medicaid,
>but you won't be charged for
>a sexual assault forensic exam.
>The Violence Against Women Act
>requires the state to pay for them.*

She looks over the paperwork.
Fills in a couple of the blanks.

>*We'll use my address and phone
>number for the time being.*

Marina hands me a scrap
of paper with a number on it.

>*Don't forget what I said. Been there.
>Call me if you need to talk.*

Conflicting emotions fountain.
"Why are you so nice to me?
I'm just a nothing."

> *Oh, Lake, no! You are quite special.*
> *Out of all the students I've taught,*
> *a handful stand out in my mind.*
>
> *You are one of them. I truly hope*
> *you'll finish school and accomplish*
> *great things. I believe you can.*

I fight useless tears.
Words stick in my throat
like a wad of gum.
"I wish . . . I wish . . ."

Stop it. Wishing's for idiots.
"Can I give you a hug?"

Despite the way I look, the way
I smell, she grants my request.
I try to keep it short.

"Thank you, Marina."

> *You're welcome. And I mean it*
> *about needing to talk. Anytime.*
> *Are you okay if I go now?*

I nod. Candace is here.

WE WATCH MARINA LEAVE

I'm still thinking about her
when a nurse calls my name.

> *I'll be right here,* says Candace.

The nurse leads me to a disinfectant-
scented cubicle, spreads a large
sheet of paper on the floor.

> *Please stand on that while you undress*
> *and put on the lovely gown that's on the table.*
> *Make sure to close it in front.*
> *The paper's to collect any loose hairs or fibers.*
> *You can leave your clothes on it, too.*
> *If it's okay, we'll take them for analysis.*

"Take them. Burn them."

> She nods. *I'll leave you to undress.*
> *The SANE will be here momentarily.*

I'm tying the flimsy hospital gown
when someone knocks and the door opens.

> *Hello, Lake. I'm Marilee, the sexual*
> *assault nurse examiner. You must*
> *be nervous, but try to relax, despite*
> *the nature of the examination.*
>
> *I've read your account of the assault,*
> *and want to start by assessing injuries*
> *you might have suffered as a result.*
> *I'll need to take pictures, okay?*

I fail at relaxing. Every poke,
every prod makes me wince.

> *The good news is nothing seems to be broken.*
> *We'll take X-rays so we know for sure,*
> *and we'll have to stitch up that forehead.*
> *Ever had a gynecological exam before?*

"No."

> *Okay, well, this is what will happen . . .*

Inspecting. Swabbing. Combing.
Scraping. Stitching. Blood drawing.
X-rays. MRI. Photos. Evidence collection.

Marilee and a tech or two work
on me for almost three hours.
It's an excruciating process.
No wonder Jaidyn refused
to put herself through it.

We finish with precautionary
measures—an injection
to combat possible STDs
and a morning-after pill.

They send me away
with antibiotics to fight
infection, and tell me
to take ibuprofen for pain.

I'm glad I'm nothing.

ALL STITCHED UP

I'm allowed to shower and dress
in the clothes Margaret gave me,
plus a pair of SANE-provided panties.
Except for the black eye and huge bandage
across my forehead, I look almost human.

But now what?
Even Candace seems unsure.

>*I've tried to find a group home placement,*
>*at least a temporary one. But they're all*
>*at capacity. For now, you'll come home with me.*

On the way, she gives me the fifth
degree. I deserve it. I tell her where
I've been, how Parker and I lived
and fed ourselves. About the dealing.

But I can't tell her what happened
to Parker, and that haunts me.
"Do you think she's okay?"

>*I think she probably got arrested.*

"I hope that's it."
Addicts, at least the few
I've interacted with, tend toward
the desperation that can lead to lockup.

>*I'll keep working on a placement,*
>*but it's going to be hard to find one.*
>*Foster has a grapevine. That necklace—*

"That was Parker all the way!
I didn't even know she did it."

What else would you say, Lake?
Even if that's the truth, who will other
foster parents believe? You or Colleen?

I sit with that for a moment.
"What do you believe?"

It doesn't matter. My job is to advocate
for you, regardless. If I thought you were
dangerous, I wouldn't be bringing you home.
But as to honesty, who knows?

"What if you can't find a placement?"

We could always look at reconciliation.

"You mean, with my mom?
No. Damn. Way."

Look. The system is overloaded. I'll give
it another try, but barring success,
it's reconciliation or detention.

"Detention? For what?"

Burglary. Colleen wants to press charges.
She doesn't care if it's Parker or you. Or both.

"Candace! I swear I had nothing to do
with that. I don't deserve detention.
And I can't go back to Mom!
Please. Give me one last chance."

SHE KEEPS HER PROMISE

To try again, and while she does,
I hang out in her sweet little house
with her two daughters and exceptionally
good-looking husband, who's a decent dad.

He cooks for the kids.

    The place smells like brownies.
Plays games with the kids.
    Their laughter sounds like little bells.
Watches TV with the kids.
    They sit close, barely touching.

They include me, though
my presence clearly makes
Kent uncomfortable.
The girls are more direct.

    What happened to your face?
    asks Kayla, who's five.

    Yeah. Did you fall down?
    guesses three-year-old Kara.

"Yes," I fib. "How did you know?"

    I fall down all the time.
    Kayla says I'm clumsy.

    Well, you are!

And now they're happy
to share their space.
I try to camouflage myself,
stay quiet, pretend I belong.

It Takes Forever

Okay, a couple of hours,
but finally, Candace appears.
She's smiling. Or grimacing.
I can't really tell which.

    Success! We'll have to stop and pick up
    some clothes and essentials for you.

I thank Kent and the girls
for Candy Land and a yummy brownie.

    I'll be gone awhile, Candace tells
    them. *The woman lives in Fairfield.*

    All the way over in Solano
    County? asks Kent.

    Yes, and we're fortunate. A girl just
    moved out and that opened up a bedroom.

Fairfield is out in the sticks
east of here. Drove by it once
on the way to Six Flags
with Molly and Pete.
I think there's some
military base near there.

Whatever.
Anywhere's better than lockup.
Or my mother's.
Or Colleen and Jay's.

I hope.

WE SHOP AT WALMART

On the state of California's dime.
I'm grateful for new clothes,
even if they're basic.

Cheap jeans, two pairs.
Long-sleeved tees, four.
Panties, two three-packs.
Two bras, straps intact.
Socks, one six-pack.
Vans for my feet.

Plus, essentials.
Toothbrush. Hairbrush.
Shampoo. Deodorant. Tampons.

Pencils.

I left the broken one
in the pants Marilee took at the hospital.
There could be some of his DNA on it.
Candace wants me to file
a police report and I guess I will.

The guy deserves prison.
If they catch him.
I doubt they'll look very hard
unless he's done it before, or does it again.

Right now, I'm just hoping
for some small sense of normalcy.
A regular roof over my head.
A regular toilet to pee in.
A regular bed where I'll feel
safe enough to close my eyes.

And school. I'm so far behind.

But I'll do whatever it takes to catch up.
"How soon can I start school?"

> *A couple of days. I'll have to round up your transcripts and register you. You missed a lot of work, so we'll need to discuss that with a counselor.*

"I messed up. I'm sorry."

> *I believe you are, Lake. And I'm sorry, too. But actions have consequences. Consider outcomes before you act.*

Logic over emotion.
Easier said than done.

"I was really in love with Parker."

She doesn't respond right away.

> *Why did you use the past tense?*

"What do you mean?"

> *If you were in love with Parker then, why aren't you now? As a rule, love is tenacious.*

Boom.

Candace Exits the Freeway

Drives a short distance
beside fields left bare for winter.
Pulls into a neighborhood
with smallish, but decent houses.

The vehicles parked on
the palm tree–lined street
tell me the people who live
here labor for a living.

Most probably work
at what Candace tells me
is Travis Air Force Base.

We stop in front of a house
that's plain but not ugly.
The grass needs mowing,
but it's nice and green.
A few flowers remain
in pots by the door, despite
the late-November weather.

I stand behind Candace,
my Walmart bags in hand.
It takes a whole minute
for the person inside
to respond to the bell.

The woman who answers
pulls the door wide open.
She fills the frame completely,
stands leaning on a cane,
eyeing me suspiciously.

I check her out the same way.

Her face says late fifties,
but her long graying hair
is tied back in a ponytail.

> *I take it you're Lake.*
> Her voice is scratchy.
> *Well, I'm Josie. Come on in.*

She steps back to let us
through, closes the door
with her cane, then limps
into the living room, which
is clutter-free but dusty.

> *You hungry? I was just fixing
> some dinner. You're welcome
> to join me, too, Candace.*

> *Thank you, but no. My family
> will be waiting for me. It's Kent's
> turn to cook tonight. I just need
> to see Lake's bedroom before I go.*

> *Right down the hall. Follow me.*

Photographs cover the walls.
There's a man, in and out
of uniform, and at different ages.

Also, kids. A boy, a girl.
From baby pics to teens,
in chronological order.

All hang perfectly straight.
And no visible dust here.

THE BEDROOM'S PRETTY

It's painted daffodil yellow.
There's a rocking chair by the window.
A table with a stained-glass lamp.
A dresser. And a bed. A double bed.

With sheets and pillows
and a star-pattern quilt
that looks homemade.

I've never slept in a double bed,
but even if it was half a single,
I'd feel like I do now.

Awed.

>*I expect you to keep the place neat.*
>*Make the bed every morning.*
>*Keep your clothes picked up.*
>*Same with the bathroom.*
>*You have one all to yourself.*

A bathroom. All to myself.

"Okay, Josie."
I put the Walmart bags
on the rocking chair.
Stare out the window,
which peeks into the fenced backyard.

>*This all looks in order,* says Candace.
>*I'd better go. I'll be in touch about school.*
>*Hopefully on Monday.*

We walk her to the front door,
where she hands Josie the antibiotics
I'm supposed to take.

> *She'll be pretty sore for a few days.*
> *Ibuprofen or acetaminophen for pain.*

We watch Candace go
 and Josie asks again if I'm hungry.
"I could eat," I admit.

> *I'm a basic cook, but if you have*
> *dietary needs, let me know.*
> *You gluten-free? Vegetarian? Hope*
> *you're not vegan. I'm a carnivore.*

"I'm not picky."

> *Good. Tonight we have chili.*

Her voice is clipped.
Not friendly, but not unkind.
I can't get a read on her.

Her body language doesn't help.
She's stiff, but that could
just be because of whatever
makes her rely on a cane.

I follow her into the kitchen.

> She points. *Silverware's there. Dishes there.*

Guess I'm setting the table.

STORM
THANKSGIVING AT THE RANCH

Is even busier than most days.
As usual, we're up by six.
Even if my roommate, Ryan,
and I didn't have to be, Pip insists
on that hour to go outside and pee.

Pip's half basset, half pit bull,
and the weirdest-looking dog.
He's also the coolest.

When I got here, Ryan had already
worked with Pip for three months.

> *Dude, you should have seen*
> *him,* Ryan told me. *He was*
> *all skinny and shaky. Scared*
> *to death someone would hurt him.*

It took Ryan days to get Pip
to believe he had a friend.
I hate to think what he went through
before he got dumped at the shelter.

Now Pip happily sits and stays,
fetches, heels, and comes on command.
All the basic obedience stuff.
His tail's always wagging.

He didn't even care when he got
another roomie. That's me.
See, new guys move in with someone
who's been in the program awhile.
The experienced dude teaches the newbie
positive reinforcement training.

It isn't too hard. I've been here

not quite two weeks, and I've got
most of it down already.

When the next batch of rescue
dogs arrives, one will be assigned
to me and we'll share quarters.
Just me and the mutt, no roomies
while we figure each other out.

Until then, I'll keep working
with Pip so he understands
Ryan isn't the only decent
person in the world.
He's already pretty good
with the other guys here.

Also, with the other dogs.
There are sixteen, and some
are ready to graduate.
People get to see them online
and apply to adopt.

One of my jobs is to upload
videos of the dogs working.
That's on top of my chores
and school and training Pip.

As Michael, who calls himself
the ranch "foreman," says,
better busy than bored.
Keeps a guy out of trouble.

I Could Find Trouble Here

If I went looking for it.
A couple of guys are what
you might call shitty.
Not necessarily overtly.

We all understand we're better
off here than in a cement cage.

There aren't even locks
on the doors to our rooms
because what if we need
to let the dogs out
in the middle of the night?

Plus, as Michael made clear,
there's a lot of wilderness
between here and civilization.
Even following the roads back
to town would take a good long while.

Plenty of time to raise an alarm
and send someone looking for you.
Then you'd be back in regular lockup.

For sure, those shitty dudes
would rather be here,
but there's something bad
in their eyes. A warning.

And something in how they move,
like everyone else should stay
the hell out of their way.
You could flip a switch and set them off.
We don't let them near the dogs.

Not that the dogs want

anything to do with those guys.
Dogs are smart about stuff
like that. They can read people
like instruction manuals.

These program dogs are super
sensitive because of how
they've been treated in the past.
They aren't about to give
shittiness a pass.

Which is totally fair.
Righteous, in fact.

Not only will the people
who apply to adopt
be screened, they'll have
to come for a couple
of visits first, to make sure
the connection's strong.

There must be mutual attraction.
The dog has to adopt the people, too.

A family that wants Pip
is coming up on Saturday.
This will be their second
bonding session.

I hope they fall in love
with each other.

But Today

Pip will enjoy a few scraps
of our Thanksgiving feast.

Everyone here must do chores,
and the responsibilities rotate.
Today, I'm playing chef.
I never realized how much
prep work went into making
a holiday meal, especially for forty people.

Peeling potatoes.
Chopping onions and celery.
Stuffing the turkey.
Scoring the ham.
Spreading brown sugar
and marshmallows over yams.
Candied yams. Who even knew
that was a real thing?

The big old camp kitchen buzzes
with activity, six of us trying to stay
out of each other's way. It's comical.
Except for the knives.
Good thing they aren't all that sharp.

My duty is pie baking.
Specifically, pumpkin.
Baking pies was not on my bucket
list, but it's kind of fun.

I only remember having pumpkin
pie at a couple of Thanksgivings—
with Molly and Pete, and
last year with Jim.

I think it's okay, but Jim

loves the stuff. He ate, like,
three huge pieces, drenched
in whipped cream.

Morley got more than a few licks, too.
Pumpkin's good for dogs.
I looked that up because he ate
so much I got worried about him.

I guess Jim and Morley
are keeping each other
company this year.
Or maybe Jim's got a new
foster. I hope he does.
I don't want him to be alone.

That must mean
I really care about him.
I should rethink that
since every person I care
about disappears.

Wonder if Lake's celebrating
Thanksgiving today.
Or if she's on the street.

Where are you, Lake?
Are you safe somewhere?

I Try Not to Dwell on Lake

As I put four pies in the oven,
clean up my gigantic mess.

Then I go to exercise Pip
while the pumpkin filling bakes.
That gives me forty-five minutes.

There's a big grassy field
behind the building.
We go for a gentle jog,
then I sit in the sun
while Pip sniffs for gophers.

I close my eyes against
the glare, and up pops
an image of a girl, haloed
in a shimmer of gold.

"Jaidyn."

She's right here, not quite solid,
but real enough. Her mouth
opens and I'm sure she'll sing.

"Oh, God, I miss you so
much, and I'll never—"

She lifts a finger to her lips.
I want to open my eyes,
make her disappear.
Want to squeeze them
tighter shut, engrave
her into my brain.

Pip starts to bark,
and for one ridiculous

instant I think he's chasing
a ghost away.

But now I open my eyes,
identify the problem.

"Pip, here. Stay!"

Together, we watch
one of the shitty guys
try to escape a big gray
honking goose.

> *Help me! Shit!*

"Stop running!" I yell at him.

> *No fucking way!*

I keep Pip close to me.
He might attempt rescue,
but we can't let the dogs
harass the livestock.
Not much I can do, either.
Nothing except laugh.

The hot pursuit continues
all the way to the dude's room.

And now it's time
to check the pies.

Best Turkey Day Meal Ever

The dogs are allowed at our feet,
as long as they're well-behaved.
The only problem that surfaces
comes when the half-humiliated,
half-pissed shitty guy walks by.

>He looks down at Pip.
>*Useless piece of crap.*

The dog visibly shrinks
back against Ryan's legs.
No way will I let this punk
destroy weeks of trust-building.
I stand. Face him square.

"Pip did exactly what I told
him to. He's a good boy."

>*Then I guess you must be
>the useless piece of crap.*

The other guys shift nervously.
I choose humor as a response.
"You know, I probably am.
My mother always said so."

The room cracks up, releasing
a collective held breath.
Even Shitty Guy smiles, scuttles away.

>*What was that all about?* asks Ryan.

"Dude had a little goose trouble.
I kept Pip out of the middle of it."
Pip wags his tail.

It's Still Wagging

Saturday morning when
the prospective adopters
arrive for their visits.

Ten program dogs, including Pip,
parade around the gym,
where their soon-to-be owners
are seated out of the cold drizzle.

It's warm in here, and the mood
is cheerful as the handlers lead
their dogs to the proper people.

Ryan offers Pip's leash
to a grinning lady with kind
eyes who's maybe thirty-five.
Her husband shakes my hand
while her not-quite-a-teen son
kneels to stroke Pip's head.

   Can I walk him? he asks.

  Sure, says Ryan. *Tell you what.*
  Let's go over there and you can
  learn all the things Pip can do.

The boy—Caleb, his mom
tells me—eagerly takes charge
of the dog, who's more than
willing to go show off a little.

   I'm so happy this will work out,
   she says. *Caleb's begged for a dog*
   since he was little and now we have
   a big fenced yard for the two of them.

"He's getting a good one,"
I tell her. "Pip's special."

> *He must be,* says the dad.
> *Caleb's never had a real friend.*
> *We hope a dog will change that.*
>
> *Our son's on the spectrum,*
> explains the mom. *High*
> *functioning, but it's rare*
> *for him to relate to a stranger.*

Caleb has definitely connected
with Ryan, not to mention Pip,
who seems to have a read on the boy.

He sits patiently, waiting
for instruction, rather than
anticipating it, which is how
he performs for Ryan and me.

"It's good Caleb's getting to learn
from Ryan. I learned from him, too.
It didn't take long. Caleb will be
an expert before you know it."

> *Caleb's mom chokes back tears.*
> *I'm—we're—incredibly grateful.*
> *To the program. To you.*
> *And to Pip, of course.*

Ryan and I must sign off
on releasing Pip into these
people's care. No-brainer.

New Dogs Arrive Monday

Which means Ryan and I will have
our own separate living quarters,
with the addition of our anxious rescues.

I can't wait.

Tonight, the room we still share is
quiet. And not only because Pip's gone.
Ryan's genuinely devastated.

> *He'll be okay, right?*
> *He's going to miss us.*

"And we're going to miss him.
But he's got a special job to do.
Did you know Caleb's autistic?
He's never really had a friend before.
But now he has a good one."

I think that makes Ryan feel
better because he says,

> *The last friend I had was in third*
> *grade. My dad was in the military,*
> *and we moved a lot. Not to mention,*
> *he drank. After a while it seemed dumb*
> *to make friends, just to lose them.*

There's a whole lot left
unsaid there. We've never
discussed our backgrounds
or why we're in lockup.

We've only talked about dogs.

THE IRONY IS

He and I could maybe be friends.
Clay and me, too. Or any one of
a handful of people who have fallen
into my orbit, for whatever reason.

But friendship requires trust,
something I'm not familiar with.
I'd guess it's the same for Ryan
and Clay. In fact, I bet Ryan's current
confession was a serious one-off.

Regardless, and I have no clue
why, my own admission slips out.
"I've only ever had one real friend.
My girlfriend, Jaidyn. She killed herself."

Blunt.

> *Seriously? That's messed up,
> dude. Why'd she do it?*

"She was raped. By her ex.
Totally screwed up her head."

Blunter.

"If I ever run into the guy
who did it, I will kill him."

> *Don't blame you. Some
> people deserve to die.*

Bluntest.
Also, accurate.

Ryan Drifts Off

Leaving me alone in the haze
of silence—no soft dog-snoring
to break it tonight—
with my renegade thoughts.

I'm a good person.
> *Consciously considering*
> *viable ways to off someone.*

Some people do deserve
to die. Lance killed Jaidyn.
> *Jaidyn killed herself.*

Her hand was only
the instrument.
> *Eye for an eye.*

She overdosed. Too easy.
It has to be slow. Painful.
> *No quick bullet to the head.*

It has to be in his face.
I want him to know why.
> *No sneaking up from behind.*

Would be the last thing I do.
They'd lock me up forever.
> *Not if there aren't any witnesses.*

Maybe I'm not . . .
such a good person . . .

WHAT HAVE I DONE?

What. Have. I. Done?
The phrase is on auto repeat,
in time with the pound of my feet
against slick pavement.

Pursuit closes in.
Hands snatch at my shoulders.

> *What have you done?*

I turn to face my accuser.
It's the guy who haunts my dreams.
The one who looks like me.
"Who are you?"

> *Come on. You know.*

I don't. But I don't ask
again. "What did I do?"

> *It's okay. He deserved it.
> Only problem is this officially
> makes you a shitty guy.*

Catapulted from turbulent sleep,
I blink, trying to discern familiar objects
in the smothering darkness.

How loudly the voice
of violence calls to me.
I'm worse than a shitty guy.
I'm ... what's the word
I'm looking for?

Wicked.   Malevolent.   Evil.

The Last One

Might be over the top.
Then again, a couple of people
on my mom's side of the family
qualify, so maybe evil's in my blood.

I've taken enough classes
to understand basic genetics.
Figure in the grandparent factor,
Beverly makes me at least
one-quarter evil.

I've always hoped my random
father might balance it out.
But what if he's just as bad?
What if he's worse?

There has to be at least
a little good in there
somewhere. Look at Lake.
And Jaidyn saw decency in me.

But what if, in the end,
the violent side of my nature
wins out? I can't always control
it. Honestly, it can feel good
to turn it loose.

I don't think I'd ever
allow it to hurt a dog.
But what if I couldn't stop it?
Maybe I don't belong in this program.

Maybe Ms. Wilson's last chance
is totally undeserved.

Seems Like Forever

Treading a sea of self-reproach
until an early slant of sun
silvers the watery darkness.

If Pip were here, he'd be asking
to go outside. But he's not,
and technically we can sleep in
until seven on Sundays.

Ryan seems willing to do
exactly that. But I haven't slept
in hours anyway. I slip into
my regulation jumpsuit,
and out into the
swelling light.

About half the dogs left with
their adopted owners yesterday.

The rest start to appear,
encouraging their handlers
toward the designated relief
spots around the grassy quad.
Some of the guys look sleepy.
None of them look angry.

Getting the dogs to this point
in their training must've led
to frustrations. Have any of them
ever felt like lashing out?
How did they reel in that monster?
Or did they? And what if I couldn't?

Maybe I'd better look into firefighting.
That nags at me all morning.

After Lunch

Michael walks me to my new quarters,
directly across the quad from Ryan's.
I don't have many possessions to carry
the short distance to a room that looks
almost exactly like the one I just left.

> *The dog's locker is already
> stocked with food and treats
> and a couple of toys*, Michael says.

"What if I decide I'd rather
not participate in the program?"

> *What are you saying? Why not?*

I can't tell him the real reason,
so I invent some lame excuse
about how hard it was letting Pip go.

> *Yes, that can be hard, but you realize
> what a special home the dog has now?*

"Yeah. But I'm not sure I'm a good fit."

Now his gaze pierces me,
like he's searching for clues.

> *Tell you what. Wait until
> the dogs get here tomorrow.
> See if you find a partner.
> Make your decision then.*

I agree, mostly so I don't have to
confess I'm worse than a shitty guy.

Monday Classes Dismiss Early

With the arrival of two vans
from the animal shelter.
The dogs will be nervous
and maybe scared, so the critical
handler meeting can't be rushed.

The shelter volunteers bring nine
dogs into the gym four at a time
(with one left over). I stand at
the back of the room, watching.
The goal is to match canine
and human personalities.
It's hysterical, and mostly works.

Clay is teamed with Roxie, a poodle
mix. Curly coat, beagle face and ears.
She's the anxious sort, but Clay brought
lots of treats in his pocket and before
long has the dog paying rapt attention.

Ryan finds himself partnered
with a big Australian shepherd.
Barney's all personality and high energy.
He pulls the shelter volunteer around
the gym, sniffing canines and humans
alike. He'll need lots of exercise
and a patient handler.

As the guys meet their dogs,
they're given as much information
about them as the shelter has.
In some cases, there isn't much.
Most were surrendered. A few
had found homes, only to be rejected.

A couple of yard mutts had never

been inside before being rescued.

Two by two, dogs and dudes peel off.
Job one: Introduce dogs to the pee spot.
Housebreaking is the first rule of order.
No owner wants to clean their carpet regularly.

Finally, the leftover dog—and I—
are all that remain. He's a big boy.

> *German shepherd and dobie,*
> says the volunteer. *Too much*
> *for his owner. Way too strong.*
> *She kept him chained to a doghouse*
> *in a little backyard.*

The animal looks at me with
suspicious eyes. When I reach
out my hand, he ducks away.
At least he didn't bite it, I guess.

"What's his name?"

> *Zero.*

Fitting. And the perfect match for me.
I mean, what am I going to do?
Send him back to a concrete cage?
I know what that feels like.
I accept his leash.

"Okay, Zero. Looks like
you're stuck with me."

LAKE
SCHOOL

Has always been my escape.
From Mom and Beverly.
From pseudo-family flack.
And now, from Josie.

Oh, she isn't like a tyrant.
More like a concrete wall.
One that has only cracked
a couple of times in the month
that I've lived in her house.

She barely talks and when she does
it's a series of barks and grunts.
I've rarely seen her smile.

She provides for my needs.
Decent food.
Decent shelter.
Decent clothing.

Transportation, if necessary,
though it's only been
a time or two: Once to register
me for school. Once for a follow-
up post-rape doctor visit.

When I come in, she doesn't ask
about my day or oversee my work.

You've got it covered, right?

Catching up means tons of labor.
One time, a chemistry assignment
frustrated me so much I threw
a pencil across the kitchen table.

> *Pointless*, mumbled Josie.
> *The pencil doesn't care.*

She must have noticed
the way my face flared.

> *Oh. If you decide to run, please
> use the door.* She lifted her cane.
> *Obviously, I won't be running after you.*

That's her way. Reminding me
I'm nothing. A big, fat zero.

I've seen one small chink in her façade,
when she checked on my forehead wound.
She peeled back the old bandage.
Gently swabbed the stitches with
hydrogen peroxide. Covered them
with a clean gauze pad. Painlessly.

Efficiently. Like she'd done
it hundreds of times before.

I still don't know her background
or have any information about
the people whose photos hang
on the walls in the hallway.

She isn't offering.
I'm not inquiring.
None of my business.
Even if I am curious.

I'VE NO DESIRE TO RUN

I do everything Josie asks of me.
Keep my bed made, my room picked
up, and the bathroom spotless.

After all those weeks using filthy
restrooms (or squatting in the dirt),
I'm grateful for a sanitary toilet.

On top of that, I dust and vacuum.
Mop floors. Wash clothes and dishes.
Clean the counters and scrub the sink.

And almost every minute
I'm surrounded by silence.
No music. No TV. Very little talking.

I don't care. I don't need conversation.
I don't need someone to listen.
I don't need to confess, or hear a confession.

I study. Read. Draw a little.
Write to Storm, hoping
Candace can learn where he is.
She promised to reach out to Jim.

Anyway, there's plenty of noise
at Rodriguez. Compared to my last
high school, this one feels welcoming.
I fit in with this crowd.

The military influence makes it diverse,
and it also means many of these
kids have moved around a lot.
Sort of like us fosters.

That doesn't mean finding

friendship is easy, however.
Understanding doesn't
necessarily translate to trust.

Fine by me.
I'm not looking for a friend.
Certainly not love, and lust
is on indefinite hold.

No, I'll concentrate on my classes,
and making up for the time I lost.

Chem.
Gov.
Algebra.
Geometry. (Online again.)
Design.
Creative writing.
Honors English.

I begged for that last one.
It took Ms. Bolton's recommendation
to a teacher friend, but
I got into Miss Ava's class.

She's younger than Ms. Bolton,
and maybe even more of a fashionista.
She's funny, and smart,
and never talks down to us.

We're reading *All the Light We Cannot See*.

An Announcement Interrupts

My time with Werner and Marie-Laure.

>**Attention, Lake Carpenter.
>Do not ride the bus today.
>Your parent will meet you
>in the office after school.**

Parent? Whatever. The final bell rings.
I tuck my book in the backpack Josie gave me.

>*Been in the closet gathering dust,*
>she told me. *But it's good as new.*

No lie. It's super-soft cocoa-colored
leather, not a scuff to mar it.
No clue who it belonged to,
but it's doubtful a foster would have left
it behind. Not even the last
girl, who apparently got pregnant
and moved in with her boyfriend.

>*If you must have sex,* Josie said,
>*be sure to use a condom.*

I didn't tell her I've written off
men forever and I don't trust
her to know I prefer girls.

I weave through the hallway herd,
find Josie waiting at the office door.
Her picking me up is surprising.
"Where are we going?"

>*Costco. Time to stock the pantry.*

I'VE NEVER BEEN IN A COSTCO

It's insane! A cavernous warehouse,
with rows and racks of everything
from produce to car tires.
Josie leads the way in her mobility
scooter, pointing her cane
at things for me to load up.

>Canned goods. Paper products.
>Cleaning supplies. Frozen meat and fish.
>Cereal. Coffee. Sugar. Baking ingredients.

Where will she put it all?
And why do the two of us need it all?
I learn when Josie pulls into the driveway,
opens the garage she never parks in.
It's floor-to-ceiling cabinets on every wall,
except the one with a big freezer.

>*I hate grocery shopping,* Josie says, *so I do most
>of it once every couple of months. Let me show
>you how it's organized, and if it's okay, I'll leave
>you to do it. I need to sit for a spell.*

Canned foods are alphabetized—
applesauce, beans, beets, corn, etc.
Dry goods go in a separate cupboard,
with assigned spots, clearly labeled.
Cleaning supplies have their own cabinet.

When it's all neatly stored, I hang
the reusable bags on the designated hook.
I start toward the door but realize
there are other cupboards.
Curiosity makes me peek inside one.

CLOTHES

Stacks of them, precisely folded.
Men's and women's. And shoes,
lined up perfectly, toes pointing out.
Also, fabric. Lots of it, and like the food,
organized according to type and color.
Plus, on a low shelf, a sewing machine.

> *What are you doing? Get out of there!*

I spin. Find Josie, scarlet with anger.
"I . . . I . . . I'm sorry. I didn't hurt
anything. I was just—"

> *Nosy. It's not a very nice way to be.*
> *Don't let me catch you in there again.*

I didn't touch anything. My temper flares.
"Why do you care so much?
It's just a bunch of clothes."

> *She's quiet for a second or two.*
> *They mean something to me, okay?*

She stands leaning on her cane.
I realize she's waiting for me
to shut the cabinet door. I do.

> *I didn't come out here to catch you snooping.*
> *I have some news. Your caseworker called—*

"Did she talk to Jim about Storm?"

> *She hasn't been able to get ahold of Jim.*
> *But the man who assaulted you has been arrested.*

"For real?"

I can't believe he was caught!

> *They want you to identify him.*

"Like a lineup? When?"
I'm terrified of seeing him again.

> *Photo ID. Tomorrow after school.*

"How do they know it's him?"

> *He had a backpack with your old school ID.*

"What about my letters, journals?"

> *Guess we'll find out tomorrow.*
> *Um . . . there's more. Your friend?*
> *She's in the hospital. There was*
> *a shooting at some street party—*

"Friend? You mean Parker?"

> *Yes. She caught a random bullet.*

"But she'll be okay, right?"

> *It's not looking good, I'm afraid.*

My throat knots. "No."
It can't be true.
And yet, I'm not surprised.
No, Parker! You can't die!

I RETRIEVE

My new old backpack from the van.
Consider the one stolen from me
in that frigid alley. Nothing valuable
inside. But everything invaluable.
My past. Or what remained of it.

Tangible memories. His stealing
them hurts nearly as much
as the physical trauma.
My body has mostly healed.
My psyche is forever scarred.

As for intangible memories, one
of them is currently in a hospital
bed, hanging on by a filament of will.

Parker. Parker. Parker.
You are an enigma.
You lifted me with joy.
You plunged me into despair.

The memories are sensual.
But they're jumbled.

> The licorice of your laughter.
> The musk of your consternation.
> The salt of your heartbeat.
> The stutter of your tongue.

In moments when I dare
think of you, I miss you.
I could never be with you again.
But please, please don't die.

WITH PARKER IN MY HEAD

My homework takes twice as long
as it should. I'm just finishing when
Josie calls dinnertime. We eat Sloppy
Joe casserole and salad in silence.

Finally, I say, "Do you think they'd let
me see Parker? The hospital, that is."

Since you're not related, I doubt it.

"That's what I thought."

You two are close.

"We love each other!"
How did that slip out?

Do you want to talk about it?

"You trying to get rid of me?"

*Even if I were, how would that
accomplish the goal?*

I shrug. "Worked for my last
'parent.'" Air quoted.

I don't understand.

"Why would you? You never
talk to me. You never talk at all."

*She sits with that for a moment.
I'm not a big talker. But I'm a good listener.*

MAYBE I DO

Need someone to listen.
When I open my mouth,
a torrent of words cascades out.
I omit the racier details and tell
Josie all about my best friend.

Maybe Parker will know I'm talking
about her and decide to hang on.

I've been quiet for so long, I can't stop.
I don't say what precipitated it,
but I mention her zoning out.
I describe her angelic singing.
Which leads me to Teddy
and our time in the homeless camp.

From there it's an easy segue to Kit,
meth, and Parker vanishing from my life.

"And now she might die."

> *How do you feel about that?*

"Like I should've stopped her!"

> *She sounds like a headstrong girl.*
> *Do you think you could've done more?*

"No."

> *You could have made the same choices*
> *as your friend. Why didn't you?*

This answer . . .

TAKES A WHILE

I keep looking for ulterior
motives. Why the probe?

"Why do you care?"

    Maybe I don't.

"Then why did you ask?"

    I'm curious, I suppose.

"What if I'm curious
about something?"

    Like what?

"Like who are the people
in the pictures in the hall?"

Her eyes wander
into some faraway place.

    My family. They're ... gone.

"You mean, they left?"

    In a manner of speaking. My husband
    was killed in Iraq in 2008.

    A couple of years later, my children and I
    were coming back from a Tahoe ski trip.
    Road was icy. Car in front of us spun out.
    I couldn't miss him. The kids didn't make it.
    I suffered a spinal cord injury.

Every word from "my husband"

on is like a headbutt to the gut.

> *My son, Eric, was about your age.*
> *Heather was a couple years older.*
> *They're buried side by side.*

I guess I knew who they were.
Maybe suspected the Air Force
took her husband from her.

The rest is too awful to consider.

> *I was a nurse, you know. But after*
> *the accident, that was impossible.*

A nurse. Of course.

> *It was months and months of rehab.*
> *At first, they insisted I'd never walk*
> *again. But I was determined to prove*
> *them wrong. It gave me something*
> *to think about, other than . . .*

So many years ago,
and still, she has tears
left to cry.

"I'm sorry, Josie."

> *Thank you, Lake. I'm sorry for*
> *the burdens you carry, too.*

BURDENS

It's like everything, from Beverly
to Parker to the pervert
in the alley, is an invisible weight.

But my back is strong.
Josie's was broken.
She survived. And so can I.

"I didn't make the same choices
as Parker because I have dreams.
If Parker ever had any, she gave up on them."

> *What makes you think she didn't?*
> *You said she has a beautiful voice.*
> *Maybe she wanted to be a singer.*

"The thing about foster kids,
at least most of the ones I've known,
is that no one supports their dreams.
After a while they figure why bother."

> *Why do you bother?*

"To prove my mother wrong
and my brother right. Mom swore
Storm and I would never amount
to anything. But Storm encouraged me."

> *Sounds like a good brother.*

"The best. I miss him so much.
The system separated us, and I didn't see
him for four years. I'd just found him
again, right before ... all this stuff happened."

> *Where's he now?*

"In lockup somewhere, I think."
I'm not going into details.
The reasons belong to him.

> *What about his dreams?*

"He never mentioned the future.
Not even in his letters."

Dinner's grown cold. Josie nukes
our plates. Once we're eating
again, she looks me in the eye.

> *Tell me about Lake's dreams.*
> *What do you want to do?*

"They're not fine-tuned yet.
I love books. I could be a librarian
or a teacher. But what I'd really
like to be is a fashion designer.
I don't draw very well, but—"

> *I imagine there are computer programs*
> *that could help you with that.*
> *So, you want to go to college, then?*

"I'm not sure how I'll make
that happen, but I want to, yes."

> *As my mom always used to say,*
> *keep your eyes on the prize.*

Eyes on the Prize

Nose to the grindstone.
Chin up. Head down.
There won't be much left
of my face by the time I graduate,
but as long as I do, I think I'll recover.

Less than six months to graduation,
putting us solidly into December.
In fact, Christmas is next week.

It's surreal, going into a police station
that's all decked out in holiday swag,
with carols playing on the speakers.
"Joy to the World" is odd background
music when you're looking at mug
shots, trying to identify your rapist.

I almost didn't go, a nagging internal
voice insisting he'll never face justice.
But Josie talked me into it.

> They need you to identify him to hold him
> until the trial. Did you see his face?

"I'll never forget it."

> Then you must. You don't want
> him out on the streets, do you?

Nope. That's why I'm here, Josie
beside me for support, flipping pages
of photos. Are all these guys rapists
or do they try to fool you with pics
of cops or how does this work?

Doesn't matter. It only takes

about five minutes to spot him.
I almost gag on the bile that rises.

"That's him," I tell the detective.
"That's that motherfu—"
I stop before I lower myself.

> *I guess you're sure, then.*

"Positive."

> *You'll sign a statement to that effect?*

"Yeah. Will I have to testify?"

> *We can't compel you to, but*
> *if you want him put away for*
> *a long time, I'd suggest you do.*

"How long until the trial?"

> *Depends. Six months, maybe.*

"My caseworker said he had
my backpack and school ID.
Was there anything else inside?"

He consults his notes.

> *Two pairs of panties.*
> *Three pencils.*
> *Some torn paper.*
> *A dried flower, in pieces.*

DRIED FLOWER, IN PIECES

I remember the day
I pressed that single small
blue-purple bloom
between pages in my journal.

> ... asters are the official September birthday
> flower. This is for you. I love you!

Parker and I made love then,
slow and sweet and warm.
Her skin smelled like
she'd been out in the sun,
and her kisses tasted of licorice.

Afterward, we lay tangled
too long, and almost got busted
when Colleen stomped down the hall
to ask for help with the groceries.
I heard her coming that time,
managed to throw on clothes.

Later that night, I noticed the aster
on my desk, the only birthday flower
I'd ever received. I decided to preserve
it the only way I knew how.

It stayed in my journal
until that son of a bitch
robbed me of everything.

> Paper. Ripped.
> Petals. Plucked.
> Flesh. Ruined.

The detective drums
his fingers against the table,

lifts me from my reverie.

"Okay, yes, I'll testify."

He nods satisfaction,
says we can go, he'll keep
us posted about the trial.

When we step outside,
where there's no Christmas
music, I take deep breaths
of iced December air.

You okay, Lake?

"Not really."

I'm seething at the guy.
Hoping his time behind bars
is miserable. Painful.

Worried about Parker.
Can't tap into her energy
stream, no matter how hard I try.

Devastated that a cherished
token of our love was totally
and so easily destroyed.

Dried flower, in pieces.
That will be the title of my memoir.
It's a metaphor for me.

STORM
ZERO

Is one hell of a dog.
He rivals Rex, although it took
Zero a lot longer to decide
I was worthy of his trust.

Oh, he never snarled or snapped.
But he had a hard time settling.
Inside, he paced. Outside, he pulled
on the leash. Hard. He wasn't with me.

Treats, which most dogs would do
anything for, did not impress him.

I'd sit on the bed, try to lure him
to "come" with dried liver bites.
He'd lurk across the room,
staring like I had to be kidding.

After four or five days,
I was getting frustrated,
and suspected he was, too.

He knew I was the food guy,
and the dude who took him
out to pee. But that was
the extent of our connection.

I did some research.
Watched YouTube videos.
Learned a lot about training.
But not how to bond.

I worried our partnership
was destined to fail.

Then Something Clicked

German shepherds are working
dogs. Dobermans, too. Zero had spent
his life chained up. Caged. And now,
walled in. No wonder he was tense.
I asked for permission to take him
running. He needed exercise. I did, too.

At first he still pulled on the leash.
But after a couple of miles, he fell in,
matching my pace. Three miles. Four.
I started to tire. But Zero insisted on five.
By the time we got back, winded,
he was walking easily beside me.
We both slept well that night.

Next morning, Zero was raring to go.
Second day, he only tugged for a half mile.
By the third, he was content at my side,
with maybe two feet of space between us.

When I wasn't breathing too hard,
I talked to Zero. Told him about Lake.
Described Jim and Morley.
Wept when I mentioned Jaidyn.

Zero was a great listener,
and while the words were mostly
meaningless to him, I believe
he recognized the emotions.
The distance between us shrank.

Within a week he started bringing
me the leash in the morning.
He even started to like treats.

WE'VE BEEN TOGETHER

For almost four weeks now.
Zero doesn't hang out at a distance.
He's by my side or at my feet,
and when he looks at me, it's with
both expectation and affection.

No more leash pulling.
No more pacing.
No more vacant-eyed staring.
We've become a team.

Training is a piece of cake.
Once he decided to trust me,
he learned the five basic commands
in a single day. Sit. Stay. Come. Heel. Down.
That mastered, we're trying new things.

Michael says of all the dogs
who've been through the program,
only a handful have moved into
the service dog arena, and even fewer
into search-and-rescue.
I know Zero can do either.
He's smart, and clever.

Christmas is the day after tomorrow,
so we're on break from classes.
That gives my dog and me
more time to work.

"Zero. Light on!"

We've repeated this trick
several times. I think he has it.

Sure enough, he goes to the switch

by the door, flips it up with his nose.

"Yes!" I toss him a liver bite.
Challenge met, reward.
"Good dog! Awesome dog."

He accepts the treat, prefers
the praise. Now, the tricky one.

"Zero! Light off!"

We worked at the "on"
for a couple of days. I just
added the "off" this morning.
I swear I can see the wheels
turning in his head. He's thinking.

Zero lifts a front paw, hits
the switch down. Light off.

"Yes! Good, good dog!"

He's a natural service animal.
We'll practice things like
opening doors and picking up
stuff off the floor. Someone
somewhere needs a dog
just like this one, or at least
the dog he'll be too soon.

Too soon, because then
he'll be lost to me.

But That's Not Today

Today I'm introducing Zero
to something brand new.
Scent training. Search-and-rescue
dogs are in hot demand, and
Zero has huge potential.

Dog training is mostly games,
and this is no exception.
Give him the scent you want him
to find, reward him every time he does.

We start by hiding an orange spice
tea bag in a TP tube. The trick is to
use strong scents the dog isn't used
to, and an empty TP tube as a decoy.

If he nose-bumps the empty tube,
he gets a yes for trying. If he bumps
the correct one, a bigger yes plus a treat.

On videos I've watched, it took dogs
several tries to become consistent.
It takes Zero five or six.

It's best not to play until boredom
sets in, so we go for a run and do
it again when we get back.

We work, on and off, all day.
By bedtime, he's got the scent
trick wired and we're both tired.
Zero sleeps on the floor next to me.

Inexplicably, Sleep Eludes Me

My body's wiped out,
but my brain doesn't care.
Maybe it's because of Christmas.

Last year I was at Jim's.
He baked gingerbread.
I'd never had it before.
Neither had Morley.

Will Jim spend Christmas alone?
I hope he isn't sick.
I hope he isn't sad.
I hope he isn't lonely.

At least he's alive. Unlike Jaidyn.

Last year I gave her a silver locket,
with one of those stupid photo
booth pics of the two of us inside.
Is she wearing it now, over my Rex shirt,
in a box in a hole in the ground?

I can't think of her dead.
I can't think of her in pain.
I can't think of her with grit in her knees.

And what about Lake?
Will she spend Christmas homeless?

"Where are you tonight, Lake?
Are you safe? Are you warm?"
I ask the questions out loud
and Zero stirs in his sleep.

I Stroke His Head

To quiet his dreams.
After a while, I tumble
into my own.

This time I'm sprinting
toward something, not
away from someone.
Zero's with me.

I can't see what's ahead.
Don't know why I want
to reach it so badly.

I tell Zero, "Hurry!"

In the distance there's laughter.
Conversation. Christmas carols.

The breeze that carries the sounds
is scented with gingerbread,
Daisy perfume, and orange spice tea.

The last is super strong
and pulls me out
of my dreamscape.

I wake to find Zero
chomping on a TP roll.
I have to laugh,
even though I never
got to see what
we were running toward.

After Breakfast

Zero and I work on a different
scent-training technique.
This one involves stashing
a scent in one of three cans.
When he sticks his nose
in the right container, reward!

He's super fast to pick up
on this trick. No surprise.

We play the game for fifteen
minutes, then go for a run.

When we get back, I'm surprised
to hear I've got a visitor.

Visitation is limited to one
day a month here, but because
tomorrow's Christmas,
they've added a day.

Most of the guys will see
a parent or grandparent, maybe.

I'm sweaty from the exercise,
but don't have time to shower,
so I wipe my armpits, smear on
some deodorant, change my shirt,
and comb my damp hair.

I bring Zero along.
Jim will enjoy meeting him,
and it's good for the dog to be
around new people.

But When We Reach

The commons, where the tables
are set up for visitation,
I don't see Jim anywhere.

Nope. Don't know him.
Nope. Don't know her.
No— Wait. Oh my god.
It can't be. But it is.

Jaidyn's mom sees me. Waves.
And when I reach the table,
she stands. Opens her arms.
I crumble into them.
Shaking like I've just seen a ghost.

Zero senses my upset.
Looks up at me, and I tell
him, "It's okay. She's a friend."

We sit perpendicular to each
other, silently taking measure.
Zero settles beside my right foot.

For the first time, I notice
how Jaidyn inherited
her mother's sharp-edged beauty.

"It's Christmas Eve," I finally say.

> She understands what I don't say.
> *We're not doing Christmas this year.*

I get it.

"Christmas was her favorite
holiday. She loved decorating

the house, shopping for gifts,
helping you bake the pies. Except
mincemeat made her want to puke."

> Her eyes—the same topaz
> as Jaidyn's—blink back tears.
> Still, she smiles. *That's right.*
> *And now that I can eat it without*
> *commentary, I never will again.*

Losing Jaidyn wrecked me.
I can't fathom how much
it has damaged her parents.
"I . . . I'm so sorry. I—"

> *I know. Storm, I want you to*
> *understand something. I'm not*
> *sure she ever told you, but Jaidyn*
> *struggled with depression for years.*
> *She took meds to keep it in check.*
>
> *The rape was a turning point.*
> *A trigger. You couldn't have*
> *changed the outcome, and neither*
> *could I. I tried so hard. I did.*

"So, the pills . . . ?"

> She nods. *I didn't see it that day.*
> *How could I have missed it?*
> *I thought she was getting better.*
> *She was cheerful that morning.*
> *I thought . . .*

Her Body Heaves

A giant sob escapes her.
Zero whines.
Gets up and circles,
sitting between
Jaidyn's mom and me.

He rubs against her
gently, sensing her grief.
She accepts the gesture,
runs her hand over his head.

> Jaidyn's father and I have decided
> to sell the house—

"No! It's your passion!"

> Every project is a reminder.
> Every room holds memories.
> Some people try to keep their loved
> ones alive by clinging to recollections.
> But she's gone. So, I've emptied her room.
>
> I came across this. I checked with
> the director here and got the okay.
> Jaidyn wanted you to have it.

She hands me an envelope
with my name on the front.
Inside is the silver locket.

And a note. Two words:
Forgive me.

My turn to lose it.

Emptied

Jaidyn's room.
Jaidyn's house.
Jaidyn's family.
Me.
All emptied
>of her laughter
>of her beauty
>of her light.

I didn't know
about her depression.
She never mentioned it.
And if I ever saw hints,
I dismissed them
as momentary lapses.

>Grades.
>Disagreements.
>Disappointments.
>Hormones.

When I think of her now
I see her smiling. Laughing.
Kissing me. Insisting
she'll love me forever.

I didn't believe in forever,
but she made me think
there was some slim chance
that one existed.

How could I know
Jaidyn's forever
might be shorter than mine?

CHRISTMAS

Has always been bittersweet.
Today, it's just plain bitter.

I thought maybe this year
would be different.
More on the sweet side.
Why would I believe a dog
or this program could
change a goddamn thing?

Jaidyn inhabited my dreams
all night, or as much of it
as I could actually sleep.
She was barely visible
in the distance and kept
pleading with me to help her.

But every time I got close,
she'd say, *Forgive me,* and
transport across the rock
moonscape expanse again,
calling, *Help me, Storm.*

Worried about my tossing
and turning, Zero kept sticking
his nose in my face, as if he could
smell the disturbance inside my head.

Finally, I yelled, "Leave me alone!"

He crept off, and is still sulking
when I give up on bed, slip into sweats.
It's cold outside, barely light,
and I'm going for a therapy run.

I'm not supposed to take off

so early, but I don't see signs
of activity, human, canine,
poultry, or otherwise. I doubt
anyone will notice or miss me.

Anyway, I'm not running off.
I'm running for my mental health.

Zero's not letting me go alone.
Once we're well away from
the compound, on the rutted fire
road up into the hills, I let him off leash.

He likes chasing squirrels
and rabbits if he can find them.
He deserves a good chase.
"Sorry I was shitty. Go for it."

I run hard. Working my body
helps my head. The rhythm
of my feet orders my thoughts.
I just wish I could sweat out
all the poisons inside me.

I never really understood
why Jaidyn loved to run.
Now I do. I wish I'd made
the effort to join her.
I always had an excuse not to.
I lost so much time I could have—

Frantic Barking

Wrenches me into the moment.
"Zero? Zero!"

The barking's behind me, to my left.
I turn and start that way, scanning.
"Holy shit!"

Zero's face-to-face
with a huge mountain lion,
who's snarling and swinging claws.
I'm not supposed to run toward
the cat, but I know it's not a fair fight.

"No, Zero! Come!"
My voice draws the dog's attention,
and that's a very bad thing.
As soon as his head turns,
the cougar takes a big swipe,
raking its giant claws down
Zero's shoulder.

He howls. Blood spurts. Fuck it!
I pick up rocks, hurl them at the cat.
"Get the fuck out of here!"

A chunk of granite connects
with the mountain lion's rib cage.
Zero keeps snapping.
I keep throwing.

Finally, the cat decides
there must be easier game
and slinks off.

"Zero?"

Ah, man. He's losing blood.
I yank off my sweatshirt,
close up the flaps of the wounds
and wrap the shirt sleeves
as tight as I can around them.

Zero's in shock, whimpering softly.
"Don't you leave me! Don't you dare!"

I'll have to carry him.
He weighs almost a hundred
pounds, but adrenaline helps me
lift him into a fireman's carry.

I move as fast as I can.
Feel the warm seep of his blood.
Hear his shallow heartbeat.

"Now you listen. You can't go
anywhere. We've got work to do."

I tell him about the tricks
we're going to learn.
I tell him about the turkey
dinner we're going to share.

I tell him he's the best
freaking dog in the universe.

"Damn it, Zero. I love you."

LAKE
IRONICALLY

The last Christmas surprise
I had was when Beverly gave Storm
and me Jenga and Memory games.
We were at Mom's for a short reunion.

I guess I've had a few decent
Christmases over the years,
with fosters like Molly and Pete,
who tried to make them nice.
But there weren't many real
surprises. Not like yesterday.

Josie didn't put up a tree,
so there wasn't one to put presents
under. Instead, after breakfast,
she led me out to the garage.
Opened the door to the forbidden cabinet.

> *These clothes belonged to my children,*
> *so there are boys' things here, too.*
> *Take your time going through them.*
> *Help yourself to any you fancy.*

"Are you serious?"

> *I'd just as soon see they get used,*
> *and I know my kids would, too.*
> *Like you, Heather enjoyed upcycling.*
> *And she was quite the seamstress.*

The sewing machine was hers, too.
For three amazing hours, I pulled
clothes out of the stacks, tried them on.

I spent much of Christmas Day
thrifting without spending a dime.

My closet and drawers are bulging.
If I ever move out of here, a garbage
bag won't do. I'll need two huge suitcases.

The whole time, I half expected
Josie to tell me she'd confused
Christmas with April Fools' Day.
But once I'd finished making
my wardrobe selections, she asked
me to carry in the sewing machine.

> *Set it there on the table against the wall.*
> *Do you know how to use it?*

"No. I wish I did."

> *Then you'll have to learn.*
> *Can't be a fashion designer*
> *if you can't thread a bobbin.*

I'm excited, and not just about
learning how to sew, but also
because she's paying attention to
something I said, taking me seriously.

Josie's been listening to me.

I doubt she believes
in me yet, but she's willing
to give me a chance.

THAT'S WORTHY OF EFFORT

Josie has me bring in a giant
basket full of an assortment
of threads and needles and pins.

> *See those little coils of thread?*
> *Those are bobbins,* she tells me.
> *I'll show you how to wind them later.*
> *For now, you can practice with these.*

She shows me where to put them
in the Singer's belly, under a metal plate.
Bigger spools go at the top of the machine.
The needle weaves upper and lower
threads together, creating stitches.
The trick is to place the stitches
perfectly, producing a straight seam.

The process reminds me of writing,
which is intertwining the exact words
to build flawless sentences and paragraphs.
Design, I think, is more like math.
Discerning patterns and finding the right
formulas to achieve the answers you seek.

The phone rings. Josie leaves me
to practice with a warning.

> *Stay focused. That sewing machine*
> *needle is sharp. I've seen them go*
> *straight through fingers, nails and all.*

I'm not sure if she's talking
as a seamstress or a nurse, but
I see her point. And that's a lousy pun.

MY SEAMS

Haven't quite risen to the level
of precision by the time Josie returns,
but they're better. She takes a quick peek.

> *Not bad, she says. Not bad.*
> *Now she changes the subject.*
> *That was Candace on the phone.*
> *Your friend Parker's improving.*
> *She's conscious and has asked for you.*

"You mean I can see her?"

> She nods. *Her doctors think it might*
> *help her psychologically. If you want*
> *to go, we should leave now. The freeway*
> *might not be bad on the way there,*
> *but the return will be lousy and*
> *heavy traffic makes me nervous.*

We're in the van in fifteen minutes.
Josie asks if I'm excited to see Parker.
"Yes and no. I'm a little afraid."

> *Because of her medical condition?*

"Yeah, but also because I'm not
sure what to say to her. I was pretty
mad at her when she disappeared."

> *Don't worry. You'll know what to say.*

I fret about it for the almost two
hours it takes to reach the hospital
and find our way to the right floor.

The nurse in charge reminds me

Parker is critically ill, and I have to
promise not to upset her.
Josie tells me to visit on my own.

> *You need me, I'm in the waiting room.*

I follow the nurse, who checks
to make sure Parker's awake.

> *Ten minutes. Tops.*

I have no idea what kind of damage
the bullet(s?) did, so I'm relieved
to see her head and face are unbandaged.

But her skin's the approximate color
of flour, and her eyes seem sunken
beneath the sharp protrusions of her cheekbones.

Street party bullet or hardcore
drug use, she resembles a corpse.
I paint on a weak smile.
"Hey, you. How you doing?"

> *How do I look?* she croaks.

"Like shit. But what else is new?"

She tries to laugh, but the attempt
is obviously painful. She shifts gears.
Her hollow eyes glisten.

> *I didn't think you'd come.*

DOES SHE NOT KNOW ME AT ALL?

"Parker, yeah, I was pissed when
you disappeared, but I was more worried.
And after you left, some bad crap went down.
When you're better, I'll tell you about it."

>*That would mean I have to get better.*
>*I'll think about it. But there's not*
>*much left for me, you know?*

"Listen. I'd totally given up hope.
But when I really needed help,
good people showed up for me.

"And guess what. I'm learning how to sew.
I'm going to be a fashion designer.
If I can do that, you can be a singer."

The smile she musters is real.
But her energy is black, and not
just because of her injuries.
I force myself to go closer.

"My ten minutes are up.
Is it okay to kiss you?"

Her lips are dry and cracked
and unflavored, and I don't
want to hurt her. I puff gently.

"I love you, Parker."

As I leave, I feel a small silver thread
snake through her darkness.

JOSIE WAS RIGHT

About the return-trip traffic.
She exits the freeway, tries alternate
routes her app promises should help.

> *Even if these roads take just as long,*
> *at least we'll be moving. Can't stomach*
> *sitting in stop-and-go, breathing exhaust.*

My eyes close against the afternoon
glare. I think about Parker, how far
she fell, and how quickly. If I'd clung
tighter, I might be in that hospital with her.

Or worse.

I hope I did give her a silver thread.
A reason to recover and work to achieve
her dreams. Whatever they are.

> *I'd better stop for gas.*

I open my eyes. Look around.
The area's familiar. Too familiar.
I catch my breath. Audibly, I guess.

> *Something wrong?*

"It's just . . . I grew up in an apartment
a couple of blocks that way.
Not a lot of good memories here."

> *I understand. Well, quick fill-up,*
> *we'll be back on the road again.*
> *As soon as I find a gas station.*

IT'S WEIRD

Just how little
things have changed.

Same streets.
Same buildings.
Same storefronts.

I guess some
of the businesses
are different.

There might be a new
restaurant or two.
I wouldn't know.
We never ate in the old ones.

What I see when I look
at these sidewalks:

Storm and me walking to school.
Storm and me walking to the store.
Storm and me walking to the park,
on the days Mom and/or Beverly
wanted us out of the apartment.

We were too little to be doing
that stuff on our own. But if
anyone noticed, they minded
their own business. Storm and I
weren't worth the bother.

Except, we were.

JOSIE TURNS INTO A GAS STATION

Locates an empty pump, pulls
a wad of bills from her purse.

> *They only take cash or debit, and I hate*
> *paying convenience fees for inconvenience.*

She hands me eight tens.

> *Would you please run in and ask them*
> *to put this on pump six?*

"Eighty bucks?"

> *Not long ago sixty would fill it.*
> *Those days are over, I'm afraid.*

Both cashiers have short lines.
I choose the closest to the door,
and am checking out the tabloids
when an uproar flares in the line to my right.

> *Eleven goddamn dollars for one pack*
> *of cigarettes? Since when? I've only got ten.*

The voice makes my skin crawl.
Don't look. Don't look. I have to.

I'd run if I could, but I need to pay
for Josie's gas. I'm standing here,
cash in one hand, when the disrupter
turns, scans the place, searching
for someone to give her a buck.

> Her eyes home in on me.
> *Hey. Lake? Is that you, baby girl?*

I pretend I don't hear, don't see.

It is! It is you, isn't it? Been a while.

She gets out of her line, pushes
in much too close to me.
Can't not acknowledge her now.

"Hi, Mom."

You're looking good, girl.

Can't say the same about her.
She has . . . shriveled. Like a raisin.
It hasn't been that long since
I last saw her. Four years exactly.
How could she deteriorate so much?

Her eyes tell me the same story
I've read in Parker's eyes. Addiction.

How you been? Where's your brother?

"Good. Not sure."
I reach the register, hand over
the money. "Pump six, please."

You heard about your grandmother?

"Yeah. Too bad."

I START TOWARD THE DOOR

Mom follows. I lie, tell her it was
good seeing her. She won't let me go.

> *Hang on. Can you spare a couple*
> *of bucks? I'm short this month.*

"I don't have any money."
I push on outside.

> *Sure you do.* Her voice is shrill.
> *I saw it! Just a little, to tide me over.*

"Mom, I don't have any!"

> She sticks her face right in mine.
> *You listen here, you little shit.*
> *I'm your mother. You owe me!*

Her hands lift. She wants to hit
me. I start to push her.

> *That's enough! You leave the girl alone!*

Josie tugs me gently back away
from my mom, steps between us.

> *I'll do what I want. That's my daughter.*

> *Afraid not. Not according to the state*
> *of California. You'd best run along.*

My mom's eyes light with rage.
She barely looks human.

She lashes out at Josie,
who lifts her cane in self-defense.

"Stop it! You've got no right!
I will so call the cops. In fact,
does anyone have a phone?"

I throw the last question
to the crowd that's gathered.
Several people offer to dial 911.
Mom deflates like a popped balloon.

> *No. No. I get the message.*
> *But you did me wrong, Lake.*

That makes me snort laugh.
"I did *you* wrong? You and Beverly
were evil to Storm and me! Evil.

"But he and I had each other.
And we decided a long time ago
that despite *you*, we'd make it.
We'd become something special.
And by God, we're going to!

"You can't hurt me anymore.
I don't wish bad things for you,
but I never want to see you again.
Can we please go, Josie?"

I turn my back, leave
my mother in my wake,
confident she'll stay there.

STORM
SIX WEEKS

Since Zero saved my life.
I'm positive that's what happened.

Michael says mountain lions
hunt at dusk and dawn,
and are more aggressive in winter,
when game is less plentiful.

Cougars prefer easier meals,
but will go for lone hikers
or joggers if they get hungry enough.
I was almost the cat's Christmas dinner.
But Zero said hell no. He almost paid
the ultimate price. For me.

Christmas Day, Michael found me
carrying Zero and loaded us both
into his truck for a rocket ride
down the hill to an emergency vet,
who gave up his own holiday
meal and was waiting for us
when we got there.

Fortunately, he had an in-house
blood bank, because Zero
was in dire need of a transfusion,
and there was a match in the fridge.

That, antibiotics, and thirty-seven
stitches to close up the wounds
gave Zero a fighting chance.
But it took extraordinary will
to bring him back to me.

He was in critical care for three
days, and I was sure I'd lose him.

But he decided to stick around.
His recovery's been slow but steady.
No complications. No relapses.
Zero got a second last chance.

We're not running yet,
but we're taking long walks.
Not at dusk. Not at dawn.

Plus, we're working on scent.
More brain exertion than physical,
but it's keeping him sharp.

He's still resting a lot,
mostly because I insist.
I have permission to keep him
in my care for as long as it takes
for him to become a great
search-and-rescue dog.

While he snoozes, I sometimes
help Ryan with Barney's training.
That Australian shepherd
has turned into one fine service dog.

Lights on/off? No problem.
Open a refrigerator door,
find something inside and
fetch it? Ditto. He'll even alert
to phones or doorbells ringing.
And he loves every minute of it.

As for the Rest

Of my time, I'm doing okay
with my schoolwork.

I'll graduate high school in June.
After that I can take college-level
courses while I serve the remainder
of my sentence. I figure I might as well
earn a few credits. I'm not sure
I need or want a degree, however.

After the episode with Zero,
I decided I don't want to be a vet.
It's not just because of the blood,
though it did make me queasy.

But veterinarians lose animals.
Sometimes they even have to help
them exit this life. Daily heartbreak
would be too hard. I'm a wuss.

I can see dog training, though.
Michael suggested, since my talents
seem more aligned with that kind
of work than fire suppression,
there might even be a path
for me to become a K9 cop.
Wouldn't that be ironic?

When I called Jim and told
him that, first he laughed.
Then he said why the hell not?

Jim's also recovering.
Turns out he needed stents
in his heart.

He was in the hospital for a while,
but he's home, on the mend,
and stays in touch, so I know
he and Morley are all right.
Jim promises they'll visit soon.

Jaidyn's locket's too small
for me to wear, so I keep it
on the wall next to my bed.
Maybe that's why I still dream
about her. Good dreams, mostly.

I only have one real piece
of unfinished business.
I need to know about Lake.

Where she is.
What she's up to.
If she's safe.

I don't know how I'll find out.
But I have faith that I will.

For now, I'm focusing on doggie
adoption day this coming weekend.
I've been posting dog videos.
Helping screen potential adopters.
Pairing those who qualify
with the proper animals.

With all that on my plate
every day, trouble can't catch
up to me. I think it stopped trying.

LAKE
I COULDN'T HAVE IMAGINED

Asking Candace for another chance
would put me on a path to happiness.
I still have a hard time embracing
that emotion or believing it can last.

All I wanted was off the street.
Food in my stomach.
A hot shower and a warm bed.
A place to heal my body and mind.

School? Yeah, I wanted that.
Would've settled for one I felt like
a freak in, as long as I could learn.
I never expected I'd find one
I'd like, or that I might make a friend
or two by joining a book club
and a sweet GSA.

When I first got here,
spending days and days in silence,
then getting reamed for opening
a cabinet in the garage, I was certain
Josie was not the parent I needed.
But was I wrong!

She's not always cheerful.
Mostly because of chronic pain.
Physical and mental.
Oh, the treasures she's lost!

I've only lost one, and there's still
a chance I can find Storm again.
Josie's are gone forever.
I'm a poor substitute.

When Josie told my mom

to leave me alone,
put her own safety on the line,
I couldn't believe it.
Only Storm has ever stood
steadfast in my corner like that.

Seeing Mom that day,
that way, was a revelation.
Whether it was because
I was too young, or too naïve
about drug abuse, I never
saw it in my mom.

The alcohol was obvious.
But she was snared by more.
Drugs might explain
some of her behaviors.
But she was our mom.
Did she ever love us?

That kind of brings me
back to Parker.
I did love her. I still do.
But I know
I could never
be with her again.
Maybe as friends.
Distant friends.

Sometimes you have to
put your own welfare first.

IT'S SATURDAY

And I'm altering this cool flannel
shirt. Sewing on leather pockets,
using fancy stitching and contrasting thread.

Creating unusual embellishments
for ordinary clothes has become a passion.
Not only do I have that opportunity
here, but Josie encourages it.
My seams are getting straighter.

Josie has been working in the spare
bedroom that serves as her office.
She's got a computer in there.
I think she's been writing.
I told her people would read
her memoir. I know I would.

At first, she said no way.
I've been working on her, though.
I told her that her story could help
other people sort through their pain.
That made her rethink.

But when she exits the room,
there's something else on her mind.

Grab your coat. We have to go.

"Where?"

Tell you in the van.

By the time we're backing out
of the driveway, curiosity
is chewing into me.

"Okay, can you tell me now?"

>We're getting a dog.

"What? Really? Since when?
I didn't know you liked dogs."

>I used to have dogs when the kids were
>little. The last one crossed the Rainbow
>Bridge shortly before my husband was killed.

>I've been on a waiting list for a service dog
>and one's become available. I won't always
>have someone around to help out, and
>my disabilities will get worse with age.

"But you never said anything.
Were you keeping it a secret?"

>I wanted to be sure it was really going
>to happen. Service dogs can be hard to find.
>But I recently came across this program
>where these kids in juvenile detention train
>rescue dogs. Not all become service dogs.
>Some just find good loving homes.

>Either way, the requirements to adopt
>are quite specific. I didn't know until
>this morning that I've been paired with
>an exceptional Australian shepherd.

She tells me his name is Barney.

AUTHOR'S NOTE

A few years ago, I established Ventana Sierra, a nonprofit whose goal was to help older teens get off the street, into safe housing, and on a path to college or career training. It was a noble cause, destined to fail—the first house opened just as the last major recession hit, and funding became impossible to secure.

But during its four-year tenure, VS was able to help more than thirty young people, several of whom had aged out of foster care. I became intimately aware of the pros and cons of the system, as well as the personal circumstances that forced these kids to live with strangers as caregivers.

Some worked hard, eager to move ahead and excel. Among our success stories: a nurse; a respiratory therapist; a comic book artist; a literary agent and novelist; a vet tech; a cosmetologist; and a real estate agent. Others left the program relatively quickly, unable to coexist with rules designed to keep the houses safe and substance-free.

Whichever way they went, almost every one experienced inner turmoil and struggled to believe their abilities could create a successful future for themselves. Due to their backgrounds, trust was difficult to establish. At school and elsewhere, the "foster child" label equaled stigma. But with rare exceptions, each had a desire to connect with others and discover love (often in all the wrong places).

Over the years, I have also had the opportunity to work with young people in juvenile detention facilities. Some had already decided there would never be anything beyond lockup, and they acted that way. Others were determined to serve their time and never return. They focused on school and the programs that could help them move forward beyond the juvenile justice system. Once in a while, it was possible to break through the veneer of the toughest ones to find some spark of hope inside.

I hope this book will shine a spotlight on the foster care and juvenile justice systems, both of which need reforms but also work very hard to support and/or rehabilitate kids who have very few choices. If we can focus on what works and change what doesn't, we can open opportunities for these young people and allow them clearer paths to a more positive future.

Acknowledgments

With heartfelt love for my Ventana Sierra kids (now adults), who opened my eyes to the intricacies of their world, and my daughter, Kelly, who invested much time and energy on their behalf. Special thanks and respect to Kelly Jesch, who has worked tirelessly to ease the way for Northern Nevada foster kids, and Sterling Raymond Miller, who offered insight into the logistics of lockup. An extra measure of thanks to Emma Dryden, who helped me slim these pages, and to Stacey Barney, who allowed me to fatten them up a little again. As always, with a rousing shout-out to Nancy Paulsen and my entire team at Penguin.

Photo Credit: Sonya Sones

ELLEN HOPKINS is a poet, a former journalist, and the award-winning author of twenty nonfiction books for young readers, fourteen bestselling young adult novels, two middle grade novels, and four novels for adult readers. *Sync* is her fifteenth YA novel in verse. After six decades in the West, Ellen recently moved with her extended family and two German shepherds to a lovely log home on five acres of Missouri woods.

EllenHopkinsBooks.com